KONRAD

Konrad fired again. Another black arrow found its target, this time in the creature's throat. Blood spurted as the arrow drove itself through the fat furry neck and into the trunk behind, nailing the beastman to the bark.

Both of its arms – the one with spiny claws, the one without – went to its neck, trying to pull the arrow free. Its body twitched spasmodically, there was a liquid gurgle deep in its throat. A final gush of blood pumped from the neck wound, both arms dropped to its sides, and then the thing became absolutely still.

Konrad had a third arrow notched, ready to let fly. The only sign of movement from the beastman was its blood trickling from the two wounds. Its blood was red, like the colour of its face, the dull sheen of its fur, the rust of its armour. It was dead.

More Warhammer from the Black Library

· GOTREK & FELIX ·

TROLLSLAYER by William King

SKAVENSLAYER by William King

DAEMONSLAYER by William King

DRAGONSLAYER by William King

BEASTSLAYER by William King

VAMPIRESLAYER by William King

· WARHAMMER NOVELS ·

DRACHENFELS by Jack Yeovil

HAMMERS OF ULRIC by Dan Abnett,
Nik Vincent & James Wallis

GILEAD'S BLOOD by Dan Abnett & Nik Vincent

THE WINE OF DREAMS by Brian Craig

· WARHAMMER FANTASY STORIES ·

REALM OF CHAOS
eds. Marc Gascoigne & Andy Jones

LORDS OF VALOUR
eds. Marc Gascoigne & Christian Dunn

A WARHAMMER NOVEL

Book 1 of the Konrad Trilogy

KONRAD

By David Ferring

A BLACK LIBRARY PUBLICATION

First published in Great Britain in 1989 by
GW Books, a division of Games Workshop Ltd., UK

First US edition published in Great Britain in 2001 by
Games Workshop Publishing,
Willow Road, Lenton, Nottingham, NG7 2WS, UK

First US edition, December 2001

10 9 8 7 6 5 4 3 2 1

Distributed by Simon & Schuster
1230 Avenue of the Americas
New York, NY 10020

Cover illustration by Karl Kopinski

ISBN 0-7434-1173-0

Set in ITC Giovanni

Printed and bound in Great Britain by
Omnia Books Ltd, Glasgow, UK

See the Black Library on the Internet at
www.blacklibrary.co.uk

Find out more about Games Workshop
and the world of Warhammer at
www.games-workshop.com

KONRAD

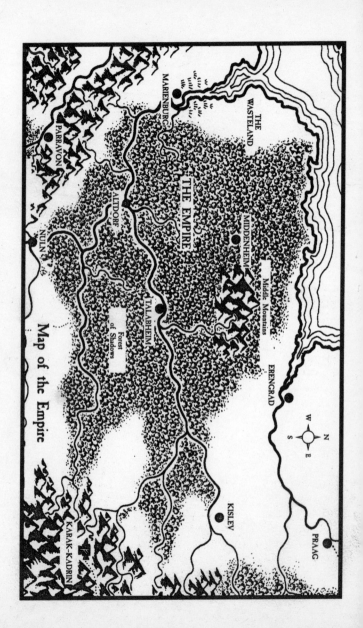

Map of the Empire

BOOK ONE

THEY CAME FROM *the west and from the east, from the south and from the north. They came from every corner of the Empire, from every land in the Old World – and from beyond.*

Many of them were human, or had once been; but many were not and had never been.

Almost all were deadly enemies. Under any other circumstances, such a rendezvous would have led to instant slaughter as every warrior instinctively fell upon his ancient foes and sworn rivals in an orgy of blood.

Yet they had not come together in peace. None knew the meaning of such a concept.

By the end of the day, there would indeed be the carnage that they all craved. But this death and destruction would not be wrought amongst those who had converged in such an unnatural alliance. Not at first. Instead they would be the dealers of death, the deliverers of destruction.

They had but one thing in common: each and every one of them was a servant of Chaos in some form or another. Between them, they worshipped every Chaos power: Khorne and Slaanesh, Nurgle and Tzeentch, and all the other dark deities.

They were united for this single unholy mission. A mission of mayhem and of murder, of mutilation and of massacre...

CHAPTER ONE

IT WAS NOT yet dawn by the time he reached the bridge and started to cross the river. The great moon, Mannslieb, had already set. Its lesser companion, Morrslieb, was at its smallest and gave even less illumination than usual.

He stopped halfway over the wooden bridge, leaning on the rail and waiting several minutes until the sky began to lighten before venturing any further. Then he headed up the hillside towards the forest, moving as slowly as the sun seemed to rise. It was a winter sun, low and dull.

His breath condensed in the cold air, and he shivered momentarily.

The rags he wore did little to keep out the chill. His old boots were padded with cloth from within, partly because they were too large for him, and wrapped in more strips of fabric on the outside, in a vain attempt to keep out the wet. But the grass was saturated with morning dew, the ground thick with mud, and his boots were still wet from the previous day.

He hardly noticed. This was how it had been all his life, or for as long as he could remember. It seemed that from the first day he could walk, he had come here alone, barefoot in the dust or trudging through the squelching mud.

It would get worse before it got better. The ice and the snow which were to come over the next month or two would make his daily task even more difficult.

He stared into the forest, trying to penetrate the thick boughs, sensing what was hiding deep inside. Even on the brightest summer day, the forest was a dark and dank place where light seldom penetrated.

Most of the trees had shed their leaves, but this somehow seemed to make them even more dangerous. Without the foliage, hiding places were fewer. Yet the trees themselves became more threatening, their thick trunks and bare branches like some kind of living creatures, waiting to pounce.

All was quiet, but he was not fooled. The woods were alive with all manner of beings. Insects and birds and animals, the normal kind of wildlife. Then there was the other kind, the kind which was anything but normal.

He was scared. Out here, he was always afraid. When he was younger, he had thought that he would lose his fear with the passing years. Instead, the opposite had happened. Then, he had been scared of the unknown. Now, he knew more of what he might be up against – and so he was even more afraid.

Probably that was why he was still alive. If he were not always alert, ever vigilant, he would have been dead long ago. Taken by one of the *things* that lurked in the depths of the twisted forest.

None of the men from the village ever came here alone. When they entered the woods, they did so in groups, and they made sure that they were heavily armed. The woodcutters were always guarded when they set about their work, felling a clump of trees to clear another area of forest.

But these precautions were not enough. Last year, a group of six woodsmen from the village had entered the trees early one morning. By evening, they had not returned. They never did. All the search parties ever found were a few scraps of bloodied clothing.

He blew on his hands for warmth, rubbing them together for a minute. His dagger was tucked inside his tunic, and he pulled it out. The knife in his right hand, the coil of rope in which to tie the firewood in his left, he finally stepped towards the trees on the edge of the forest.

Every day he entered at the same point, took the same route. He knew each tree and root, every sapling and bush. If something were not right, he would know instantly. But every day he had to diverge more from his regular path in the search for wood.

It was always a search. There was no point in breaking off branches because, even at this time of year when they seemed so dead, they would not be dry enough to burn. He was as much a hunter as those who stalked wild animals for food, shooting the elk or the boar with their arrows.

The trees at the edge of the woods were widely spaced. The deeper one went, the more closely packed were the ancient boughs, as though they too huddled close for protection from the beings that dwelled within their depths.

But such defence seemed no more successful for the trees than it was for the woodcutters, because every so often one of the mighty trunks lay stretched out on the ground, as if a victim of the forest's unknown predators.

He had seen the *things* many times, sensed them far more frequently. He had no idea what they were or what they were called, and he did not want to find out.

To him, they were all monsters, and he preferred to keep as far away as possible.

Neither human nor animal, they were like a hideous cross between the two, as though spawned from some obscene mating. Creatures of fur and flesh and feather, hands and hooves and horns. Yet they were stupid. Their mutations seemed to have bred out all their natural senses. They had neither the brains of humans nor the instinctive awareness of animals.

Many a time he had been within a few yards of such loathsome creatures, with only the trunk of a narrow tree for protection, but they had neither seen him nor heard him nor smelled him.

If one ever had, then he would have been dead. This was why he had grown ever more cautious. His luck could not hold for ever.

His pulse began to race as he reached the edge of the forest, and he gripped the hilt of his knife even tighter in his sweaty palm. All thoughts of the cold were banished from his mind. He moved slowly, but his head kept turning from side to side, listening, while his eyes darted about even faster.

There was nothing to hear, nothing to see – but he knew something was there.

Not too far ahead, one of the *things* lay in wait. Perhaps it was lurking in ambush, knowing that he came this way every dawn. Or perhaps it was simply chance that had brought the being to this point in the forest, some fifty yards away.

Although out of sight because of the trees that stood between, he could visualize it crouching near the gnarled roots of a forked trunk.

He also waited. He had learned to be patient. That too had saved his life on many an occasion.

He stood motionless, hardly daring to breathe in case the vapour from his nostrils signalled his location, his heart thudding faster than ever, his mouth dry but his body damp with sweat.

The creatures were mostly inhabitants of the night. During the hours of darkness they crept towards the village, searching for any unpenned animals. With the arrival of daylight, they retreated to the forest. But day or night, they were equally deadly.

After what happened the previous year, a hunt had been organized to clear the forest. There had even been soldiers brought in. He had never seen such a wonderful sight. They had ridden into the village, the sun sparkling on their armour, their bright pennants flowing behind them. Until that day, he had hardly considered what existed beyond the village. He wished he could have been a soldier.

Some of the troops were billeted in the inn, much to his master's displeasure, whose contribution to the clearing of the forest was to pay for their board.

But he was delighted, because he could listen to the soldiers' tales of life outside the valley, of things he had never heard or imagined could exist. He had happily polished their helmets, burnished their armour, groomed their horses.

Some of them even gave him pennies, the first money he ever owned. He buried the brass coins in the stable, near where he slept, because he knew his master would take the money from him and beat him. He had been beaten regardless, but he had kept the money.

He had also kept a dagger, which he stole from a captain who had never rewarded him even with a word of thanks, despite all the work he had done. He wanted something from the outside world – and he had never seen such a strange knife, either before or since.

The handle was made of some kind of white bone, carved into the shape of a serpent's head, but it was the blade which made the weapon unique. Instead of having straight sides from hilt to point, both cutting edges were made up of a series of curves which rippled closer to one another until they met at the tip.

The troopers had swept through the forest, clearing the woodlands of the creatures. But the forest stretched for ever, and before long the *things* returned again.

Now there was one nearby, waiting as he waited.

He heard a sound and he spun around, because it came from behind him, towards the village. It was the sound of a horse, its shod hooves clattering across the wooden bridge a few hundred yards away.

He narrowed his eyes, focusing on the rider. It was very rare for anyone else to be up so early. Often, he would have collected a huge bundle of firewood and been back in the village before anyone else was about. This was more rare in winter, however. Because of the fewer daylight hours, more people were awake at dawn.

He recognized the rider – he recognized everyone from the village – and she was the most unlikely person to see at this hour of the morning.

He would have expected her to lie in bed very late, while her father's servants did all the work and tended to her every whim. She lived in the manor house at the head of the valley. Her father owned that, as he owned the rest of the valley. Everyone in the village lived on his land; even the innkeeper had to pay rent for the tavern.

She was dressed in white furs, and her horse snorted as it cantered over the narrow bridge. She halted for a few seconds, looking back in the direction she had come, then tugged on the reins, turning her mount's head. But she did not turn the steed completely and return to the village. Instead, she rode towards where he was.

And where the *thing* was!

ALTHOUGH HE HAD been watching her, he had not forgotten the creature. He was totally aware of it – while it, in turn, was totally oblivious of him. But it had heard the rider, and it started moving towards the edge of the forest.

The boundary had been pushed back over the years, further and further from the river, to leave a wide area of hillside stretching up from the water's edge.

The rider could have chosen to keep to the track by the side of the river. She did not. For some reason, she rode up the slope.

Her route took her parallel to the forest itself, closer to him, while the *thing* closed upon her.

It was still beyond his line of sight, but he could tell that the being was cutting diagonally through the trees in a route that would take it towards the rider.

She rode on quickly, confidently. He watched, waiting for her to realize what was happening, to wheel her horse and gallop away. But she kept on coming, as though unaware of the danger.

What was she doing? Why was she out here all alone?

He continued to watch, trying to work out what was happening. The creature was very close now. She would have to flee almost immediately, or else it would be too late.

Then, suddenly, he guessed the awful truth: she did not know! She had absolutely no idea what was about to happen.

But he did. He knew exactly what would occur. His head turned as he followed the track that the *thing* must take. In a few seconds the creature would be upon her, leaping high and toppling her from her mount.

He sprang from the trees and into the open, and he ran, dropping the rope, shouting out a warning, heading straight for where the inhuman assailant would launch itself at its helpless victim, yelling out again, telling her to get back, back, closing the gap, wondering if he could possibly reach her before the creature did, but knowing that he could not achieve the impossible – because what he had observed was inevitable.

She saw and heard him, because she reined in her horse as he sped towards her. But it was too late, already much too late.

He had halved the distance between himself and her by the time the monster burst from the forest. Then he saw it for the first time, really saw it, as it leapt into the air.

It was repulsive, a mockery of both the human form and a parody of all animals: a huge body covered in matted dark grey fur; a face like that of a dog, but with horns and long fangs; short limbs, ending in claws and talons – but it also gripped a rusty sword.

It roared as it jumped, springing up at the rider. She was leaning back, tugging on the reins, and instead of carrying her straight out of the saddle, the *thing* knocked her aside. She toppled to the ground as her terrified horse reared up and then bolted.

The monster also landed on the soft earth – but before it could turn upon its defenceless prey, he was there.

He dived upon its back, his left arm going around its neck, tugging its head upwards, and his dagger plunged into the creature's throat.

It screamed and writhed as its blood fountained from the wound.

He drove the knife into its tough hide again, then again. At each stroke, the creature screeched out its anger and its agony, and it twisted and turned, finally throwing him off.

It was far bigger than he was. Even without its blade, a single blow from one mighty paw would have crushed him.

He rolled aside as it staggered upright. One forearm went to the gash in its neck, as if trying to staunch the flow of blood. The blood was as unnatural as the being itself, a sickly yellow-green colour.

The brute stared at the wetness on its paw, seeming not to understand what it was. It opened its mouth to bellow out its rage, and more vile blood trickled from between its canine jaws. Its eyes narrowed as it stared at its tormentor, and it lurched towards him.

He felt the fetid odour of its hot breath, and he gagged. He was smaller, but he was faster. He dodged aside, avoiding the slicing sword. He had seen the blow coming.

But what he did not see was the whiplash of the creature's long, thin tail, which caught him around the ankle and dragged him to the ground. He landed with a thud, tried to roll away – but could not. The snake-like tail had him gripped tightly.

The creature had become still, glaring down at him. Its blood dripped onto his tunic, the liquid hissing as it burned like acid into the worn fabric. He wriggled and squirmed, unable to tear himself free from the snare around his foot.

The nameless predator loomed above him, its bulk blocking out the dawn sun. Trapped by its ominous shadow, he felt cold, colder than he had ever felt in his whole life, colder than he would ever feel again – because surely this was the end of his life.

All was dark. He could see nothing, nothing now and nothing ahead, nothing but the monstrous shape above him.

But he refused to surrender without a fight. Instead of trying to pull away from the tail which held him chained down, he slid through the mud towards the creature, kicking his leg forward, gaining a little bit of slack, then grabbing the slimy tail in his left hand – and hacking at it with the knife in his right.

One slash, two, three. Three more cries of agony, each louder and longer than the previous one. Then the tail was severed. Blood spurted and splashed over his hands, but he ignored the pain as the foul liquid ate into his skin.

The monster lurched towards him, its sword swinging wildly. Instead of attempting to dive away, he sprang upwards to meet it, holding his dagger in both hands – and the thing impaled itself on the point of the blade.

The knife sank into the tough hide up to its hilt, and the being's wounded scream was more agonized and fearsome than ever. It dropped its own weapon, and its razor-sharp talons clawed frantically towards him.

He weaved away, slipping beyond the reach of the creature's final clawing grab. It slammed heavily into the ground, and the whole forest seemed to shake with the impact.

It lay on its side, still and silent.

He stood several yards away, also still and silent, ready to leap away if it should so much as twitch a single muscle. Its eyes were still open, staring at him, but after a few seconds they began to glaze over.

He rubbed his hands on his clothes, trying to ease the pain of the liquid fire which had burned into his flesh.

He wondered what to do, and he glanced around warily. If there were more of the creatures near, they would soon smell the blood. They had no loyalty to their kind, and here was a feast for them.

His knife was embedded in the being's chest. He had to retrieve the weapon, but he still did not want to go too close to the monster.

HE HEARD A movement behind him, and he spun around rapidly, poised for escape. But it was only the rider, who was by now sitting up.

'My clothes!' she said. 'They're ruined!'

She was clad in rare white furs. Her coat, trousers and boots were covered in mud. Would she have preferred blood? Her own?

'Help me up!'

For the first time he wondered why he had done what he had, risking his life to save her. It was such a stupid way to behave, he thought. He had not thought, however – that was the answer.

He had acted instinctively, his body controlling his behaviour, not his mind.

'Did you hear me? Help me up!'

She was human. That was another part of the answer. All humans were allies against every other living being in the world.

'Where's my horse?'

He ignored her and stepped towards the dead creature. He had to retrieve the dagger. It was all he had.

She suddenly screamed, and he sprang back in surprise, thinking she had seen the monster move.

'Is it dead?'

She had become totally still, her eyes fixed on the thing's corpse. It seemed that she had only just noticed it.

He picked up a stick and moved closer again, prodding the creature. There was no response. It was dead. It had not the brains to pretend.

'What happened?'

The fall must have stunned her. As well as not seeing the fight, she could not remember the creature knocking her from her mount.

He heard the suction of the mud as she lifted herself up, then the squelch of her boots as she walked slowly towards him. He bent down over the creature, holding his breath because of its obnoxious stink. He seized the dagger hilt with both hands and tugged as hard as he could. It would not budge.

He turned his head for a breath of fresh air, braced his feet against the dead monster's torso, then tried again.

'What are you doing?' She moved closer for an answer to her own question.

There was a slight movement of the knife. He wrenched again. Then he felt a pair of arms around his waist, pulling him, pulling the dagger, and the blade began to slide slowly free. Suddenly it was out. They both toppled over backwards.

He prevented himself from falling and managed to retain his balance, but she let go and ended up on her back in the dirt again. He ignored her, examining the knife.

The weapon seemed undamaged. He had never used it before, not like this. He had only ever pretended, played at fighting, attacking logs and ambushing trees. But he had never risked blunting the rippled metal by cutting wood or even stabbing the point into a sapling.

He stared down at the dead creature, and he felt triumphant. He had fought with a being much bigger than himself, and he had been victorious. He leaned forward and carefully wiped his blade on the monster's dark fur. When it was clean, he tucked it into his belt.

He prodded the sword with his foot. It was chipped and corroded. He did not need it, did not want it.

Then he turned and looked at the girl. She was about twelve years old, which was his own age – or so he believed. Her hair was short and jet black, her eyes dark, her skin very pale – where it was not splattered with mud.

This time he did help her up, his bare hands around her gloved ones, and he winced as her fingers gripped his injuries.

'Oh!' she gasped, staring at the fresh wounds.

He tried to pull away, but she kept hold of his hands, then she stared into his eyes. He looked away, not meeting her gaze.

'You're the boy from the inn. They say you can't speak, but you shouted to me. It was a warning, wasn't it?'

He made no response. He tried to pull loose, but she was holding his wrists.

'Wasn't it?' she prompted.

He nodded.

'You have my eternal gratitude,' she told him. 'You saved my life.'

He shook himself free. He had to go. He had firewood to collect. He should not be here, not with her.

If his master found out, he would be beaten, beaten more than usual.

'Give me your hands!'

It was a direct command, the kind he had obeyed all his life. He held out his hands to her.

She tugged her white kidskin glooves off with her teeth, then took his right hand between hers. She was almost the same height as he was, although her hands were smaller – and warmer.

She raised his hand to her mouth, blowing between her fingers onto his sore flesh. It seemed that her palms became warmer still, heating his hand as if it were in front of a fire.

She said something, a few soft words which were too quiet for him to hear. After a few seconds, she opened her eyes and released his hand. The warmth had numbed the pain caused by the creature's venomous blood. She took his left hand and repeated her actions.

He looked down at his hands and gasped in amazement. The wounds had closed up, scar tissue had formed: they were already healing!

He stumbled back a few paces, in a way more afraid of the girl than he had been of the monster. She was as unnatural as the creature had been: she was a magician...

'Don't tell anyone,' she warned, and put the index finger of her right hand to her lips. Then she smiled. 'If you can tell anyone, I mean. You shouted a warning, but did you use any real words? Or was it just a senseless cry, like an animal? Can you speak, boy?'

'I... I speak,' he whispered.

'What?'

'I speak,' he said louder, defiantly.

He spoke to himself when he was alone in the forest, but this was the first time he had ever let anyone else know that he could do so.

Until now, the only sounds that he permitted to escape from his lips were the yells of pain when he was whipped. Not that the beatings hurt very much any more; he was used to them.

'My father will reward you,' the girl told him.

'No! Tell no one!'

'Why?'

He shook his head, not wanting to explain, not knowing how to. No one must know what had happened. His master must not find out that he had a knife, that he could speak. He glanced over at the dead creature.

'A beastman,' said the girl.

Beastman. He remembered now. That was the name the soldiers had used when they had hunted for the creatures which had slain the woodsmen.

'Part man, part beast,' she continued. 'There are all sorts of them in the Forest of Shadows, I've been told.' She glanced into the closely packed ranks of dark trees. 'I hope there aren't any more of them around.'

'None near,' he said.

'You can't be sure,' she answered, then she looked away from the woods and back at him. 'But you are sure, aren't you? You know. You knew where that one was before it could even be seen. How?'

'I saw.'

He had seen it – but she had not. That was why the creature had been able to come so close to her.

And that, he realized, was why those six tree cutters had died. They had not seen the beastmen which had stalked them through the forest. The same must have been true of all the others who had been abducted and murdered by such creatures.

She was watching him, looking into his eyes again. He glanced away, and after a moment she did the same.

'Where's my horse?' she asked.

He turned, searching for it. 'By river,' he said, pointing.

'Good,' she said. 'I'll be in real trouble if I lose that animal.' She glanced down at her mud-encrusted furs. 'I shouldn't be out here, so maybe it would be best if we both kept quiet. But what about that?' She gestured towards the corpse of the beastman.

'Soon gone,' he told her.

The creature was nothing but dead meat. Within a few hours, the bones would have been picked clean by the carrion eaters. A few hours more, and even the bones would have been devoured.

'Will you come with me to my horse?'

It was more than a question, less than an order. He nodded his agreement. She picked up her fur cap from the dirt and walked away.

He glanced at the sword. He did not want to touch it, but neither did he want to leave it there. Some other beastman would find it and use it. He tugged his sleeve down over his palm, then picked up the weapon.

He followed the girl to the river bank, then threw the blade into the middle of the river.

When they reached the grazing horse, he cupped his hands so that she could use them as a step up into the saddle. She did not move. He raised his eyes and saw that she was looking into them once more. Her gaze flickered from his left eye to his right, then back again. He stared down at the ground, waiting for her to step into his hands. She finally did and mounted her horse.

He wiped the mud from his palms on the sides of his leggings, then glanced at the scars on his hands. When he looked up at the girl, she put her finger to her lips again, bidding him to remain silent.

But he was always silent. Or had been until this morning.

Even though she was splattered with filth and mud, she seemed so poised and elegant. In comparison, he was like a beggar dressed in filthy rags – yet he supposed that was almost what he was.

'I won't forget this,' she told him. 'My father can't reward you if he doesn't know, but I can. Is there anything you need, anything you want?'

He shrugged, not knowing what to say. He had nothing, had never needed more than that. He did have his dagger, however, and that was what prompted the thought.

'Arrows,' he said. 'And bow.'

She nodded, a half smile on her pale and muddy face.

'You shall have them,' she told him. 'My name is Elyssa. What's your name?'

THEY WERE UNITED *for this single unholy mission. A mission of mayhem and of murder, of mutilation and of massacre. Allied as never before, the events of this day should be recorded in the annals of history – had there been anyone left alive to chronicle such events.*

By the time the sun had finally set on today's foul deeds, as red as the blood which stained the fields and the crops within them, the streets and the homes within them, and by the time the long shadows of night crept across the scorched earth and the smoking ruins, there would be no trace of any life in the valley below.

It would be as though the place had never existed, its inhabitants had never been born, had never lived.

The vanquished could never say what had transpired, and neither would the victors – because even the conquerors would not survive this day.

Once the common enemy was slain, it was inevitable that the marauders would turn upon each other in a frenzied feud. And then the blood would flow even more freely, more crimson and scarlet, darkly shading the midnight landscape as they slew and sacrificed one another to their own lords of Chaos.

Thus what had occurred would be completely forgotten, erased from all knowledge as absolutely as the village had been obliterated from the face of the world, its inhabitants annihilated.

No one would ever know what had been – or what might have been...

CHAPTER TWO

HE HAD NOTHING. Not even a name.

It was always 'boy!' or 'you!' or 'hey!' or 'vermin!' or 'little rat!' or some more obscene description. Names were for people who had a real home, a true family, a proper place to sleep. For those who did not live in a barn with the animals, for those who did not have to fight off the dogs for the scraps of meat from discarded bones – bones meant for the hounds. His master treated his dogs better than his 'boy'.

Names were given by parents, but parents were something else he did not have. Adolf Brandenheimer was his master, but he was sure that the innkeeper was not his father. No father would treat his son in such a fashion.

Nor could Eva Brandenheimer be his mother, for the same reason. If anything, she treated him worse then her husband did. It was she who used to chain him up with the pigs when he was a child. One of his earliest memories was of crying and of her beating him with a leather strap. The more he cried, the more she beat him.

He had learned not to cry, just as later he had become immune to punishment.

Children resembled parents, he knew, and he was glad that he looked nothing like the overweight Brandenheimers and their six fat children. Even if he had been properly fed, there would be no similarities between him and the tavern owner's family. He knew that he could not possibly be related to them.

But who were his parents? And why was he with the Brandenheimers?

Those were questions which had often puzzled him, but there was no way of discovering the answers. No one ever told him and he had no intention of asking. There had never been any reason to speak to the Brandenheimers, which was why he had never done so. To them, he was merely another of their animals, a beast of burden.

Animals did not speak; he did not speak.

Animals did not have names; he did not have a name.

MANY WEEKS PASSED, so many that he thought Elyssa had forgotten him. Their paths had crossed in the village on two or three occasions, but they had ignored one another, as they had always done previously. That was the way he assumed things would continue until he heard her horse upon the wooden bridge one cold and icy morning.

He was used to being ignored or treated with contempt by everyone else in the village. He was the lowest of the low, and she was the complete opposite – the only daughter of Wilhelm Kastring, the richest and most powerful man in the whole valley.

IT WAS PAST mid-winter, the second week of Nachexen. The sun had ceased its southward drift and slowly, inexorably, the days had begun to grow longer. On each one, as ever, he had been collecting firewood from the forest.

For him, every day was the same. He began each day by collecting wood and lighting the fires; he ended each one by making sure that the embers in every hearth had been damped down. It was all he could remember – and all that lay ahead of him.

Sometimes, however, it seemed that he had lived out his whole life in a dream. It was as though his memories were those of another person, that he had been told of his life, not experienced it.

Elyssa halted her mount once she was across the river, and she stared around. It could have been that she was out for a dawn ride, deliberately disobeying her father's wishes as she had done on the day when they first encountered one another.

He stepped into the open, even though he had not finished collecting that morning's quota of kindling. He did not call out. If she wanted him, then she would see him.

She kicked her heels into her mount's flanks and rode towards him. A minute later she reined in her horse by his side.

'I'm glad you're here,' she said.

'Always,' he told her. 'At dawn.'

'This is the first time I could get away.' There was a bundle tied to her saddle; she passed it down to him. 'These are for you.'

He unwound the linen and found a bow, a quiver, ten arrows. They were magnificent. They were the weapons of a warrior, not of a huntsman. They were meant for war, for killing enemies, not for stocking the larder with animal carcasses.

They were all black. The bow was of sleek black wood, the grip bound in soft black leather. At each tip, near the notch for the string, a golden crest was embossed in the wood. It showed two crossed arrows, and between the points was a mailed fist. Even the bowstring was black. The same gold arrows and fist design was wrought into the rippled black hide of the quiver.

He examined each of the shafts in turn, taking his time while he tried to think of something to say. They were identical. Ebony shafts, coal black feathers, heads of midnight metal. A single narrow band of gold encircled the centre of each of the yards, and the crossed arrows and clenched fist motif was etched out to show the black wood beneath.

He stared up at Elyssa. All he could do was shake his head in bewilderment. He wanted to speak, but could not find any words.

The girl was smiling as she watched him, and he noticed her gaze shift from one of his eyes to the other. He glanced away quickly, pretending to examine the perfectly matched feathers of the flights.

What could she see? It seemed as though she knew about his eyes. No one else did, so how could Elyssa? Then he remembered: she was a magician...

'They belong to my father,' she told him, as she dismounted. 'But he's never used them, he's probably forgotten that he even has them. Look at all the dust.'

She ran her fingers across the soft leather of the quiver, then showed him the dirt on her glove. He imitated her action, studying the dust on his fingertips.

'How are your hands?' she asked.

He showed her. There was no sign of the wounds which the beastman's foul blood had burned so painfully into his flesh. He had been hurt many times before, but injuries which had been much less serious had left scars that would always mark his body.

Elyssa pulled off her right glove with her teeth, and she touched the backs of his hands with her warm fingers. Her eyes were wide with wonder, as though she could not believe she had healed him. But she said nothing, and he did not ask. He preferred not to think of it.

She asked: 'What's your name?'

She had asked the same question on their first meeting, and he had not replied. This time he said: 'No name.'

'You must have a name. Everyone has a name.'

'No.'

'But what do you call yourself?'

'Me,' he said, and he laughed. It was a strange noise and he surprised himself with it. It was strange because it was a sound he had never made before. He had never had a reason to laugh until now.

Elyssa also laughed. 'I must call you something,' she said. 'Don't you want a name?'

He shrugged. He had managed so far without one. Until she had asked him several weeks ago, he had never really been aware that he had no name.

'Can I give you one?'

He looked at the bow, the quiver, the arrows. They were the first things anyone had ever given to him, and he was delighted with the gift. If Elyssa also wished to give him a name, then she could. He nodded his head.

Her horse had begun to crop at the sparse grass, and she stroked the animal's neck as she spoke.

'When I was very young I used to have a friend. Not a real friend, I've never had a real friend. He was a boy who was always there when I wanted him. But he didn't exist, not to anyone but me. I made him up. I haven't seen him for a long time.'

She paused and looked at him. 'Will you be my friend?'

He looked at her, meeting her gaze, staring into her dark eyes. He was totally in awe of Elyssa. They were exact opposites. She had everything, he had nothing. He had saved her life and she had repaid him, but why did she still want to know him? And why had he spoken to her, broken his silence for the first time?

She was a wizard. That was why. He was under her spell. She had enchanted him, and there was only one thing he could say.

'Yes,' he said.

'Then you can have the name of my friend,' she told him. 'Your name is Konrad.'

'Konrad,' he whispered, slowly speaking the two unfamiliar syllables for the first time. 'Konrad,' he said, louder, liking the sound.

It was a name he had never heard, but a name he had always known. And it was his name, his very own, the name that had been awaiting him all his life.

'Konrad!' he yelled, raising the bow in one hand, the quiverful of arrows in the other. '*Konrad!*'

THE BOW AND arrows were not as easy to hide as the dagger. He found a place for the bow and half the arrows beneath the bridge, tying them to a ledge under the timbers. He kept the other five shafts in the barn behind the inn, where they would be protected from the worst of the weather.

He did not even tell Elyssa where he had hidden them. In the beginning he was very cautious, unsure of the girl. He had never trusted anyone in his life, and at first he believed that she might betray him. She could easily tell her father that he had stolen the bow, the quiver, the arrows.

The entire village was Wilhelm Kastring's domain. The fate of everyone within the valley was in his hands. Life or death, it was Kastring's decision.

Elyssa was not meant to leave the grounds of the manor alone, without an armed guard. He was the only one who knew that she did.

If necessary, she could ensure his silence with the evidence of the black weapons.

But there was no necessity. He was always silent, except to her. Elyssa had used the word 'friend' – which was what they became, over the weeks, the months, the years...

And he became Konrad.

Only Elyssa ever used the name, of course, because no one else knew. But that was also how he thought of himself. She had given him a name, and it was as though his life had truly begun once he had his own identity.

Elyssa said that she had invented a boy called Konrad as a playmate when she was young. In a way, it was as though she had also created him, the second Konrad.

Elyssa, too, had been reborn, because without him – without Konrad – she would have had no life. Had he not slain the beastman, the creature would have stolen her life. Thanks to one another, they had both been born anew.

THE BOW WAS too big for Konrad at first, but in time he grew to match its size. He practised with the five arrows, morning after morning, targeting the trees, week after week, until he became an expert, month after month.

The first shafts became warped by the cold and damp, the points blunted by so much use, the flights damaged. But he left the other five where he had first hidden them, although he inspected them regularly, running his fingers across the wood and metal and feathers, admiring the craftsmanship which had welded the three into a single unity.

He polished the quiver, keeping the leather supple. He wondered what kind of weird creature had such skin, and he wondered about the arrow and fist design which was emblazoned on each item of the set of weapons. It was not the Kastring crest.

The animal with the weird hide must have been one of those semi-mythical beasts which existed at the far end of the world. Or perhaps even in the next valley. To Konrad, they were equally as distant.

Like his strange knife, the black leather and the unfamiliar crest were symbols of the unknown lands that lay beyond the forest, the river, the hills. The thought of such wonders both fascinated him and made him uneasy.

He began teaching himself archery by firing his arrows into tree boughs. Trees, however, did not move. He finally decided he needed a living target, to try his skills against one of the inhabitants of the forest.

A beastman was the obvious prey, but he did not want to tangle with one unless it was absolutely necessary. He knew how fortunate he had been that day long ago, managing to slay one of the tough monsters with only his dagger. There was no purpose in asking for trouble. If they left him alone, he would do the same.

Before he had the bow, he used to snare rabbits to supplement his meagre rations at the inn. Thus a rabbit became the first victim of his archery skills. As he became more proficient, he was able to shoot birds out of trees and even to hit fast-moving targets such as squirrels.

That was how he lost the first of his arrows; it vanished high in the trees and he was unable to find it despite climbing into the tallest branches.

He could have lived out in the forest, he realized. There was plenty of food, if one knew where to look. There were edible plants, birds' eggs, seeds. Even without his bow, he could trap small animals and catch fish from the river.

He preyed on the smaller creatures – but if he tried to survive out in the wilds, he would have become prey for the larger beasts that dwelled in the darkest reaches of the woodland. He killed a wild boar, the largest creature he had ever aimed at. It took two well-placed arrows to fell the beast. But before he could reach the animal, it was pounced upon by three pack wolves. They tore it apart, eating what they could, before dragging the carcass away to devour at their leisure.

That was how he lost two more arrows. All Konrad could do was watch. He was unable to move in case one of the wolves should notice him and decide he was a tastier meal. He had not even known that they were near. Could he have been so intent on stalking the boar that he had not sensed them?

The bowstring snapped several times over the years, and he renewed it, although he could not replace the black twine. Even the bow itself finally splintered and broke. It was black all the way through, not stained with some dark dye. He mourned its loss and dug a grave, burying it near the place where he had first encountered Elyssa and the beastman.

By the following dawn, some nocturnal forest creature had dug up the broken bow, searching for dead flesh. It could have found none, but there had been no sign of the black wood.

Although he was able to carve himself a new bow, he could not replace the precious arrows. The shaft of another broke, which left only one – and the five he had hidden.

He could not replace the arrows, but Elyssa could. Although they were not nearly as good as the originals, it meant that he could save the other five. He was not certain why he was saving them, but he was convinced that one day they would serve a purpose.

The seasons passed, and so did the years. Very little changed. Elyssa came to meet him at dawn every so often. Perhaps she would be there for a few consecutive days, perhaps once a week, perhaps every month or so. She told him that he was her only friend; he knew that she was his.

Her visits were the only thing he had to look forward to. He was disappointed when she did not arrive, always sad when they had to part.

She once referred to a feast at the manor house, held in honour of a neighbouring landowner. Konrad told her what he had been eating at the same time, and she had been both horrified and disgusted.

After that, she always brought him a package of food whenever they met – sweet delicacies the like of which he had never tasted, spicy meats and savoury pastries.

'Sometimes I think you prefer the food to my company,' Elyssa often joked.

'True,' he would agree.

For the first few minutes, he did not have time for much conversation; he was always too busy eating.

They talked together, because they had no one else to talk with, and they grew together. Konrad became taller with every passing month, growing from boyhood towards a man.

Elyssa was tall for a girl, but her height could never match Konrad's. Although still slim, her shape filled out as she developed into a woman.

Whenever she was with him, Konrad became less punctual about returning with the morning's firewood. He preferred to spend more time with Elyssa and risk the anger of his master. Sometimes he did not even bother taking back any kindling.

One morning he noticed the innkeeper's expression as he swore at Konrad, beating him for returning both late and empty-handed. He had always believed that his master hated him, but the look in his eyes that morning was not of hatred – it was of fear.

Until then, Konrad had still been scared of the landlord. But not any more. Brandenheimer's whip had even less effect on Konrad's broader, stronger back, and the regular beatings became little more than a meaningless routine.

Konrad knew that his life would not continue like this for ever. The past had been the same, but the future would not be.

He could not foresee what would happen, yet he was convinced that something would occur. It might not be soon, not that year, perhaps not even the one after, but he was positive that everything would change.

'I ASKED MY father about you,' said Elyssa.

No matter the time of year, Elyssa always wore a cloak. She would spread it on the ground so that her clothes did not become soiled by the dirt or stained by the grass. Dirt and

stains, however, made little difference to the castoffs that
Konrad always wore.

But this was Vorgeheim, the height of summer, and neither
of them was wearing anything. They had been swimming
together in the river, and now the morning sun was drying
their bodies.

The bow lay by Konrad's side. It could be strung in a second, an arrow notched in a second more. The beastmen were
fewer during the summer, and it was several months since he
had been aware of any in the vicinity.

Konrad watched as Elyssa continued combing out her black
hair; it had grown longer as she had grown older.

'Asked him what?' he said tensely.

'Who you were,' she replied.

Suddenly his heart was racing, as though he sensed that
there were some deadly predator lurking in the forest two
hundred yards beyond them. He grabbed the hilt of his knife,
clenching it tightly.

She glanced at him and smiled. It was one of her wicked
smiles. Elyssa had a streak of maliciousness in her character.
She could also be very capricious, her mood changing for no
apparent reason. Sometimes she came across the bridge on
her horse, then turned back before reaching him; sometimes
she did not bring any food, and she offered no explanation;
sometimes she hardly spoke a word while they were
together.

'You don't know about your past,' she told him. 'But my
father ought to. He knows everything that happens in the valley.' She studied Konrad, then added: 'Or almost everything.'

Konrad's heart pounded, and he could feel the blood puls-
ing through his veins. His body was damp, and not with river
water. Although he wanted to hear what Elyssa had discovered, equally he did not want to know.

This was something they had discussed several times, the
way that Konrad could not possibly be one of the innkeeper's
family. But who was he? No one else in the village had someone who was treated so badly, like a slave. Even Wilhelm
Kastring, the wealthiest man in the region, employed all his
servants and paid them a wage; he did not own them.

Konrad said nothing, waiting for Elyssa to continue. But she was teasing him, wanting to be prompted.

'And?' he demanded anxiously. 'What happened? What did he say?'

'He asked how I knew about you. I said I'd seen you in the village, that you were treated like some kind of animal. I wondered why and who you were.'

'What did he say?'

'He said I was to keep clear of you, that I shouldn't speak to you. I told him that you couldn't speak. When he asked how I knew, I said it was well known that you were dumb and stupid.' Her eyes sparkled with amusement.

'What else?'

Elyssa frowned, becoming serious. 'It's odd, because when I pressed him more, he was very uneasy. It was almost as if he was... scared. He didn't want to answer. He warned me again that I should avoid you.' She forced a laugh. 'I always obey my father. That's why I'm not here.'

Konrad dug his dagger angrily into the dirt. He wished that Elyssa had not asked her father, wished that she had not told him – not that she had really told him anything at all. Such lack of information was somehow worse. From his reaction, it seemed that Wilhelm Kastring did know something.

'Scared,' Elyssa had said, and that was similar to what he had seen in Adolf Brandenheimer's expression. People in the village avoided him, they always had. Could that be out of fear, not contempt?

And if so – why?

Elyssa put her hand on his arm, but he shrugged her off. 'Don't be angry,' she said. 'I wasn't expecting that kind of response from him. I'll be prepared next time. I can usually get around my father; I'm his favourite daughter.'

Elyssa was Kastring's only daughter. She had three elder brothers.

'There's more,' she added. 'The next day he asked me about the bow and quiver of arrows I gave you.'

'What? He knows?'

'No!' Elyssa shook her head rapidly. 'He doesn't know you have them. He must have gone down into the cellars looking for them. That's one of the places where I used to play. They were hidden in a small room, the only things there. The lock had rusted away, that was how I found my way in.'

'What did you say?'

'I said I didn't know what he was talking about. I didn't know anything about bows and arrows, that he should ask my brothers.' She shrugged. 'It's just coincidence.'

Konrad glanced at the last black arrow, at the tiny crest carved out of the gold band.

'Don't worry,' Elyssa said. 'He knows nothing. He'd forgotten all about them.'

'Until you mentioned me.' He shivered, and not because he was cold. She moved behind Konrad and started to comb his hair. He tried to block all thoughts of the black weapons from his mind, instead remembering when Elyssa had originally combed his hair.

That was after they had been in the river together for the first time, almost in this exact spot, downstream and out of sight of the village. It was the summer after he had saved her from the beastman.

Konrad had always hated water and avoided it, but the girl had persuaded him to shed his clothes and enter the river with her. She was always very persuasive – and still was. Because of her, he had learned to swim.

'I've not seen you without any dirt before. You're quite good looking,' she had told him that day, after they emerged from the water, then she laughed and added: 'For a peasant.' She had examined his body, running her fingers over the pale scars on his back and on his limbs. 'Was that the innkeeper? Did he do that?'

'Or his wife. Or his children.'

'These are too old for me to heal,' she said. 'I can't do that – yet.'

He looked at the girl, waiting for her to continue, but she simply smiled and put her index finger to her lips, then reached for her comb.

She dragged the comb through his knotted hair. It was the first time it had ever been combed. She was treating him like a doll, he realized, like her imaginary Konrad. But he did not

mind. He enjoyed every moment of her company. For the first
time in his life he was not alone, and every dawn he hoped
for her return.

When they parted that day, he rolled in the filth, tangling
his hair and dirtying his face. He had not wanted his master
to know that anything out of the ordinary had happened.

Nowadays, however, he returned to the tavern neat and
clean, although still clad in rags. He no longer cared. There
was nothing that Brandenheimer could do to him that he
could not take.

That day on the riverbank was also when Elyssa first mentioned his eyes. He had been aware of her looking at them on
several occasions, and he had always turned away.

'You have the strangest eyes, Konrad,' she had said.

Immediately he had shielded them with his hands, even
though it was a futile gesture. It was far too late – and she was
a wizard, she could see through his hands.

'You shouldn't hide them,' she said, tugging his protective
palms away.

'What do you know about my eyes?' he asked, pressing his
face closer to hers than ever before, staring deep into her dark
eyes – almost as black as her hair, as black as the arrows she
had given him. 'What can you see?'

'What can you see?' she echoed.

'Nothing!' he asserted, closing his eyes as tightly as he
could. 'Everything,' he whispered.

She had never referred to his eyes again.

Until today. Everything was exactly the same. Almost. The
time, the place. All that had changed was them. They had
both grown, physically as well as emotionally. They were
closer than ever, knew the other better than they did anyone
else. But they were also further apart, aware of how separate
they were in all things except their friendship.

'You have the strangest eyes, Konrad,' said Elyssa. Again.

In so saying, she broke their unspoken pact. He had never
mentioned her magic, the minor feats of wizardry that she
could perform with such apparent ease, and she had never
mentioned his eyes – or, more particularly, his left eye.

His blind eye.

No one would *ever know what had been – or what might have been.*

The future of the whole world lay in a combination of minor factors, all relatively trivial when compared to the greater whole. But each of these insignificant elements comprised a part of the overall scheme of things, and few could say which would prove more important in the centuries to follow.

After today, the world would continue on its ordained path towards the ultimate triumph of Chaos. Another obstacle on that glorious route would have been eradicated as surely as the village itself had been totally eliminated.

Most of the attackers knew not what the effect of their raid would be or why it should occur, neither did they care. For the vast majority, all that mattered was the conflict itself – the battle that was to come.

Even if it were no real battle, but more akin to the gory work of a butcher in a slaughterhouse, it made no difference. The end result was the same: pain and agony, torture and death. Death of one's enemies, one's allies, one's self, all were aspects of the same eternal war.

The one certainty in life was ultimate death, and in this the brutal invaders would not be disappointed. They lived for death – and they must die...

CHAPTER THREE

KONRAD COULD NOT see what Elyssa could see, what everyone else could see. He could not see his own face, his own eyes.

That was what she had meant by him having strange eyes. She was referring to their appearance, although she may also have meant more. Elyssa's own dark eyes were deep whirlpools, and with them she could see far more than she ever told him – just as he could see far more than he had ever revealed to her.

The following day Elyssa returned, and she brought a mirror. She came soon after dawn, as ever. There was seldom anyone else around so early, at least in this vicinity.

The area where the beastman had been killed was now in a clearing, the forest having been pushed back over the years by the tree cutters and woodsmen.

Elyssa and Konrad met further away from the bridge, where there was less chance of them being observed by anyone from the village.

'You've never seen yourself, have you?' she said, as she gazed at her own image in the mirror. She pushed a lock of jet black hair away from her forehead, over her left ear. 'Here.'

She held the mirror towards him. 'But be careful, I don't want your ugly face cracking the glass!'

He was not really listening to her words. All his attention was focused on the thing she held in her hands. It was oval in shape, framed by what seemed to be a silver border. Even the handle and backing were of silver, studded with glittering red and yellow pieces of tiny glass. He saw the sky reflected in the smooth glass as she offered him the handle.

'What?' he said, not accepting.

'It was a joke.' She pushed the mirror towards him even more.

'A joke?' He drew back further, shaking his head.

'An ugly face is supposed to break glass.'

The mirror must have been worth a fortune. The red and yellow decorations were not glass, he realized, but some kind of precious stones. Silver and jewels – and all so that Elyssa could look at herself.

'You're scared, aren't you? Scared, scared, scared!'

In a way, Elyssa was right, but Konrad refused to admit it. He grabbed the handle, then slowly raised the face of the mirror to his own face, not knowing what to expect.

He had first seen his reflection in the surface of the river. That gave him no true idea of his appearance, or – more importantly – of the way that his eyes appeared. As far as he could tell, they were the same, but it was difficult to be sure when only his right eye could truly see anything.

The polished surface of a soldier's shield, several years ago, had been of no more help. It served more to distort his features than to define them.

Glass itself was a rarity. There was no such thing as a mirror in the tavern, or probably anywhere else in the whole village except at the manor house. He had only heard the word from Elyssa, and her mirror must have been fabricated in some distant land.

Konrad looked at himself for the first time.

He gasped in surprise, blinking at the young stranger who blinked back at him. The first thing he noticed was the mane of untamed hair, neither fair nor red, but somewhere in between. He had held clumps of his hair in his hands previously, when it grew too long and he had cut it with his knife, but this was the first time he had seen himself – or anyone – with hair of such a colour.

He glanced over the top of the mirror and noticed Elyssa grinning at him.

He raised the mirror to hide her from view, bringing it closer towards his face – towards his eyes.

They looked identical, no different, both pupils pale green. But the early morning sun was behind him, the mirror reflecting red into both his dilated irises, and he shifted his position so that he was no longer dazzled by the bright rays of light.

As he moved the mirror, as his pupils widened, he saw that one of them became darker, more green, while the other became lighter, yellower – turning into gold...

His eyes were different colours.

One was gold. One was green. That was what Elyssa must have meant by him having strange eyes.

But one could see. And one could not.

He was holding the mirror in his right hand, and he raised the fingers of his left to his eyes. His image did the same. He touched the skin beneath his left eye. But his reflection did not – it touched the skin below his image's right eye. He frowned.

Elyssa had been watching this, and she laughed. He caught a glimpse of her reflection as she moved around behind him. She stood on tiptoe and leaned over his right shoulder, and he saw her face by his face.

It was different somehow, not an accurate picture of the way she looked. She was like her own twin, whose hair was swept back over her right ear instead of her left.

And although she stood to his right, her image was on the left of his image...

He saw her reflection smile, watched as her lips mouthed the words that he heard in his right ear: 'It's a mirror image, Konrad. Left isn't left, right isn't right. I don't look like that, not exactly, and you don't look like that, not exactly. Watch.'

She moved to his other side, from right to left. But her image switched from the left side of the reflection to its right side.

'What you see in the mirror as your left,' she explained, 'is really your right.' The image of her eyes met his. 'And what you see as your right is really your left.'

He had one good eye. One blind eye. One of his eyes was gold. One was green. But which was which? He looked away from Elyssa's image, instead concentrating on his own reflection, trying to work out what he could see.

He saw a young man in his late teens, the stranger who already seemed familiar, who looked perplexed more than worried – and who had eyes of different colours.

Konrad could only see properly out of his right eye, and so he gradually closed his left. It was the gold eye that his image slowly shut, although it seemed it was the right one.

That was a distortion caused by the glass, he now knew. He could not trust the mirror, but he could trust the evidence of his right eye, his green eye.

With only one eye open, he could see exactly the same picture in the mirror as he had been able to with both eyes open. That was what he had anticipated. The right eye was his one good eye. He could see nothing with his left because whenever he closed his right, it was as though he shut both eyes. Almost.

'See?' said Elyssa.

He saw her. He saw himself. He nodded, and he saw his image nod. He opened his other eye, saw it glint golden.

He knew that his eyes were different, although he had never imagined that they would appear different in such a way. At first glance, the green and the gold were not that dissimilar; but on closer inspection, the difference was readily apparent.

Elyssa was the only person ever to have mentioned this, which was only to be expected. She was the only person ever to have spoken with him, instead of at him, the only person ever to have looked at him long enough to have noticed the apparent difference.

Then he closed his right eye. And, as ever, it was like closing them both. He could see nothing, nothing that was happening *now*...

In the darkness there was a brief glimmer of light, faint and distant. If he concentrated, focused his left eye, his golden eye, his blind eye, he could make out an outline. It was an oval, the shape of the mirror that he still held. And within the mirror was the refection of a face.

What he saw, he realized, was the image that he still held in his brain. It was the last thing he had seen. The mirror. Within it a face staring back at him, both eyes open. Two different eyes, one green, one gold.

But it was the face of someone else!

It was an older man, his face lined and bloody, shadowed and bearded. It was a face that Konrad had never seen before, yet it was a face that he could not fail to recognize.

It was his own face. He was staring at himself as he would be many years from now.

He was staring into the future.

'No!' he yelled, squeezing both his eyes further shut to dispel the image, then opening them wide, catching a brief glimpse of his own – young – reflection in the glass, before hurling the mirror as far away from him as possible.

He heard the glass shatter then Elyssa cry out in anger and disbelief, felt the blow against the side of his head as the girl hit him as hard as she could with the palm of her hand, saw her hurry over to where the mirror had landed and begin picking up the scattered fragments of fractured glass, all the time yelling at him.

Konrad was aware of exactly what was going on, but he felt completely removed from it all, as though it were happening at some other time – as though he were remembering.

Remembering what had happened.

Or what was yet to happen...

ELYSSA HELD THE unbroken mirror in her lap, and they sat side by side on the riverbank, near to one another, but not as near as they usually sat.

It was as though she had just arrived and was about to show him the silver mirror, that none of the events of several minutes ago had happened – yet.

He felt totally confused, his mind and his senses completely mixed up. Past, present and future seemed inextricably intertwined, and he could not tell which was which.

He knew exactly what would happen. But that was because it had already happened. This was now. There would be no repeat. Elyssa had shown him the mirror, and he had thrown it away.

He preferred not to consider what had occurred in between, when he had stared into the mirror and seen the reflection of himself – the image of his future self.

The mirror had broken. But Elyssa had found every shard of glass, fitted them all back within the silver frame, then rubbed her hands across the splintered surface, her fingertips becoming red with blood as she smoothed away the roughness, all the time whispering enchantments.

Although he was vaguely aware of what she was doing, there had been too much else on Konrad's mind. He had been thinking about his left eye: his golden eye, his blind eye. His blind eye that could see, that could tell him what was going to happen – and that had done so for most of his life.

The minutes dragged by while his respiration and heartbeat slowed almost to normal. He felt calmer now, no longer on the verge of panic.

Elyssa had said nothing to him directly since cursing him for throwing away the mirror. She must have realized that something serious had occurred for Konrad to have behaved in such a manner.

She looked down into the mirror, either studying her own reflection or else checking that the glass showed no sign of damage, then glanced over at Konrad. Their eyes met for the first time since they had looked at each other's image in the mirror.

'It was only a joke about your face breaking the glass, I told you that,' she said. 'You didn't have to take me at my word. Too much of a shock, was it, seeing yourself?' she added, and she smiled ironically.

He shook his head slowly, put his hands over his eyes and rubbed them, while he wondered what to say.

'What did you see?' asked Elyssa.

He stared at her. She could not have been referring to his own image. How did she know he had seen something strange? Then he realized that she was guessing.

His vision was a subject they had never spoken about, no matter how important it was to him. He kept it within himself, partly because he did not understand, partly because he did not want Elyssa to know. It was something he could do, a talent he had which she did not possess – and which it seemed no one else did. In a way, it was the one thing that he had of his own. He did not want to share it with her, and he was unsure why.

She was his only friend, they ought to have been able to talk about anything and everything. They never discussed her wizardry, however, although she did not mind him knowing of her talents.

He glanced at her fingertips. He was unsure whether she had cut herself on the broken glass, or whether the spilled blood was the price for the magic she had expended to repair the mirror.

Just as she kept her skills to herself, so it was with what he could do.

There was another factor: even after all this time, he still did not fully trust Elyssa. He had no evidence for this belief, and such a notion was beyond any reasoning. She was the one person in the world that he knew, had total faith and confidence in, would have done anything for – yet there was an almost infinitesimal trace of suspicion.

He had not wanted to open up to her fully, because then she would know everything about him and would have a hold over him.

The idea made no sense, he knew, but rationality and feeling could not be reconciled.

And it was all to do with his eyes, or one of them. It seemed that his left eye was blind – yet he could still see from it. See not what was happening *now* but what *would* happen...

Most of the time there was hardly any difference, his left eye was ahead of his right – ahead of what was actually happening – by a fraction of a second.

That was how he had been able to avoid Brandenheimer's boot or his whip. He knew where it would strike an instant before it did, and thus he had been able to avoid the full force of every blow.

He noticed Elyssa was studying herself in the mirror again. As she did so, she idly licked the blood from her fingers.

By now, he was beginning to doubt that there had been any different image in the mirror. It must have been a trick of the light – except that there had been no light, because his eyes were shut. Then it must have been a trick of his eyes.

He could not possibly have seen his future self; he had never been able to foresee anything further ahead than a minute. He refused to believe it, therefore it could not have happened.

He would not tell Elyssa what he had mistakenly thought he had seen, but he had to say something.

'I'd never seen my eyes before,' he told her. 'I didn't know they were a different colour. That was what surprised me. I didn't mean to break the mirror. I didn't know glass was so easy to break.'

She was watching him, and he could tell from her expression that she did not believe him. The best way to convince her was to tell the truth, up until a point.

'When I close my right eye,' he explained, 'my left eye becomes blind. When my right eye is open, I can see out of my left – but what I see isn't precisely the same. I don't see what *is* happening, but what *will* happen.'

'You have the gift of foresight? You can see the future?'

Konrad shrugged. 'I suppose so, but it isn't any great talent. At best, I know what will happen within a few seconds, perhaps even a minute, which means I can act accordingly.'

'That's what happened when we first met? You *saw* the beastman?'

'I knew it was lurking in the forest. When you rode up, I realized that you didn't know it was there, you couldn't see it like I could. I'd already watched it spring out of the trees and knock you from your horse. Then I saw it happen again a few moments later. Luckily, it didn't kill you with its leap.'

'That was because you warned me.'

Konrad shrugged. 'Possibly.'

'Can you *see* anything now?'

'Nothing.' He shook his head. 'Nothing any different, I mean. I can see you sitting there, that's all.' He stared beyond the girl, at the forest. 'There's no danger.'

'So it's danger that you sense? You can see if something dangerous is about to happen, and you can stop it?'

'I can't stop it. I can see what will happen, and I can make the best of it. If there's a wild animal near, I can avoid it. I know which route it will take, and so I choose another path.'

Elyssa was correct: he could see danger. It might be relatively trivial, such as the angle of the stick with which Adolf Brandenheimer was about to thrash him. Or it might be far more important. This was what had saved his life so many times in the forest.

And sometimes it had almost killed him.

He could not rely on his foresight, because he had been let down on two vital occasions. The first was when he had fought with the beastman that had attacked Elyssa. It was as if he had suddenly become blind, because he did not know what the creature was going to do next, which way it would strike.

His right eye had told him what was happening now, but his left had told him nothing. Everything had become black, the future consisted of an empty void – and he thought he was going to die. It appeared that he had seen no future because there was no future for him to see.

He had not died. Instead, it was the beastman that had been killed. In a way, the most frightening aspect of the fight had been his sudden blindness to what was about to happen.

The second time was when he had killed the wild boar. The creature had then been pounced upon by three pack wolves – and yet he had no idea that the wolves were in the vicinity. He had almost fallen victim to the three predators.

It was danger that extended his range of vision. But too much seemed to overload his senses, making him as vulnerable as anyone else.

His foresight could only be measured in seconds – until today, when he had seen many years ahead.

Elyssa was still watching him, waiting for him to continue, to tell her what he had seen in the mirror.

He had been confused, astonished at seeing his own reflection for the very first time. That was all. He had seen nothing else, because there was nothing to see.

'If you can only see danger,' said Elyssa, 'then you don't know what's going to happen next...'

KONRAD STARED AT her, wondering what she meant. Her face was totally expressionless as she put the mirror down on the grass behind her.

She leaned forward and unfastened one of her sandals, kicking it towards him. It landed by his side. Then she untied the other one, and sent that flying through the air at him. Konrad caught the leather sandal before it could hit his chest.

She was wearing a silk blouse and a long velvet skirt. The pale blue blouse was fastened by a series of ribbons. One by one, she slowly undid each of them, alternating her left hand and her right, working her way down from her neck to her waist.

The front of her blouse hung loose, and Konrad glimpsed her breasts as she stood up. There was a narrow silver belt around her waist, but it was there purely as an ornament, because her turquoise skirt was secured by a bow at the hip. She undid the bow.

The garment consisted of a single piece of fabric that was wrapped twice around the lower half of her body – and Elyssa began to unwrap it.

Facing him, she gradually unfolded her skirt until her left leg was bare from waist to ankle. Her left hand rested on her hip, holding both edges of the garment. Then she lifted her hand, letting it fall free. As she did so, she spun around until her back was to him.

She glanced at Konrad over her shoulder. All she wore was her blue blouse, which she slowly peeled down over her arms and allowed to drop to the ground.

He had seen her naked many times before, but never like this. She had always pulled off her clothes as quickly as possible, never so teasingly.

Very slowly, she turned to face him. All she wore was her jewellery – the silver necklace and belt, and the matching bracelets around her wrists and ankles. Otherwise, she was completely nude.

She stood with her hands on her hips, her legs astride. What always amazed Konrad was how pale Elyssa's long-limbed body was. Apart from the jet black of her hair and the soft pink of her nipples, her body was completely white.

He licked at his dry lips as he gazed at the girl. 'You want to go for a swim?' he said.

She shook her head. She raised her right hand, beckoning to him with her index finger.

Konrad obeyed. He stood up and walked forward, stopping in front of her. Elyssa lifted her other hand, and she tugged at Konrad's ragged shirt. It came off easily, except that the sleeve became caught on his right wrist because he was still holding her leather sandal. Elyssa took the sandal, cast it aside, pulled the shirt free, then reached for the string that held up his old breeches.

They stood a foot apart, staring into each other's eyes. Elyssa's were so dark that it was hard to tell where the pupil became the iris.

Konrad's breeches dropped around his ankles. He was even more naked than Elyssa; he wore no silver. 'Are you sure you don't want to go for a swim?' he managed to ask.

Elyssa's face showed the first flicker of movement: she smiled for a moment. 'There's something else I want,' she said, and she leaned towards him.

Konrad gasped in surprise and pleasure. They had often touched each other before, but only by accident or in play. This was completely different. As she held him, he moved slightly nearer, and he lifted his hands to Elyssa's breasts. As he gently caressed them, he remembered the first time he had touched her soft female flesh.

A few years ago, she had asked him to teach her archery. He had stood behind her, showing her how to hold the bow and arrow. While he did, her budding breasts had pushed against his arms. He had rubbed himself against her, hoping she would not notice. But she had – and when he drew away, she had pressed herself up against him, urging him to hold her tighter. Since then, they had come into physical contact many times, either clothed or nude. Sometimes it had been in fun, but lately such encounters had become more serious.

They kissed.

They had kissed before, although never like this. Until now, their lips had merely brushed lightly together when they said farewell. But suddenly their mouths were locked eagerly together.

Elyssa's lips parted, and he felt her wet tongue against his lips. Konrad opened his mouth, his own tongue darting out to meet hers.

Their bodies were pressed as close as their lips. They were in contact from head to toe, trying to hold each other even nearer. Elyssa's naked body felt warmer than the heat from the sun, and Konrad was unable to tell if it was her racing heartbeat that he could feel or his own.

Simultaneously, they both pulled away, panting for breath. They gazed at each other for several seconds. There was no need for words. They both smiled, then sank down to the ground.

Elyssa lay upon her satin cloak, and Konrad lay upon her.

They melted together, becoming as one.

KONRAD GAZED UP at the clear blue sky; Elyssa was stretched out on her side, watching him. He chewed a stalk of grass and tried not to smile.

Elyssa picked up the mirror and caught the reflection of the sun, shining it in Konrad's eyes.

He put his hand in front of his face, trying to block out the dazzling light, and he turned to look at her. He could not see her very well because of the brightness of the mirror, but it seemed that she was staring at him with an expression he did not recognize. Then he noticed that it was more than her expression which was unfamiliar.

Just as Konrad had seemed to see his older self in the mirror a while ago, for an instant it was as if he were observing another Elyssa. No longer a girl, she had become a woman. Her mischievous features were twisted, exaggerated into a malevolent stare.

And he saw more than that. Worse than that...

He looked away immediately, squeezing his eyes tightly shut, but it was too late.

Absolute love had turned to total hatred.

The paradise of the present had become tomorrow's hell.

Konrad did not need his eyes to know the future, did not need a silvered mirror to foresee what would be. Even without them, he was aware that his only friend would some day betray him and cause his ultimate destruction.

THE ONE CERTAINTY in life was ultimate death, and in this the brutal invaders would not be disappointed. They lived for death – and they must die.

Today everyone and everything must die. The victors would themselves become victims when ally turned upon ally.

There would be no mistakes, as there had been two and a half thousand years ago.

That day there was a survivor, and because of this one oversight the inevitable ascendancy of Chaos had been delayed.

The one who had escaped was named Sigmar – Sigmar Heldenhammer, who had founded the Empire...

CHAPTER FOUR

THE DAYS OF summer were longer than those of winter, which meant that Konrad worked more hours at this time of year. In winter, he was usually up before the sun because he needed all the time there was. In summer, he sometimes slept on a few extra minutes.

As ever, he spent his nights in one of the barns behind the inn, lying among the straw which would become the fodder for the livestock. At least he did not have to eat grass and hay; it was about the only thing that he did not share with the animals.

He lay still for a while, staring up through the cracks in the roof, watching as the sky lightened. He was thinking about what Elyssa had told him last year, about her father being worried that the black bow and arrows had gone missing. She had not mentioned this since, and he was unsure what had reminded him of the subject.

He yawned and sat up, gazing over to the far side of the barn, to where he kept the quiver and arrows. It was several weeks since he had checked them. He clambered down from the loft, pulled the ladder away and set it up against the opposite wall. Then he climbed again, up into the rafters, hauled himself onto one of the beams and worked his way along to the strut where the quiver was tied.

It was still in the same piece of linen in which it had been wrapped when Elyssa gave it to him, all those years ago. He sat down, balancing himself on the beam, and loosened the package from its hiding place.

As he untied the final knot, he paused, listening, *seeing*…

THERE WAS A rider approaching.

Elyssa?

He caught a glimpse of her, also, a distant vision. But the first rider was someone else, a stranger. A dangerous stranger…

There had to be great danger for Konrad to have become aware of the newcomer and for him also to have been conscious of Elyssa's whereabouts.

She was about to leave the grounds of the manor house, to head across the bridge to meet up with Konrad. But if she came this way, as she must, she would instead encounter the other rider.

Without needing to think, Konrad had already acted. He was down the ladder, rushing across the barn and out of the side door. He did not need to look around to know that the stranger was less than a hundred yards away, approaching the well in the central square.

Konrad sprinted through the empty village, along the cobbled street which led up to the manor.

He had not seen the horseman intercept Elyssa; it was only an assumption. But he was between them now, he could head off the girl, and the two riders would not meet.

He heard hooves on the cobbles. They were ahead of him. Elyssa's horse. He had not heard the stranger's horse yet, he realized. The newcomer was too far away to be heard, still too far away to be seen with normal vision.

Elyssa was just ahead of him, reaching the first of the cottages at the bend on the incline. He dashed around the corner, seeing her, really seeing her for the first time.

She reined in her mount as soon as she noticed him.

'Back!' he called, trying not to shout too loud in case the intruder should hear.

'What is it?'

He grabbed her horse's bridle with his left hand, and for the first time he noticed that he was still carrying the linen bundle which contained the quiver and five black arrows. He tugged at the animal's head, trying to turn it.

'You've got to get out of sight,' he warned, his breath coming in short bursts. He looked back over his shoulder and saw – nothing.

He saw the curve in the street, the houses on either side. The rider was not in view yet and should not have been for several seconds, but Konrad was unable to tell where the horseman would be when he appeared.

It was as if he had vanished. He had not, that was impossible, but this was further evidence of the extreme danger that the intruder presented – like the time with the beastman, the time with the pack wolves, the two previous occasions when Konrad's talent had deserted him.

'Come on!'

Elyssa did not question him or argue. She recognized the look of anxiety in his face. She held out her hand, reaching down to him. Konrad took it, pulling himself up behind her. She spun the horse, kicking her heels into its flanks. They galloped up the hill, towards the walls of the manor. The shod hooves seemed very noisy in the still morning air.

Konrad glanced anxiously back, yet there was still nothing to be seen, nothing to be heard, no sign that there was anything amiss.

He tried to picture what he had seen. A single rider, the dawn sun glinting from the bronze armour which completely covered him.

Even the horse was totally hidden by its own matching armour.

Elyssa's steed reached the manor. The drawbridge was down, the wooden gates stood open and they rode in. The manor was not designed as a fortress. The bridge was little more than an ornament. Even if it could have been raised, the narrow moat would provide little obstacle to any determined attackers. The gates could easily have been battered down, the walls breached.

Konrad had never been inside the grounds of the residence before. It was forbidden territory to most of the peasants. At the moment, he preferred to be there than to be outside.

He leapt from the back of the horse, then ran behind one of the gates while Elyssa dismounted and tied up her horse out of sight.

The rider was finally in view, unhurriedly coming up the centre of the narrow road towards the manor. His mount's hooves made not a sound upon the cobbles. He rode closer and closer in total silence. It was as if the whole world had become quiet.

There was nothing to be heard anywhere in the village: no dog barked, no animal in any of the barns made a sound. Beyond the village, there was not even the cry of a bird or a wild beast in the distant forest.

'Who is he?' whispered Elyssa, by his side.

'I don't know.' He kept his voice as low as hers. The knight was too far away to hear them, but it would have seemed unnatural to break the eerie silence.

'He's like a ghost.'

Konrad shivered. She was exactly right, he realized. It was as if both rider and horse were dead, because surely no living creatures could move with such absolute quiet.

He had five arrows, but no bow. Even with a bow, he would not have been tempted to shoot at the rider. His extra sight had sensed danger, but what use was an arrow against a supernatural entity?

'Should I call my father? Summon the guards?'

Konrad shook his head. That would be futile.

As the horseman came closer, Konrad could see more detail. Rider and steed were clad in matching plated armour, all of burnished bronze. The armour was elaborately wrought, the helmet patterned with intricate designs. There was the narrowest slit in the visor to give vision for the eyes within – if there were any eyes within.

It seemed that he was mounted upon some fantastic beast, whose carapace was of shining metal. The head of the horse, if such it was – could any horse carry the weight of so much metal as well as its armoured rider? – the animal's head, was protected by a helmet from which protruded two long spikes, just above the eye slot.

Similarly, a double spike emerged from the crown of the knight's helmet, making the wearer also resemble some horned beast. There were more spikes at the knuckles and knees, toes and elbows. The armour was damaged in a few places, dented and buckled, showing signs of previous combat.

The rider carried a circular shield, bronzed, with a heavy central spike. A sword hung at his side, bronze handled, scabbarded in bronze. He also carried a long war lance, also of bronze, held vertically in one gauntleted and spiked fist.

'What does he want?' asked Elyssa.

The rider's head had been slowly turning from side to side as he approached the manor. Not out of caution, because it seemed that he had nothing to fear, but because he appeared to be taking in every detail of his surroundings. He halted on the other side of the drawbridge, and he looked directly at where Konrad and Elyssa were hiding.

He could not possibly see them, but Konrad felt the stranger's eyes on him – and it seemed as though he had come here for Konrad, that was the sole reason for his incursion.

'I'm not frightened of him,' said Elyssa. There was no bravado in her voice. She meant exactly what she said, which made Konrad feel even more nervous.

She stepped forward, and he hurriedly grabbed hold of her, pulling her back behind the ancient wooden door.

'I want to talk to him!' she protested.

He put his hand over her mouth to silence her. 'But he doesn't want to talk to us. That isn't why he's here.'

She shook her head free. 'How do you know? You don't know anything! You're just a stupid peasant!'

He stared at her, not because of what she had said. Her words meant nothing. But for a moment he had caught a distant glimpse within her dark eyes, a glimpse beyond her anger, beyond this moment.

He *saw*...

He saw death. Real death. Elyssa's death.

For an instant, less than the blink of an eye, he had witnessed Elyssa totally devoid of life, robbed of the essence of
being. It was more than death, it was worse than death, it was
a descent into the deepest abyss of ultimate despair and
depravity.

Involuntarily, he loosened his grip. It was as though he did
not wish to touch Elyssa for fear of contaminating himself,
that he might also become a victim.

He closed both his eyes, hoping to erase all memory of the
brief but absolutely horrifying image – but knowing even
now that he could never succeed. The vision might fade with
time, but it would live with him forever. The memory would
live on, but Elyssa would not.

She had sprung away and into the open, and he heard her
call out: 'What do you want? Who are you looking for?'

Konrad rushed after Elyssa, drawing his knife to protect her
from the rider. It was a futile gesture, he knew. He could not
save the girl from the knight as easily as he had rescued her
from the beastman so many years ago.

Even as he leapt out, he saw that he was not needed. The
stranger had turned and was riding slowly back down the hill.
The armour rattled and squeaked, the hooves clattered on the
cobbles. Horse and mount were not ghosts, thought Konrad,
as he watched them vanish through the deserted village. Then
he turned to look at Elyssa.

The stranger was not dead, but Elyssa soon would be.

He was leaving. Konrad had no idea where he could go, but
he could not stay in the village any longer.

He had been considering the idea for some time, prompted
by various reasons. He was going because he could no longer
stay, and today's events were the deciding factor.

It was very rare for a stranger to arrive in the village. It was
not on any trading route or major highway, even the river was
not navigable, it was too narrow and treacherous. Nobody
ever passed through. The only people who arrived came
solely to visit the village itself, and there were very few of
them.

Today all that seemed to have changed. The knight was like no visitor, and he had not stayed. After riding through the village, as if conducting a tour of inspection, the horseman had withdrawn.

It seemed as though his arrival and departure had gone completely unnoticed except by Konrad and Elyssa. Konrad had believed that everyone in the village was hiding away from the stranger, and he expected they would appear once the bronze knight had gone. Instead, the morning was no different from any other.

It was no different for the rest of the village – but very different for Konrad. For the first time that he could remember, he did not set off for the forest to collect firewood for the inn – because he would never return there again.

By chance, he had already collected the quiver and five arrows.

But was it chance? It was the arrival of the stranger which had caused him to keep hold of the linen bundle; and it was the arrival of the stranger that had finally spurred him to quit the village.

The quiver and arrows were almost all he owned, all he needed. The few coins he had been given or found over the years were no longer buried near the tavern. He had changed their hiding place, and they were now tied under the wooden bridge, along with his bow and the other arrows that Elyssa had given him.

'You shouldn't be here,' Elyssa had said, once the knight had disappeared from their sight.

She looked back, anxiously gazing towards the manor house. There was no sign of anyone else. He had never expected that the place would be like this. He had imagined there would be armed guards posted on the walls, at the gates, that whenever Elyssa came to meet him she somehow escaped via a secret passageway.

Perhaps sentries always patrolled the grounds – on every day except this. Today, like the villagers, they were all hidden away in fear of the strange horseman.

Konrad did not really know. He knew very little about Wilhelm Kastring and where he lived, and Elyssa rarely spoke about her father or her home. Kastring was the most important person in the whole village, and so Konrad had assumed that the manor house would be like a fortress. Until today, he had only seen the house and its walled grounds at a distance.

It was the largest building he had ever seen, built totally of stone. Even the roof was tiled, not thatched like most of the village. There were several smaller buildings within the grounds of the manor, and even the least of them was built of brick, far more substantial than most of the other village constructions.

'Then I'll go,' Konrad replied.

He had dropped his quiver when he had let go of Elyssa a few minutes previously, and now he picked up the linen-wrapped bundle. He noticed she was watching him.

'Remember this?' he asked

She nodded. 'My father will kill you if he knows you have it.'

'How will he know?'

Konrad looked at her. She appeared no different from the way she always had. Or almost always had. A few minutes ago he had visualized her as being dead, or worse than dead. Last year, he remembered, his mind had filled with a vision of how she would appear when she was older – and when she would betray him.

The two images were incompatible. Elyssa must either die or grow older, she could not do both. In either case she could betray him, but her treachery would be over nothing so trivial as a black quiver and a few arrows with a strange gold emblem.

Konrad could trust no one, nothing, not even his own perceptions. That was why he must leave, although by leaving he could not avoid his own senses.

Elyssa did not reply, and Konrad turned away. He walked through the wooden gates, over the drawbridge, and started to make his way down towards the village. The main street would lead him to the bridge, then across the river. There was a route beyond the bridge, through the forest. It was only a dirt track, but it must lead somewhere.

He did not look back. A few seconds later, there was no need, because he heard Elyssa's horse following. She rode far enough behind so that it did not appear they were together – although Konrad was unsure whether they were together or not.

The village was beginning to come alive at last, doors and shutters opening, people moving around. Barn doors stood ajar, and animals were being herded out into the fields. Now that it was daytime, there was less danger from the predators that lurked within the woods. Guarded by the herdsmen, the cattle and the sheep could feed in relative safety.

Konrad passed near to the tavern, but the building was still and silent. The inn was the last place in the village to sleep at night, the last to blow out the candles and oil lamps, and it was always the last to awaken each morning.

When he reached the bridge over the river, he clambered beneath and retrieved his bow, his arrows, his money.

They reached the place where they usually met, and Elyssa dismounted, spreading her latest cloak on the ground.

Konrad sat down nearby. There was only one reason for him to share Elyssa's cloak. And this was not the day for that.

'I've no food for you,' she said. 'The cook has disappeared. No one has seen him since yesterday. My father is very angry and has been complaining ever since about the awful meals that he's been served.'

Konrad had often seen the cook buying provisions in the village. He was an odd looking person, very small and round. It was only recently that Konrad had discovered why he looked so strange: he was a halfling, the only non-human in the village.

'Who was he?' Elyssa asked, after a while, and it was obvious she was not referring to the cook at the manor house.

'That's what I was going to ask you.'

'Perhaps we would know the answer if you'd let me speak to him.'

'You think you'd have been given a reply?'

Elyssa shrugged. 'I didn't mean what I said. About you being a stupid peasant.'

He glanced at her, and their eyes met for the first time since they had left the manor house. Her eyes were as dark and enigmatic as ever, but they sparkled with life, not death.

'Even if you are!' she added.

He grabbed her foot, pulled, and she fell onto her back. They both laughed, and suddenly all the tension between them was gone. They were friends again, the way they usually were.

Elyssa sat up, then said: 'I'm getting married.'

'What?'

'You heard. I'm getting married. I've known for a while, but I didn't mention it before because I didn't want to think about it.'

'Who are you marrying?'

'Someone my father knows. He lives in Ferlangen. He owns Ferlangen.'

Konrad had heard the name. Ferlangen was the nearest town, or so he believed, but he was not sure how far away it was or in what direction it lay.

'So,' Elyssa added, 'it looks as though I'll be seeing some of the world at last.'

He was sure she suspected that he planned to leave, because it was a subject that she had often mentioned. She had frequently urged him to go, saying that if she was in his position she would have quit the village without hesitation.

He had no family, she often said, no reason to stay. He owed nobody anything. Why did he not simply leave? If she were a man, she would have gone long ago. But it was different for her because she was a girl, she argued, and because of who she was.

Now that he intended to take Elyssa's advice, he was unsure whether or not to tell her. Having made up his mind to go, he did not want her to dissuade him. She had suggested the idea when there was no likelihood that he would depart. In a way, it was as though she were trying to foist her own ambitions upon Konrad. But he knew how changeable she could be – and how persuasive.

'Have you met him?' Konrad asked.

She shook her head.

'Do you know anything about him?'

'He's old, nearly forty. But he's rich, very rich.' She shrugged. 'A girl can't have everything.'

She looked away and, more quietly, added: 'A girl can't have anything.'

'Do you have to marry him?'

She looked at Konrad. 'Does the sun have to rise every day? That's what it does. It can do nothing else. I have to marry Otto Krieshmier. I can do nothing else.'

'Do you want to?'

'What I want has nothing to do with it.'

'That isn't fair.'

Elyssa smiled, then she laughed, laughed out loud for almost a minute until she was finally able to control herself. She used her silk scarf to wipe the tears from the corners of her eyes. Konrad could not tell whether they were tears of laughter or sadness.

'Fair?' she said. 'You talk to me about fairness? What about your life? Has that been fair? Has it? Nothing is fair, Konrad. There is no such thing. You should know that. I have no complaints. How long is it since you saved my life? Five years? Nearly six? Maybe that was when my life should have ended, that was my destiny. Every day since then has been extra. I have no complaints. Even if I died tomorrow, I have been grateful for every extra day – thanks to you.'

As she spoke, she took hold of Konrad's hand – and for the first time ever, her fingers were cold, icy cold. As if she were already dead...

'What's wrong?' she asked, staring at him.

'Nothing,' he answered, squeezing her cold hand.

He was lying, and they both knew it.

He had thought of asking her to go with him. It would be less of a wrench if they fled together, because he would be taking the only thing that he cared about, the only thing that he did not want to leave.

But, paradoxically, she was also the major reason that he must go. He was not simply leaving in order to escape the village, he was leaving to escape Elyssa.

He could not pretend he had not experienced the visions that he had seen. Leaving with her could not change what he had witnessed, could not save her.

Perhaps Elyssa was correct. She had been destined to die.

Saving her from the beastman had extended her allotted span
of life, that was all. One's fate could not be avoided.

'I don't know why, but I had a strange feeling that the rider
we saw was my husband-to-be,' Elyssa said, suddenly. 'I think
that's why I wanted to talk to him. It was as though he was
someone I knew – or would know. I had this silly idea that he
had come to carry me away on his horse, to abduct me before
the wedding.'

'But you said he was like a ghost.'

'Well, someone nearly forty is nearly dead.' She forced a
laugh, and it was a laugh that sounded forced.

Konrad was thinking about the rider. Elyssa had been correct. At first, he did seem like a ghost, riding silently through
the village on his phantom horse.

Konrad and Elyssa must have been mistaken, it was their
imaginations which had invested the bronze knight with
spectral abilities. Everything had not really become silent, all
sounds totally frozen, it was only that they were too terrified
to hear any noise.

At least, that was what Konrad preferred to think. The
horseman was a rare visitor from the world beyond the village, the world into which Konrad soon intended to venture.
He preferred not to contemplate the prospect that the outside
world could be so dramatically different – that beyond the
safety of the valley, life was not as simple and straightforward
as it was within the village and its environs.

'So, who was he?' asked Elyssa.

'Who knows? Maybe he was lost. No one comes here without a reason. If he was lost, that must have been his reason.'

Elyssa was looking at him, unconvinced.

Konrad continued: 'He rode to the head of the valley, up to
the manor, realized that he couldn't get through, then rode
back the way he'd come.'

Konrad could not persuade himself, and so he doubted
that Elyssa believed his reasoning.

She glanced at the sun. Although it had only risen within
the last hour, already it was burning fiercely in the cloudless
sky. She unfastened the buttons at the top of her blouse.

'Do you know what it is tomorrow?' she asked.

Even after all these years, he could never get used to the way she changed the subject so frequently.

The days made very little difference to him. Sometimes he did not even know what month it was. 'Festag,' he guessed.

'I didn't mean the day of the week. But you're wrong, it's Backertag. It's the eighteenth of Sigmarzeit, the first day of summer!'

'Oh.'

'I can tell that doesn't seem important to you. Am I right?'

Konrad gestured widely and wildly with both arms, as if to encompass the whole of the world. 'But it's summer already,' he said. 'It's been hot for weeks.'

How could anyone say when summer started? As if it began on exactly the same day each year. People tried to impose their will upon the seasons, but they were never successful. Sometimes it was hotter in spring than summer, colder in autumn than winter. Nature refused to be tamed. The climate could not be confined into neat sections, the way that different crops could be grown in different fields.

Elyssa shook her head despairingly, as if Konrad could not be reasoned with.

'Much more importantly,' she said, 'tomorrow is the holy day of Sigmar.'

'Oh,' he said again.

He had heard the name of Sigmar many times in his life. At first, it was just a name, used as an oath by the men at the inn. 'By Sigmar!' they would swear. It meant nothing to Konrad.

Later, he came to know that the strange building at the very heart of the village was a temple to Sigmar. Even later, he heard something about how Sigmar had founded the Empire, but he had not paid much attention. He had not even heard of the Empire, had no idea where it could be. He had finally learned from Elyssa that the village was a part of the Empire – Elyssa was the source of most of his information.

'Everyone in the whole village goes to the temple tomorrow,' Elyssa said. 'Rich and poor, they all stand side by side in worship and praise. Everyone except you, Konrad. Why? Don't you believe Sigmar is a god?'

Konrad shrugged. What everyone else in the village did was no concern of his. The Brandenheimers had never taken him to the temple when he was young, and he had never given the matter any thought.

'Or is it because you worship someone else?' Elyssa continued. 'Ulric?'

He shrugged again, totally uninterested. He had never even heard the name.

'Or,' Elyssa pressed on, 'do you worship the other gods, the Dark Gods?'

'Who?' demanded Konrad, impatiently. 'What are you talking about?'

'I don't know,' she admitted. 'I've sometimes overheard my father talking about other gods. I can't remember the names. But I could tell it was something he was reluctant to mention, as though he was frightened. The only other time I've ever seen him scared like that was when he asked about the weapons I gave you.' She bit her lower lip as she remembered. 'I thought you might know about the Dark Gods.'

'I don't even know about Sigmar, so why ask me? I'm only a stupid peasant, remember?'

This time it was Elyssa who seized Konrad's leg, pulling quickly and sending him sprawling. As he sat up, she stood.

'So you won't be at the temple tomorrow?' she asked.

'No,' he replied, as he rose to his feet.

'I must be going,' said Elyssa.

She stood by her horse, and Konrad cupped his hands. They looked at one another, Elyssa's gaze moving from one of Konrad's eyes to the other. It was a long time since she had done that. Then she stepped into his interwoven fingers, and he helped her into the saddle.

They looked at one another. They said nothing, because there was nothing to say. Both knew they would never see each other again. Elyssa must have believed that the reason was because Konrad was going to leave; but Konrad knew it was because she was going to die.

They kept looking silently at each other. Words would not have been enough. Elyssa smiled briefly; Konrad nodded slightly. It was their only goodbye.

He watched her ride away, and he followed at a distance for a while, keeping her in sight until she crossed the bridge and entered the village.

She did not look back.

THE ONE WHO *had escaped was named Sigmar – Sigmar Heldenhammer, who had founded the Empire.*

By the end of this day, there would be but one individual who emerged alive and unscathed from the field of battle.

And this time, that was as it should be.

The lone survivor was he who now contemplated the scene of impending carnage, he who had planned and schemed to make this glorious day come about, he whose manipulations would continue until every one of his erstwhile allies had become a bloody corpse, as much a victim as those they had earlier defeated and destroyed.

He was no longer human, but not yet daemon – although he was in command of both – and after today's inevitable triumph he would be rewarded with a higher role in the pantheon of Chaos.

He gazed down at the village laid out like a sacrificial offering beneath him, anticipating the prospect both of absolute victory and of total annihilation, and he smiled.

It was a smile that betrayed not a trace of his lost humanity.

The people in the valley below worshipped Sigmar as a god, whose holy day they believed this was.

Let them all pray to Sigmar. He could not save them.

Nothing could...

CHAPTER FIVE

BUT KONRAD DID not leave. He could not. It was as if he did not know how. The dirt road led away to the south. It was the main access route to and from the village, but he did not take it.

He had lived in the valley all his life. He had never been more than an hour's walk from the village. It was not that easy to go, he discovered.

If Elyssa had asked him to return with her, he would have done so. She had not. It was as though she wanted him to leave, wanted to be rid of him.

He kept expecting Adolf Brandenheimer or one of his fat children to come after him, to order him back to the inn, but no one came.

He sat watching the village for hours, where life went on as ever. It made no difference that he was not there. He was not needed, not missed.

Instead, he was the one who missed the village, missed the tavern. For every day of his life, there had been an invariable routine that he had followed. Without that habitual order, he felt lost and more alone than ever.

By a great effort of will, he had forced himself to abandon his daily routine. Having succeeded, he kept fighting the urge to collect firewood from the forest and carry it back to the inn.

A part of him wanted to continue as though today were no different from any other. Another part urged him to leave, to go now while he had the opportunity. Torn between these two conflicting impulses, he did nothing.

Konrad sat still, and all that moved was his shadow as the day passed. When he became thirsty, he drank from the river. When he became hungry, he ignored the pangs. Throughout his life, he was more often hungry than not.

He waited and waited, and he wondered what he was waiting for. Some kind of motivation, some external force which would make the decision for him.

It seemed that he had spent his whole life waiting, knowing that one day something different was going to happen, something which would change the whole course of his existence. Today must be that day, and yet he was unwilling to face the unknown future.

The longer he stayed away, the less likely it became that he would return to the village. While he did nothing, the hour became later, the day shorter. He should have left when he had a chance to reach the next village while it was still daylight.

He had no idea how far the nearest outpost of habitation was – but in between lay the forest, the dark, deep forest and all the unknown terrors that dwelled within. There were miles and miles ahead of him, hours and hours of darkness. And still he did not make a move, postponing the inevitable for yet another minute, another hour...

But if he did wait for another hour, it really would be too late. The sun was low and sinking fast, the light fading. Darkness meant danger. His foresight could not give him an extra few seconds, the seconds he needed for survival, not in the dark.

Konrad could not fire an arrow when he was unable to see what he was aiming at. Night was the time when the forest came alive, and the nocturnal creatures that prowled the woods were not hampered by lack of vision. To them, the night was as bright as day. The darkness was their ally, but Konrad's enemy.

It was now or never, he realized. And it could not be never, because that was not his destiny. Just as he saw, so he knew that there would be more to his life than this.

He stood, and he looked at the village for what must be the final time. At all the thatched cottages that lined the main street, at the watermill upstream, at the fields with the crops, the pastures with the grazing animals, at all the barns and dwellings, at the temple to Sigmar, even at the tavern, and finally at the walls of the manor house, where Elyssa must have been.

He spun around and strode away. Instead of taking the dirt road away from the village, he headed directly into the forest. The worn and rutted track was unfamiliar territory, but the woods were not.

It was much darker within the forest than in the clearing behind, but he did not have to rely on what he could see even with his normal sight. For the first few hundred yards he knew every root and bush and sapling and tree trunk. He trod through the dense thickets without having to think, letting his instincts guide him.

The deeper into the forest that he went, the more diseased became the trees, the more of them that were covered in fungus and malign growths. Over the years it seemed that the infection had been spreading faster, blighting ever more of the forest.

Konrad did not travel very far. It would be dark within the hour, unsafe to venture any further. He stopped next to a huge tree that he had often noticed. Some fifteen feet up, there was a narrow slit in the trunk, and within was a hollow space. He had once climbed up to explore and discovered that it made an ideal hiding place.

Konrad was not the only one who had come to such a conclusion, having found the hollow lined with feathers and dried bones. Some kind of bird had used the tree as its nest. And it was no small bird of prey, because some of the white bones were over a foot long. He had been unable to identify either the bird or the bones.

He threw a stone into the split in the trunk, to find out if any other creature had taken up residence. There was no answering screech or squeal, howl or hiss.

Gripping his dagger between his teeth, he hauled himself up. There were no branches to aid his climb, and this lack of accessibility made it an even more desirable residence.

Balancing himself with one arm, holding his knife in his free hand, he looked inside the hollow. There was nothing to see. More importantly, it seemed that there was nothing inside to see him. He reached in, stabbing wildly with his knife, but the blade met with no resistance.

He shinned down the tree, collected his bow, his arrows, the linen bundle, then climbed back up and in through the opening. It was a much tighter squeeze than it had been last time; he had grown since then.

There were still bones and feathers within, but it smelled no worse than the stable where he had always slept until now. He would spend the night here.

Konrad had wasted a day, but he was determined that the next day would not also be lost. Tomorrow, at dawn, he would really begin his journey. Today he had done less than on any other day in his whole life, although he felt far more exhausted than usual.

He stared out through the narrow breach, watching as night fell. The forest was an eerie place even during daylight, but in the gathering darkness the trees seemed to move – their branches like limbs, their trunks like bodies.

The Forest of Shadows, that was what Elyssa had called it, and he wondered how far the woods and the shadows would spread. He had never been further than the top of the steep hill.

Konrad yawned. Perhaps during the night the woods did indeed become alive. The darkness was like some magic spell which cast itself across the whole of the forest, transforming it from inanimate to animate. Maybe the most feared creatures of the night were the trees themselves.

He might even have willingly ventured into an arboreal trap. The hollow where he had secreted himself was the stomach of a carnivorous tree. The bones and feathers all around him were the leftovers of previous undigested meals, all that remained of creatures which had previously taken refuge here.

He smiled at the notion. It was only a crazy idea, the product of his exhaustion. Even if it were true, he did not really care. He felt too tired to escape.

He was cold, there was no straw to bury himself beneath as in the barn where he always slept. Neither was there enough room to lie down; he had to remain in a sitting position. Despite all this, he was soon asleep.

It was not a peaceful sleep. He was haunted by the worst nightmares he had ever experienced. He dreamed that the woods all around him were full of the most bizarre and hideous creatures, impossible beings that made even the most deformed and repulsive beastman seem as innocent as a newborn child.

When he awoke, he discovered there had been no nightmares.

Everything that he dreamed was true.

KONRAD AWOKE TO the sound of a voice. There was only one at first, at a distance. After a few seconds he heard another, closer. And another, even closer. Then footsteps, the tramp of feet through the undergrowth. More and more of them, heavily trudging through the forest.

It was still night, as dark outside as it was within the hollow where he had sought shelter, and so there was nothing to be seen. But it seemed as if there were a whole army going by, and the tree shook with the vibration. They passed slowly, their progress impeded by the closeness of the twisted trees.

He heard the sounds of armour, of weapons, of animals, as well as the voices. Voices speaking a language he could not understand, which must have originated in a far-off land.

And from the sounds he heard, those speaking the strange tongue must also have had strange tongues of their own. They did not seem to be human.

What was going on? He could tell from the direction that the inhuman legions took that they must be heading towards the village.

Konrad dared not move a muscle for fear of betraying his presence. All he could do was sit motionless, waiting until the alien cohorts had passed by.

It was an eternity until the last straggler had gone beneath the tree. And not merely beneath. As the first rays of dawn light filtered through the leaves and branches above, Konrad thought he saw a movement on a level with the hollow – five yards high!

But it must have been a trick of the light, he realized. Nothing could be that tall, no living creature. If he had seen anything at such a height, it must have been the top of a weapon, the point of a spear or a lance.

Although the army of the night had passed by, silence did not return and neither was the forest empty. The mysterious invaders were still within a few hundred yards, he could tell. They had come to a halt at the very border of the woods, lurking in the shadows as the sun rose.

He had seen nothing, nothing but an imagined movement at an impossible height, but there was something about the creatures that had gone by which reminded Konrad of the beastman. Perhaps it was the smell, the odious stench of the monstrous beings.

But surely the forest could not be full of beastmen, an army of them – an army in the literal sense, with weapons and armour? It was all he could think of. And, senseless though it was, it was the only thing that made sense.

At this very moment, hundreds of feral eyes must have been gazing hungrily down at the valley and the sleeping village. On their own, most beastmen fled into the depths of the forest at dawn. Together, it seemed that they had no fear of the light. They must have joined forces in order to destroy the village. That could be the only reason they were here now.

Konrad's first thought was that he had to warn the villagers. But there was no way through, he realized. The creatures were between him and the houses.

Then he wondered why he should want to issue a warning. What had anyone in the village ever done for him? They had never cared whether he lived or died, so why should he care about them?

Except for Elyssa.

When he had saved her life all those years ago, that had been an instinctive reaction. One human aiding another, they were allies against the inhuman creature that had attacked her. This was how he felt now about the people in the village. He was more like them than the beings who lay in wait, about to pounce upon them.

Yet this time he was not acting without thought, boldly leaping into the attack against a single beastman. Then, there had been no time to think – but it turned out that he did have a chance.

Now, he reasoned, he had none. There was no point in getting killed for no reason – or even for any reason.

His only reason would have been Elyssa. He had saved her once, but he could not do so again. She was dead, he had seen it. And seeing it was what had prompted him to quit the village. Because of that, he was beyond the ring of marauding beastmen – or whatever they were.

He could do nothing for anyone. Anyone except himself.

He remained where he was until it became fully light, and wondered whether to try and slip furtively away. He felt safe where he was. He had not been noticed when the nocturnal regiment had gone by. But he might not be safe when they returned. If they became aware of him, he was caught in a trap. Now that the creatures were behind him, this would probably be the best time to make his escape – and maybe the only time.

Warily, Konrad peered out through the hollow. He could see nothing except the trees of the forest. There was not a trace of movement. All was still, even in the direction of the village, the beastmen – or whatever they were – hidden by the dense array of trees.

He eased his bow out of the split in the trunk, followed by the bundle that held the quiver and five black arrows. His other arrows, the ones that Elyssa had given him later, he had always carried loose.

Climbing up the tree while encumbered by his weapons had been difficult enough, and climbing down was no more simple. He could have dropped them all to the earth, but he feared that the slight sound they might make would betray his presence. Instead, he worked his way cautiously to the ground.

He leaned back against the trunk for a minute to ensure he had not been noticed. He had to be doubly careful. He was on edge because of the inhuman entities that were so close, and also because he would soon be stepping into a part of the forest where he had never previously ventured.

He unwrapped the quiver, adding his other arrows to the five of his originals. He had grown used to the newer shafts, but when he compared the two sets they were as different as could be. The black arrows were like works of art, fashioned by a master craftsman. The others were functional, that was all.

Tucking the linen wrapping into his tunic, not wanting to leave any evidence that he had been here, Konrad slung the black quiver diagonally across his back. He had never worn it before, but it did not seem so. The black leather fitted comfortably, as though it belonged there, the flights of the arrows protruding over his left shoulder.

He bent his supple bow into its reassuring curve, slipping the string into the notches he had carved at either end. A bow was a simple thing when compared to an arrow, which was why he had been able to fabricate his own with just his dagger. Once, that had been his only possession, his only weapon. With his other armament, he felt like a warrior.

Arrow and bow, they were part of the same, both needed one another – and both needed an archer. The bow was useless without an arrow, and so Konrad drew one from the quiver, notching it into the bowstring and holding it loosely in his grip.

Thus armed, he began slowly walking up the hill and through the woods, resuming his interrupted journey away from the village. No purpose would be served by looking back, of thinking what was happening behind him. There was nothing he could do even if he wanted to.

He was alone now. It was no use remembering Elyssa. She had been his only friend, but the time they had spent together over the years added up to very little. He had always been alone.

As he glanced down at the arrow in his hand, he noticed that by chance he had chosen one of the black shafts.

Then when he glanced back up and saw the hideous creature a few yards ahead of him, he knew that it had not been chance at all.

IT WAS A beastman, that was all it could be. An animal that walked like a man. But it was unlike any beastman he had ever previously seen. Its deformed appearance made it unlike any animal; but its weapons made it more than any wild beast.

In either case, it was far less than human.

It was not much taller than Konrad, but it seemed far bigger because of its width. Covered in thick reddish fur, it was also clad in pieces of rusty armour which were worn seemingly at random, and around its fat belly was a belt from which hung a variety of knives, saws, cleavers – the tools of a butcher.

What drew Konrad's immediate attention was the creature's face. At first, he thought that it must have been wearing some kind of mask, a mask that was a parody of a human face. Yet its head really was like that – crimson of flesh, without fur. It had a nose, a mouth, two eyes – but the eyes were where the mouth should have been, and the mouth was in its forehead!

Its ears were huge and folded back like those of a dog, and its bald head was covered in warts, hung with loose folds of flesh which made it seem like a reptile. Pink slime oozed from its mouth and nostrils.

Its sudden appearance startled Konrad – because he had not known it was there, that he was about to encounter it. His foresight had let him down, perhaps because his senses had become overloaded by his concentration on the dangers of the bestial clans behind him.

The creature looked as surprised to see Konrad as he was to see it, and they both froze, staring at each other – although the beastman's eyes were completely white, without any pupil. The moment stretched into eternity, then the being rapidly raised its right arm, in which it held a massive axe. It roared out a blood-curdling war cry and hurtled towards Konrad.

As the arm rose up, Konrad realized with horror that the monster was not holding an axe – the axe was part of its arm! The weapon seemed fused to the creature's limb, and he supposed that the axe must have been made from bone. Instead of having a hand, the fiend's fingers had ossified into the whitened blade which now threatened Konrad.

He noticed all this in but a moment, and by then he had raised his bow, drawn back the string, released the arrow and sent it shooting straight into the beastman's chest.

The inhuman did not halt at once, although its yell was cut short. It slowed, gazing down at the shaft buried in its torso, sticking out from between two of its corroded plates of armour. Then its forward momentum ceased and it staggered drunkenly backwards, colliding with a tree.

Konrad fired again. Another black arrow found its target, this time in the creature's throat.

Blood spurted as the arrow drove itself through the fat furry neck and into the trunk behind, nailing the beastman to the bark.

Both of its arms – the one with spiny claws, the one without – went to its neck, trying to pull the arrow free. Its body twitched spasmodically, there was a liquid gurgle deep in its throat. A final gush of blood pumped from the neck wound, both arms dropped to its sides, and then the thing became absolutely still.

Konrad had a third arrow notched, ready to let fly. The only sign of movement from the beastman was its blood trickling from the two wounds. Its blood was red, like the colour of its face, the dull sheen of its fur, the rust of its armour. It was dead.

It seemed that it was a part of the tree against which it was transfixed. The tree was crooked and decayed, and the creature was distorted and corrupted.

Although he had not been aware of this particular brute, Konrad now *saw* that there were many more of the predators about.

They were not merely behind him, the forest was full of them – and there was another heading towards him at this very moment, less than twenty yards away.

He also heard it coming. There was no way that such a lumbering beast, such an impossible creature, could move silently through the woods.

The only place to hide was behind the tree on which the dead beastman was impaled, and Konrad sprinted the few yards in an instant, quickly ducking around the back of the broad trunk as the other monster came thudding into view.

It was like two creatures in one, twins which had been born together and were still intertwined. One huge body, but surmounted by two tiny heads, supported upon four legs, and with four arms, each of which was carrying a different weapon – a sword, a mace, an axe, a spear.

Hairless, its black body covered with patches of yellow flesh, it swayed from side to side as it proceeded on its four crooked lower limbs. Walking neither like a man, nor like a horse or any similar creature, its legs seemed completely uncoordinated, as though it were trying to go in two directions at once and instead ended up taking the middle course.

Konrad peered out from behind the tree as the ungainly giant lurched towards him. He had to decide which of the two heads would be the target of his first arrow, which of the four eyes to aim at.

The nearest of the two black heads turned to gaze at the dead beastman as the huge being weaved between the trees. Its mouth opened and it screeched out some incomprehensible message, waving the two closest limbs and their weapons.

That was the head which would receive the first shaft, Konrad concluded. But the beastman kept on moving, and a few seconds later it had disappeared from view, although it could still be heard crashing through the woods.

It must have thought that the dead raider was still alive, Konrad realized, as he lowered his bow. He might not be so fortunate next time – and judging by the activity within the forest, there would be many next times.

He moved around the tree and stared at the creature that he had slain. Even dead and immobile, it was an unnerving sight.

He tried not to breathe in the stench of death, to avoid inhaling the fetid odour that was like a shield around the disgusting creature.

That was the kind of protection Konrad needed. Only a beastman was safe in the forest today. A human stood no chance.

And so he would have to become a beastman.

He drew his knife.

KONRAD HAD SKINNED many animals before, but never a creature like this. The smell was utterly repulsive. Had he eaten lately, he would have thrown up. Even so, his stomach turned at the abominable odour, and his throat was filled with the foul taste of his own bile.

There was was no time to retrieve his arrows. He snapped off the black shaft in the creature's chest, then broke the one in its throat, and the body fell away from the tree.

He stripped off the pieces of armour before slipping the point of his knife into the tough hide, then he began to slit the corpse open. He peeled its fur off in a single piece, and it was as red on the inside as the outside. It was the body which would attract the other predators, and so he carried his gory trophy away until he was out of sight of the flayed corpse.

Although he had been in a desperate hurry, it was an efficient piece of handiwork. He had managed to peel the skin away from the limbs almost intact, cutting off only the clawed feet, the clawed hand – and the bone axe.

Now he stepped into the furry legs of his victim, pulled its upper limbs over his arms. Because his arms and legs were shorter than those of the thing, his hands and bare feet were hidden by pieces of fur. He folded its hide around his torso. The creature had been much fatter than Konrad, but he wrapped the loose skin tight around his waist with the brute's weapon belt, doing his best to cover the join with the various plates of rusted armour.

Despite the clothes he wore, his victim's blood oozed through onto his flesh, warm and sticky. He was covered in so much blood and gore that he felt like a corpse. If he did not endure this ordeal, then soon the feeling would become reality. He wondered if there could be much difference.

He slung his quiver over his shoulder, held the bow in his left hand. His dagger was still in his right, stained and dripping blood.

A flap of skin hung behind his neck, like a hood. It was the fur of the beastman's head, and now he drew it up over his own head, almost covering his face. He had believed that the stench could not possibly get any worse, but it did. He gagged, his stomach heaving dryly. Nothing came up except saliva, which dribbled from his lips. Just like the slime from the beastman's mouth, he thought – but at least his own mouth was where it should have been.

He spat away the foul taste and wiped his mouth with his sleeve. Except it was not his sleeve, it was the furry forearm of his vanquished foe – and the taste was infinitely worse than the one he was trying to get rid of.

He looked like a beastman, he stank like a beastman. But could he pass as one?

He would discover that in a moment, he thought, as he suddenly became aware of another creature lumbering through the forest towards him.

Konrad turned to face the thing. It had only one head, two arms, two legs, and its face was the right way up. But its fur was very pale, almost white, and its skull was so elaborately horned that the horns almost formed a helmet.

It seemed to be clad in armour plates the same colour as its flesh, but then Konrad realized that fur and armour were one and the same, both a part of its hunched body. The creature was armed with two massive curved swords, one gripped in each of its pincered forelimbs.

It paused, gazing at Konrad, its huge green eyes staring through its complex horns.

Konrad waved his dagger in what he hoped was a non-threatening but comradely gesture. The creature replied by raising both its arms, both its swords – in what Konrad hoped was also a non-threatening but comradely gesture...

The beastman made a sound, a deep grating rattle, which may have been a form of greeting. It made no sense to

Konrad, and he reciprocated by bellowing out a nonsensical string of vowels which made an equal lack of sense.

The sound seemed to satisfy the furred and armoured being, which resumed its journey through the woods, heading in the direction of the village.

Konrad took the opposite route, trying not to think about the two beastmen he had encountered. Although inhuman, they were far more than animals. They were armed – and it seemed that they could also speak.

He did not get far before his path was blocked again. This time there were three of the vile creatures, all of them very similar in appearance. Most of the beastmen he had seen throughout his life were very different, and it was hard to say what kind of animal they resembled, what their ancestors may have been. But with these three there was absolutely no doubt.

They were rats, giant rats.

They were not as tall as he, and he might have fancied his chances in combat against any one of them. Not against all three, however, and it was clear that they were suspicious of him. Their noses twitched as they sniffed at him.

They stood upright on their hind legs, which seemed proportionally much longer that the legs of a normal sized rat. And their teeth were definitely longer.

Their fur was brown, covered in various pieces of chain mail and clothing and the skins of other animals, none of which seemed to match. Rats were notorious scavengers, and these ratmen were no different.

Their dark outfits were decorated with a zigzag emblem. One of the creatures also had the same design branded onto its chest, and another had it gaudily painted on its snout.

Two of them were armed with short saw-bladed swords; the third carried a similar weapon, its longer blade mounted on a pole. Each bore a round shield emblazoned with the same zigzag pattern.

One of them said something, its voice rapid and unfathomable. It raised its serrated sword threateningly. The other two joined in, chattering unintelligibly and pointing their blades at him, then in the direction of the village.

Konrad did not understand what they said, but he did not have to be a linguist to guess what their gestures meant. According to them, he was going the wrong way.

He gazed at the furred beasts, and they stared menacingly back at him, their tails twitching. It was clear that he could not get past them, and it was equally evident that they had no intention of going on and leaving him there. If he even tried to move forward, they would jump him. They suspected him of being a deserter.

He had killed countless rats during his life, but they had all been the proper size, the small size. He stood no chance against these three giants.

All he could do was turn and head back the way he had come, making sure he steered well clear of the skinned body of the beastman that he had slain. He heard the rat-things close behind him, swiftly speaking to one another in their shrill voices.

He was on edge, anticipating that they would attack him now that his back was turned. Rats were devious, scheming creatures – and these would be no different.

He could see nothing of what would happen, but under these circumstances that was of no consequence. When he most needed to be warned of danger, it seemed that he could no longer rely on his advanced vision.

There was no retreat. If he tried to go back, even if he managed to evade the armed rodents, there were too many other impossible creatures prowling the forest. He would soon be identified as an outsider – and soon be dead.

There was safety in numbers, and for the moment he would only be safe with the beastmen, as one of them.

Ahead of him, the light of day was filtering through the labyrinth of trees. It was growing brighter. They were almost out of the forest. In the gloom, his disguise had held up to cursory inspection. But in the bright daylight, it would soon become apparent that he was an impostor, a human in their inhuman midst.

He slowed his pace, heard one of the ratmen hiss a warning, felt the jab of a blade in his rear. He jumped forward, hearing what could only have been rodent laughter.

David Ferring

Then the sound of rat glee was drowned out by the sudden heart-stopping roar as thousands of menacing battle cries ripped through the clear morning air, shattering the serenity of the valley.

The heathen horde erupted from the woods and cascaded down the valley, screaming and brandishing their weapons.

Their lethal assault upon the defenceless village had begun.

CHAPTER SIX

KONRAD WATCHED IN hypnotized horror as the heathen hordes hurtled down the hill towards the huddled houses.

The invasion was not merely by those who had been lurking within this area of the forest. As if on a given signal, the village was attacked from all sides. The valley had been completely encircled, and now the circle was tightening, like the noose of a hangman's rope.

Every manner of creature took part in the assault. Beastmen were like the spawn of human and beast, but there were many other abhorrent mutations: creatures that ran, creatures that crawled, creatures that slithered, creatures that flew, creatures that rode on the backs of other beasts – and others that seemed to be an integral part of the animal upon which they rode: such as horses that had human bodies growing from their necks – while from those human necks grew totally inhuman heads.

And every one of them was as loathsome as the vile entities that Konrad had encountered in the woods.

He stood rooted to the spot, immobilized by the amazing spectacle. There were far more assailants than inhabitants of the village. No one who lived in the valley below stood even the remotest chance of survival.

There was no sign of movement in the village, even though it was well past dawn. Then Konrad remembered what Elyssa had told him yesterday, although it seemed far longer ago than that.

Today was the first day of summer. It was Sigmar's holy day, and everyone would be in the temple. Konrad could see the gilded cupola in the very centre of the village. Trapped within the temple, the inhabitants would be easy prey for the renegades.

But whatever the circumstances, the villagers would be helpless victims. They were not soldiers, few had weapons, and they were vastly outnumbered.

Like an uncontrolled pack of wild dogs, although a thousandfold more deadly, the impossible beasts of every shape and size raced down the valley slopes.

The river lay between the village and those marauders who had erupted from this part of the forest. The bridge was too narrow to carry more than a few, and so most of the creatures charged directly into the water. At this time of the year, the river level was low and it was easy to wade across – for a human, at least.

The invaders pushed and shoved in their haste, knocking their allies aside, using them as stepping stones, so that it appeared as if a new bridge had been constructed to span the river – a bridge of flesh, of fur, of scales, of feathers, of armour, of chain mail, of every type of weapon and armament.

And still there was no sign that anyone in the village knew what was happening.

Konrad could not move, could hardly think. The whole experience was beyond his comprehension. He understood what was happening – but why? What were all the creatures? Where did they come from? Why did they want to destroy the village?

He felt the point of a sword jab at him, so viciously that it sliced through the fur he was wearing and cut into his own skin. He twisted around angrily, raising the knife which was still in his hand. The blood of the dead beastman seemed to have fused his palm and the hilt together, just as one of the creature's own limbs had been a weapon.

The three ratmen were still with him. He could not read the expressions on their faces, but he recognized the malicious glints in their black eyes. They were trying to provoke him. They wanted to kill him, but it seemed they needed an excuse.

All his anger and hatred and frustration suddenly flared up within him. There was nothing he wanted more than to oblige the rodents, to attack them. He could kill one, maybe two, but he would also die – die like everyone else in the village.

That would be futile. He had quit the valley yesterday in order that he might live. He was back here already, but he was not back to die.

It was because of the ratmen that he had not escaped, that he had been forced to return. They would pay the price. He could not kill them on their own terms, in hand to hand combat – or hand to paw...

But if he could put some distance between himself and them, it would be a very different story: three ratmen, three arrows, three corpses.

Konrad glared at the rat-things, staring into each hated pair of beady eyes in turn, and then he swiftly spun around and began sprinting down the slope.

He knew that he could outrun the overgrown vermin. Their legs, although they imitated those of a man, were not designed for running. He had been up and down this incline countless thousands of times. He belonged here, the invaders did not, and he resented their presence.

Konrad had never considered himself as a villager, that he was a part of the valley. He had lived here all his life, but it was not his home. He believed that he had none, that he belonged nowhere. But as he sped down the hill, he recognized that he was on his own territory.

The forest had always been the dividing line between the human and the non-human, as had the division between day and night. The beastmen had their own place, their own time, but now they had broken the unwritten law, that inviolable rule of nature. They did not belong here.

It was an insult to all humanity that they dared show their ugly faces and disgusting bodies, that they polluted the air with their obnoxious stenches, that they screamed and yelled in their gibberish tongues, as if mocking the humans that they wished they could be.

There were so many of them, and still they poured down the hill. Some had such a bizarre appearance that it seemed impossible they could ever have survived their birth. Maybe they had not been born. Could such savage travesties of life ever have entered the world in the normal manner?

Often, they appeared to be two halves of different creatures, as if joined together by some giant with a malicious sense of humour.

Perhaps they had emerged from eggs, like birds, or been transformed from one kind of being into another – from fish to amphibian, like tadpoles into frogs. Maybe they had been created out of rotten food or dung, born in middens the way that flies were.

Konrad felt both fascinated and repulsed by many of the ghastly apparitions. He tried not to look at any of them directly, for fear of attracting their attention. All he could do was act as they did, continue the charade of being one of them. It was either that or die.

He remembered when he was younger and had seen the first soldiers in the village, how he had wanted to be like them. And now he was part of a vast army – but he was with the forces that those troops had come to destroy.

Could that be the reason for this attack? Was it a reprisal for the way that the troopers had scoured the forest for beast-men, all that time ago?

Konrad had no intention of imitating the raiders exactly, following them over the river, and his course veered to the left, away from both the bridges – the wooden one, and the one fabricated from inhuman flesh.

All the other invaders were armed with clubs and spears, swords and maces, flails and axes, daggers and lances, the kind of armaments that he knew. But many of the weapons carried by the festering multitude seemed to have no human equivalent, or else they were instruments of which Konrad had no knowledge.

There were so many weapons being waved menacingly by so many creatures that Konrad did not feel conspicuous when he slipped his dagger into his belt, drew one black arrow from the quiver, notched it, and began drawing back on the bowstring.

The only thing that he did which might have appeared out of the ordinary was turn around and aim uphill, back the way he had come...

He had expected the ratmen to follow him, but there was no sign of them. He scanned the slope above, his eyes sweeping the area the rodent trio could have reached by now. He did not see them; they were lost among the teeming rabble.

He turned back, but none of the beasts seemed to have noticed him. He was far away from most of them, but neither did this seem to matter. They had other things on their minds – if they had minds. That must have been what had become of the ratmen, he realized. They were so anxious to join in the assault that they no longer cared about Konrad.

He stared at the turmoil in the river, where so many of the creatures were still crossing the water. His bowstring was still drawn back. He had to vent his frustration, take a small measure of vengeance. It did not matter what his target was. They were all the same. If he fired into the solid mass that swarmed over the river, it was impossible to miss.

Yet he had one of his black arrows notched, and such a work of master craftsmanship deserved a better fate than being fired at random.

He gazed across the river, at the hordes which by now surged through the village. As he did so, for the first time he heard what could only be a human cry.

None of the invaders could have made such a sound, even those that seemed almost human. The cry was that of a villager, a cry of torment, of torture, of despair – of death.

Then Konrad saw his target. One of the rat-beings. It could not have been one of the three which had prevented his escape, but that made no difference. The rodent was far away, almost at the limit of Konrad's bow, and it was scurrying rapidly among the buildings.

He drew back the string fully, aiming high, across the river, concentrating, visualizing the flight of the arrow, imagining where the rat-thing would be by the time the shaft angled down.

He released the arrow, watching for a second time as it arced through the sky, up and over then down – and directly into the creature's verminous back. It fell dead, a streak of red staining its brown fur.

By then, Konrad already had another arrow notched, expecting that he would have been observed, that by his actions he had betrayed himself. He stared around intently, watching for some creature to come charging at him, but none did.

It was not one of the last two yards of black wood with the golden crest that he had chosen, but one of the inferior shafts. He did not need the best to pick off his next target, whatever it would be. He wanted to save his final two original arrows.

He caught the thought, wondering where it had come from. Why did he need the last black arrows? He narrowed his eyes, trying to concentrate, which was difficult because he was distracted by all the sounds of death and destruction coming from the village.

No image would resolve in his mind. It never did when he tried to force one, so instead he let his eyes focus on a different subject – the next beastman that he would slay.

HIS TARGET WAS using its armoured head as a battering ram against the door of the barn where Konrad had always slept, until last night. It had the legs of a man, but the dark body of an insect, with four articulated limbs instead of arms.

The arrow split open the creature's shell, which could not have been as hard as its head. But the shot did not kill the beast. It staggered away, clawing vainly at the shaft in its back, unable to reach it.

Another of the invaders rushed up to the insectman. This was a being that seemed especially ugly because it was basically

humanoid in shape, and so its deformities were more apparent
– such as its green-tinged skin.

The newcomer was well armed and armoured, and Konrad
thought that it was about to help the wounded brute. Instead,
it swung its heavy sword and with a single sweep detached
the writhing insectman's head from its body. The attacker had
struck almost without missing a step, before continuing its
rampage through the village.

Even so, the wounded creature did not drop. It continued
staggering around, trying to remove the arrow, as if unaware
that it had lost its head.

Then yet another of the marauders, a beaked and antlered
creature, attacked the acephalous insect-thing, knocking it to
the ground with its spiked mace. The black carapace splintered and shattered under a succession of blows.

Konrad turned his attention elsewhere, notching another
arrow. Another arrow, another target, another victim – this
time a creature with a crested head, leathery wings, taloned
tentacles in which it wielded two axes.

It was easy, almost too easy, and Konrad was drawn even
closer, down to the water's edge, searching for his next victim.

The centre of the village was where most of the creatures
were gathered, but it was just out of range. The heart of the
village was the focus of their murderous attention because
that was where the temple lay – with everyone inside.

Including Elyssa.

No! Elyssa was dead. Dead or dying, fated to become a
corpse very soon. There was nothing he could do, no way that
her destiny could be changed.

That was why he had left the valley, but now – against his
will – he had returned. Perhaps that was his own destiny, that
was why he had been forced back.

He was so near to the temple, yet so far. He had to discover
if she was still amongst the living. And if he died finding out,
then that was the way it must be.

He began wading through the water, his bow held high to
keep the string dry – and because he had another arrow
already notched. By now, all the marauders that were going to
reach the other side had done so. Many of the creatures that

had ventured into the river before him had not made it across. Not alive.

Many had drowned, and their bodies floated past him. Dead, they looked even more hideous and impossible than they had ever done whilst alive – if alive was what they had been.

The river was stained with streaks of blood, but it was not merely red in colour. Black and green, blue and yellow, a rainbow of death hues. The blood could not have resulted from drowning, it could only have come from from battle wounds.

The spectrum of blood must have been caused by the invaders having fought and slain one another as they crossed the river.

The benighted armies were in such a frenzied state of death-lust that they would even kill their allies – as Konrad had already witnessed when two of the fiends had set upon the insectman that he had wounded.

The air reeked of the suppurating odours of disease and decay, the nauseating stench of the bodies of so many of the invaders, some of which stank as if they had long been dead and rotting.

Maybe that was the answer: they had recently been corpses, and this was the day the dead sought vengeance against the living. All the beastmen slain by humans over the centuries had returned to wreak their revenge.

When he waded up onto the other shore, Konrad recognized another smell. The smell of burning wood – and of burning flesh. Human flesh!

The savages had set fire to Sigmar's temple, in an attempt either to smoke out the villagers who hid there – or else to burn them alive.

He had been deafened by the cries and shrieks of the malformed creatures – the barks, the roars, the howls, the yelps, the screeches, the growls, the snarls – but now Konrad heard more and more other voices: the screams of the humans who were their prey.

Not wanting to, but unable not to, Konrad made his way from the river and up the road which led to the temple. The village was small, he knew every street, every building. Each street was full of the inhuman invaders, each building under seige.

Even though no one could have been inside them, every house was the subject of an insane assault by a variety of the beasts.

Because it was Sigmar's holy day, none of the farm animals had yet been taken out into the fields. They were still penned up inside the stables and barns – or were until the raiders attacked. Now they were all being butchered, and the pitiful lowing of cattle and the pathetic bleating of sheep were added to all the other sounds of mayhem and massacre.

And in the centre of the village, the temple was like a furnace, blackened and blazing. Konrad could not get very near because of the temperature and the press of monstrous bodies, and neither did he really wish to. He could hear more than he needed, glimpse more than he wanted.

He heard the screams of the villagers who were being immolated, and he saw the fate of some of those who had tried to flee the funeral pyre.

Those who were slain immediately were the fortunate ones. Those less lucky were tortured and abused, ripped apart and killed. And even that was better than what happened to those who were greedily devoured, eaten alive...

Everyone who had been within the temple was as good as dead. There could be no survival for those who remained inside, and there could be no escape for those who fled the flames.

The only hope for Elyssa was that she had avoided going to the temple that morning. Although she had said she would be there, that did not mean she had kept her word. Many a time she had broken her most faithful promise to Konrad, telling him that she would return the following day but not reappearing for weeks.

It was the smallest of chances, but it was the only chance there was.

Konrad skirted the crowd of creatures that packed the area around the inferno, all of them trying to join in the murder and mutilation. He made his way up the road that led to the manor house, avoiding the other malevolent beings who were ransacking the houses, throwing out all the contents into the street in wanton fury.

He passed a pack of green humanoid creatures that were playing football in the street. Konrad had often seen the village boys play the game, but he had never been invited to join in.

The players were like the being he had seen attack the insectman. Tall and broad, with oversized arms and heads, they had pointed ears, sloped-back foreheads and fangs that jutted up from their heavy lower jaws, and their game seemed to have different rules from that of the village boys.

They threw their football as well as kicked it, hurling it at the houses and letting it bounce down the road. There were dozens and dozens of the renegades playing the game. The teams – if they could be called that – viciously fought and bit and punched and kicked each other on the pretext of trying to gain posession of the ball.

The main difference, however, was that they were using a human head as their football.

Konrad carefully avoided their sport, but just as he thought he had passed them by, the head rebounded off a wall near his side. It rolled down the cobbles and came to a halt at his feet.

He looked down – and he recognized the head. It was that of Adolf Brandenheimer, the innkeeper, his master. His ex-master...

Konrad gazed in horrified fascination. The head was bruised and bloody, but the eyes were still open, and they seemed to be staring accusingly up at Konrad, as if blaming him for every misfortune that had been suffered.

Then he heard roars and yells, a thunder of feet on the cobbles, and he glanced up in time to see a horde of the humanoids bearing down upon him.

HE HAD BEEN carrying his bow, an arrow notched in the string, since before he crossed the river. But there was not time to bring up the weapon before the creatures were upon him.

He managed to step back a pace, away from the tavern owner's head. Even so, he was knocked aside and fell to the ground. The invaders pounced on the head and on each other, bodies piling up, limbs flying as they punched and clawed in search of their grisly trophy.

That was what they had been after, not Konrad, and he was able to crawl quietly away. He had lost the arrow, but he retrieved the bow. Then slowly, cautiously, hoping not to provoke the brutes, he backed further away. The players had no interest in him, however: they were all too involved in their parody of a game.

Still not turning his back, Konrad stood up, picked another arrow from his quiver, fitted it in the bow – and noticed that he had selected one of his final pair of black shafts.

The noise and activity within the melee had been increasing, but then most of the ugly humanoids suddenly began pulling away from the huddled pack, and the shouting and yelling reduced.

Konrad raised his bow. If they came for him, he would take at least one of the creatures with him.

As the inhumans drew back, he saw that Brandenheimer's head lay in two halves, as if cloven apart by an axe. That was the reason for the relative quiet – the players had lost their ball...

They had fought when they had a head to fight over. After a temporary break for a change of tactics, they began to fight again. Now it was no longer any kind of game. The fighting had turned serious, deadly serious.

Instead of feet and hands, the belligerents reached for their weapons – knives and swords and axes – and launched themselves back into the fray. Sparks flew as weapons were parried or impacted with armour, screams rent the air as they found their mark.

In a matter of moments, all the players had become combatants. So had the spectators, all the other creatures who had been idly watching while the temple blazed, while the cottages were engulfed in flames. With no more humans to kill, they turned upon each other.

Conflict between the invaders had been relatively rare until now. But not any more.

Konrad's disguise had been for protection. It had made him one of the beastmen, one of the marauders. That was now no defence, and he backed away even more quickly until he was beyond the final burning house.

In the middle of the battle between the former allies, he caught sight of a serpentlike creature, slithering through the fracas. It resembled a huge snake, except that it had a human head growing from its sinuous yellow and blue striped body.

It rapidly wriggled between the feet and talons and hooves of the skirmishers, towards the split skull of Adolf Brandenheimer. Then from its human head flickered out its long forked snake tongue, yellow and blue, lapping at the spilled brains of the dead innkeeper.

'Ahhh!' screamed out Konrad, giving voice to all his caged-up rage for the very first time.

He did not care that Brandenheimer was dead. The innkeeper meant nothing to him. He had been repelled at the sight of his severed head, but his reaction would have been the same no matter who the victim. Watching the snakeman feasting upon human brains was the most repulsive sight Konrad had ever witnessed.

Even while he screamed out his hatred, his anger, his total disgust, the arrow was in flight. It took the serpent through its left eye, the so human eye of its so abhorrently inhuman shape.

The creature screeched in agony, its whole body twisting wildly, sending many of the other beings flying, knocking them to the ground so that they were leapt upon and slain by their opponents.

Another arrow notched, the final black arrow, Konrad turned and sprinted away, towards the manor house.

As soon as he looked up the hill, he saw that it was futile. If there had ever been a chance, there was no longer. Smoke drifted up from behind the walls of the manor. Like the rest of the village, Wilhelm Kastring's home was now ablaze.

The village had been a slaughterhouse for its inhabitants. Now it became a battleground as the invaders fought each other, fought to the death – their own and every other being's.

Swords hacked off limbs, axes severed tentacles, claws snapped bones, jaws bit through both flesh and fur. The battle was acted out against the background of the burning village. The heat was almost unbearable. Smoke drifted everywhere, becoming thicker, making it difficult to see. The cobbles were slick with blood of all colours. The stink of charred flesh and alien blood, and all the other odours that the marauders had brought with them, was overpowering.

There was no retreat through the village, Konrad realized. Even in the poor visibility, there were so many enemies that one was bound to see him endeavouring to pass safely by.

His eyes streamed, and he coughed on the choking fumes. The only escape from the suffocating smoke was up the hill, towards the manor. That was not, however, a route away from the invaders. There must have been yet more of them in the manor house, but he had no alternative. Whether he remained here, or whether he went back, he would die.

He made his way up the hill. Every moment, he looked around, watching for some warning of attack, for one of the abominations that would notice him as potential prey.

There was no need for him to make for the manor house, he then realized. Now that he was away from the conflict, from the smoke, he could have headed off in any other direction.

Yet he kept going, almost against his will. Against all reason, he was still hoping that Elyssa could be in the manor house. Alive. He could see the flames, smell the blaze, but he continued onwards.

He reached the drawbridge and entered the gates of the manor. The last time he had been here, the sole time he had been here, was with Elyssa. It seemed a lifetime ago, yet it had only been yesterday morning.

There was still no trace of life within the walls, human or inhuman, no trace either of life or of death. The house was ablaze, tongues of brilliant red and yellow flames leaping up from the doors and the windows, plumes of thick black smoke curling upwards.

Compared to the scene down in the village, however, the burning manor house was like a welcoming hearth fire in winter. No stench of burning flesh assailed his nostrils. No unspeakable atrocities were committed against men and women and children and animals.

No impossible creatures squirmed or crawled or prowled in front of the blaze. No savage humanoids suddenly turned upon one another in a manic blood feud. There was no sign of the foul beings who must have set the manor ablaze, as they had the rest of the village.

Drawn by he knew not what, Konrad went nearer and nearer. He saw something move within the burning house. At first he thought he was mistaken, his eyes deceived by the flames, but then he saw another movement inside.

Had it been night, he would have described what he perceived as a shadow. Within the inferno, however, there was no such thing as a shadow. There was a dark shape in the hallway, a dark human shape. Someone was trapped inside!

When he was twenty yards away, he saw that the figure was coming towards the blazing doorway. Konrad slowed, and he moved towards a row of bushes to protect himself from the blast of heat that washed over him.

He watched as the shape stepped out into the open – and it was a person, a normal human. For a moment, he believed that it was someone whose clothes had been burned off them, but there was no sign of injury or pain. The figure calmly walked out of the manor house as though nothing were wrong.

It was a man, a tall slender man, naked from the waist up, his face impossibly thin. He was bald, his cheeks hollow, his eyes deep set, and his head looked almost like a skull.

Konrad did not recognize him; he was not a villager, which meant that he could only be one of the invaders.

He looked nothing like any of the others, however. He was too human. He had no weapons, wore no armour, carried no trophies such as bones or scalps, bore no marks of combat or ritual mutilation.

Despite everything that Konrad had witnessed today, this lone man was the most frightening sight that he had ever seen.

He had walked through the flames as though they were harmless. He seemed quite at home, as if fire were his natural environment. Even now, he did not hurry away from the blazing entrance. It was of no concern that the manor house was even hotter than the furnace of the village smithy.

Yesterday, Konrad had watched as the bronze warrior had ridden up to the manor. That had been strange enough, but now this other figure was even more awesome.

Kneeling between the bushes, Konrad watched as the skull-faced man surveyed the grounds of the manor, while the flames flickered all around him. Around – because it seemed as though he were wearing invisible armour that deflected both the heat and the flames.

He seemed like an entity straight from hell.

Konrad took careful aim with his last black arrow. His target was the infernal creature's heart. At such a range he could not miss.

He did not. The arrow buried itself deep in Skullface's bare chest.

But the victim did not even move!

He did not fall, he was not even forced to take a backward step because of the impact. All he did was glance down at where the black shaft was jutting from his heart, as if it had caused him no more inconvenience than a wasp sting.

Then he took hold of the arrow in his right hand, and he pulled. He yanked the shaft quickly out – and there was no trace of a wound in his chest, not even a hint of blood.

He rolled the arrow between the fingers of both hands, inspecting it. When he noticed the crest carved out of the gold band, he looked up.

Skullface stared straight at where Konrad wa standing, and broke the black arrow in two. It snapped like a dry twig. The sound was what Konrad had often heard in the forest, a sound that had frequently warned him of danger. It galvanized him into action. He sprang up, turned and ran.

And ran and ran and ran.

CHAPTER SEVEN

KONRAD COULD REMEMBER very little of his frantic flight from the manor house – and from the inhuman human who could not die.

All he knew was that he had run and run and somehow must have reached the river. He had managed to evade the village and all the creatures who rampaged through the burning buildings, intent on destroying everything there and also each other.

He could recall plunging into the cold waters of the river and letting himself be washed downstream. The fur in which he had earlier disguised himself soon filled with water, weighing him down, and he had almost drowned before freeing himself from the beastman's skin.

Then he had half-swum, half-floated downriver, away from the village and from the carnage. All the time he was expecting that a group of marauders would suddenly appear on the river bank, drag him out of the water and slaughter him as brutally as they had slain everyone else.

He drifted downstream for what seemed like hours, crashing against the rocks which occasionally thrust themselves up out of the river bed, hitting the long roots of the trees which grew near the water's edge, thudding against the boughs which had toppled into the river, colliding with the corpses of the dead invaders which shared the river with him, until his body was bruised and grazed and cut in dozens of places. He hardly noticed.

Even in the height of summer, the river was always cold, and it had sucked all the heat from his body. The reason he could feel no pain from his injuries was because he was freezing.

Eventually he was forced to wade into the shallows and drag himself up onto the bank. He must indeed have been in the water for hours, he now realized: when he noticed the position of the sun, he judged that it was around midday.

The trees almost came to the side of the river, but he found a space where he could lie in the sun, shivering, trying to become both warm and dry. He felt tired, cold, hungry, sore – but he found he was unable to lie still. His body was exhausted, not his mind. He felt restless and it was impossible to do nothing.

His money had gone, he discovered, the few coins had vanished from his pocket at some time during the day. The piece of linen in which the black bow had originally been wrapped was no longer tucked inside his tunic.

His replacement bow had also been lost, he did not know when, although he still had his quiver. It hung around his neck, somehow not having come right off when he had shed the fur. His arrows were missing. There was nothing inside the quiver except water.

He had let the beastman's belt, and all its weapons, sink to the bottom of the river, but he had made sure that he had not lost his own dagger. It had been clutched tightly in his fist all the time he had been in the water, and now his fingers felt very numb.

He stuck the blade in the ground, massaging the palm and knuckles of his right hand with the fingers of his left. He removed the quiver, poured out the water, then stripped off his wet clothes. That was the best way to warm his body, he reasoned.

Despite being in the water for so long, his ragged tunic and worn breeches were still stained with the splattered blood of the beastman that he had slain. But at least his own skin and hair had been sluiced clean by the river.

The thought of the beastmen made him glance into the forest behind him. He could not sense any danger, but he knew that he could not rely totally on his extra vision. In any case, an ordinary beastman was the least of his worries. After what had happened this morning, such once-frightening creatures seemed relatively harmless.

He tried to avoid considering what he had witnessed, but inevitably his mind kept returning to the massacre. He had known that the world was full of weird and terrifying beings. He had heard the strange tales of the occasional traveller who stayed at the inn, and Elyssa had passed on a few stories of the lands beyond the valley that her father had narrated to her.

Elyssa...

She was dead. There could no longer be any room for doubt, for remote possibilities that the girl may have lived. He had known she would die, and she had. But being forewarned did not make him any less sad.

She had died, as had all the others in the village. He had not known how she would meet her terrible end, only that she would do so. Yet he had believed that she would be the only one to suffer such a fate. He had been totally oblivious to the fact that everyone else who dwelled in the valley would also die.

Everyone except himself.

Why had he alone survived? Because he did not really belong there? That made no sense, but neither did anything else, and he tried not to think at all.

But his thoughts kept focusing on Skullface, the impossible man who walked through fire and who was immune to an arrow in the heart. That was the most unbelievable episode of all, and already Konrad found it hard to convince himself of what he had seen.

All the other fantastic sights he could accept – perhaps for the very reason that so many of them were beyond his comprehension, and had no basis in rationality. But fire he knew, arrows he knew. And no man could survive the flames of such an inferno, no man could be unaffected by a fatal arrow. No man. Thus Skullface could not have been a man.

Yet none of the other marauders had been totally human – most had been the exact opposite – so why did Skullface occupy so much of his attention?

Hoping to blank his mind of such unnerving and futile contemplations, Konrad picked up his clothes and returned to the water's edge. As he did so, as if in mockery of his attempts to forget, the body of one of the brutes that had attacked the village floated past.

It had webbed feet, he noticed, but that had been no help to it in the water. At first he thought that the corpse must have been trapped upstream for a while by a tree or a rock, then he realized that it had nothing to do with the massacre.

It must have been dead for days, because its putrid body could not have reached such an advanced state of decomposition after only a few hours in the water.

It was floating face down, most of it submerged, and he could not see it very well. Even so, he saw more than enough. The marauder had been multi-coloured, green and yellow and brown, with long sharp spikes sticking up from its spine and the back of its skull. Like Konrad, it seemed that it had held onto its weapon – except that it was another of those monsters whose forelimb had mutated into a blade, a hooked sword. Its other front limb ended in a pair of powerful pincers.

He waited until the bloated corpse had drifted out of sight, then began washing the last traces of blood and gore from his garments. He would be like the bait in a trap if he wore them. Even diluted, the scent of spilled blood would be a lure to the predators that prowled the woods.

Rubbing the fabric together in the water, pounding it on the rocks, squeezing as much moisture out as possible, also warmed him up. By the time he finished, he was no longer shivering and only his hands and his hair were still wet. He spread his clothes on a large rock to dry, and he wondered what to do.

What to do now – and what to do for the rest of his life.

He had been tired, but he could ignore the fatigue. He had been cold, but now he was warm. He had been in pain, but his injuries were only superficial. He had been hungry, and he still was. Food was his first priority. If he ate something, that would also help his weariness.

There would be fish in the river, but catching them without a net or line was always a long process. Neither did Konrad particularly want to enter the river again, not for a while.

The forest always contained things that could be eaten, if one was careful. Over the years, Konrad had become very careful. He could not have survived on what he was given at the inn, even when he supplemented his diet with what Elyssa used to bring, and he had always foraged and hunted in the woods. That was what he had intended to do this morning, until he had encountered the beastman with the axe growing from its arm.

The trees where he had emerged from the river were subtly different from the ones he was used to. Maybe it was his imagination, but they seemed somehow healthier and straighter, not so rotten and twisted. That meant it should be easier to find sustenance, that there should be fewer poisoned and tainted plants which masqueraded as nourishment.

Leaving his clothes where they lay, he picked up his knife and entered the forest, in search of edible fungi, of tender young shoots, of seeds and berries and nuts – of anything that he could find to fill his empty belly.

By the time he had found enough to satisfy his craving, his clothes were dry. They were even more torn and threadbare after the beating he had given them, and they were still stained with old marks, but every trace of recent gore seemed to have gone.

He dressed, turned to go, then looked back, remembering the black quiver. It was useless without any arrows, but there seemed no reason to leave it behind. He slung it over his shoulder.

Konrad had never been in this part of the forest before, and he did not want to risk taking the wrong direction and finding himself back in the village, and so there was only one way he could go.

Knife in hand, he began making his way along the side of the river, heading further downstream.

THAT NIGHT HE slept peacefully and dreamlessly.

Because he was on unfamiliar territory, he had spent a few hours looking for a safe resting place. He had been unable to find a tree with a suitable hollow, but he located one whose wide trunk forked into three, and the junction provided an almost level area that was just the right size in which to curl up.

As ever, he woke before dawn. He was cold and stiff, and he stretched and rubbed at his aching limbs. He inspected his wounds, all of which seemed to be scabbing over. When they healed, he would have a few more scars on his body.

He waited until it was light before he climbed down the tree. He drank from the river, then returned to the woods in search of food.

After an hour of foraging, his hunger pangs were temporarily quelled, but he would need something more substantial before long. If he had been back at the village, he could have eaten some of the animal feed.

He smiled at the idea. It was the first time he had thought of the village this morning, and instead of remembering its destruction he was considering food.

That was the way it should have been, he supposed. All the village had ever meant to him was food and shelter. It had never given him anything else. He did not care that the village had been attacked, did not care that everyone had been killed.

With one exception...

He blanked out the image of Elyssa that began to form in his mind, instead forcing himself to concentrate on where he could find his next meal. He could not hunt because he had no arrows, so that meant either wading into the shallows in the hope of catching a fish, or else setting snares.

He chose some pieces of fallen wood that would be suitable as pegs. Then, as he walked along the river bank he collected strands of the long fine grass growing there, and he wove them into lengths of string.

As it had been yesterday, his progress was slow because of the density of trees, which grew right up to the water's edge. He tried to keep close to the river, because it must lead somewhere. As long as he knew where the river was, he did not consider that he was lost.

The landscape resembled that of the valley, although it was not so steep and the woodlands had not been cleared as they had been around the village, but the same kind of wildlife must have inhabited the vicinity.

When he finally came to an open space, where no trees grew, he was suspicious at first. He then realized that the ground was very rocky, and the soil was not deep enough for the trees to set down roots. But there was plenty of grass for rabbits to eat – and so there should be plenty of rabbits for him to eat.

He searched the area, scanning the ground as he walked, looking for droppings, the sign that there was a warren nearby. Finally, he saw what he had known must be there.

Rabbits always followed the same routes, like people taking a road, and so he only had to set his snares along the tracks that they had made previously and they would be caught.

By this time, he had enough plaited grass to make four traps. He tied the makeshift string to the pegs, pushed the pegs deep into the ground, propped up the grass loops with twigs. Then he went away to wait.

Waiting, he discovered, was something he was not very good at. He had never had to do it, not for more than a few minutes. At the inn, he never had a moment's rest. The only time he had ever waited was whenever he was in the forest and a beastman had been near. He had always been forced to hide and wait for it to move on.

He had also spent a lot of time waiting for Elyssa, he supposed. Often he had waited weeks between her visits, but that was not the same as having to wait in the woods until a rabbit had sacrificed itself for his dinner.

There was no point in going on further, exploring what lay ahead, because he would only have to return to examine his snares.

Time passed. He watched as the sun completed its long slow climb towards its zenith. Half the day was over, half the day was yet to be. Konrad decided that he could not wait his whole life for a rabbit. If he had caught nothing, then he would continue with his trek along the river. Instead, when he returned to where he had placed his traps, he discovered that he had caught two of them.

One rabbit was dead, having strangled itself. The other had managed to trap its hind leg in the loop of grass. Konrad broke its neck with a quick twist of his wrist.

He felt pleased with himself, and he went back to the river to cut the rabbits open. He threw their entrails into the water so that the smell of blood would not attract any of the larger local creatures.

Making a fire seemed to take almost as long as catching the rabbits had done. Although he would have eaten them raw if he were desperate, he was not yet that hungry. He decided it would be best to make a fire in the very centre of the clearing, because that would give him the best chance of seeing any creature that was drawn to the scent.

He collected plenty of twigs and sticks. That was something he was good at. He made up a bow from a short stick and twisted grass, looped the bowstring around a vertical stick, and began rotating the end of the stick against a piece of wood that he held on the ground.

Finally, the friction produced smoke, charring, a tiny flicker of flame, and he managed to ignite a piece of dry grass. When he at last had a proper blaze, he hung the skinned body of the first rabbit over the flames.

He waited again.

The animal was black and burned on the outside, almost raw in the inside, but it tasted fine to Konrad.

While the rabbit had been cooking, he had scraped its pelt clean. It might come in useful. When he resumed his journey, he tucked the skin in his belt. He tied the hind legs of the other rabbit together with a plait of grass, hanging it from his belt. He carried his snares in the quiver.

Within a few minutes of leaving the clearing, he came to a bridge over the river and a road which led off from it in either direction. The bridge was nothing like the one at the village. It stood higher out of the water, was broader – and made of stone. The road was also much wider than the dirt track that led from the village's wooden bridge.

Konrad climbed up from the riverbank and onto the bridge, and he stood in the centre of the span. He had known that the river must lead somewhere, and this was what it had led him to. Having found the bridge, that meant he must make a decision.

At first, all he had wanted to do was escape from the doomed village. He had succeeded, but now what did he do?

He could not live in the forest forever. There were too many dangerous beings within the woods. Yet he did not particularly want to go and live in another village, not after the way he had always been treated. He had no trade, no skills, he would most likely end up working in another tavern. But at least he would be paid, he supposed.

Then he remembered that he did have a skill. He was a hunter. He could trap small animals, he could shoot larger ones with his bow and arrows – if he had a bow and arrows. Perhaps he could trap more rabbits, exchange them for some arrows. He could make another bow for himself.

There was an alternative to choosing between the forest or a village, he realized. He could choose both.

Konrad looked to the left, then to the right. Both roads seemed the same, both must lead somewhere. It made no difference which route he took, and so he took one of them.

HE HAD HALF-EXPECTED that he would encounter a village very quickly, that it would be situated near the bridge, by the river. When after about half an hour he had come across no sign of habitation, he considered returning, thinking that he had picked the wrong direction. Yet he was in no hurry, and so he continued on his chosen route.

The road was only made of dirt, but a ditch ran on one side. He guessed it was there to drain off the water in winter, to prevent the surface becoming a quagmire of mud. The trees had been cut back in a wide swathe on either side, making it less easy for travellers to be ambushed. Even so, he walked in the centre, and his knife never left his hand.

Hearing a noise behind him, back down the road, Konrad spun around. He did not recognize the sound. Whatever it was, it was growing louder, coming quickly closer.

Although he could see nothing yet, neither did he want to be seen. He left the road and jumped the ditch, hurrying out of sight behind the nearest broad tree. Then he watched and listened while the unknown sound grew louder, nearer.

It rattled and panted, creaked and cantered, and then came level with his hiding place. A wagon of some sort, pulled by four horses. An enclosed wagon, with people inside, while two more people sat on the top, driving the team of horses.

There had been wagons in the village, but they had been used for carrying crops and logs. Konrad had never seen anything like this, a vehicle whose only cargo was people.

It was soon past him, and he hurried back to the road so that he could see the wagon vanish, but it was hidden by the dust that the wheels had disturbed.

Konrad walked on, waving his hand in front of his face to clear the dirt from the air.

And then, ahead of him, out of nowhere, he saw two men walking in his direction.

His immediate reaction was to freeze, and he did so. His first thought was to flee, but both men carried bows. Although they did not have arrows notched, they probably knew these woods and would be able to pursue and shoot him if he tried to run.

They must have been from the next village. Either that or they were outlaws. But he had nothing for them to steal.

He could not hide away from everyone. He would have to face people when he eventually reached habitation, and so he walked towards the two men. At least he presumed they were men. They looked human, although after what he had witnessed yesterday he knew it was impossible to be certain.

The men had slowed when they saw him. They were both older than Konrad, bearded, dressed like woodsmen from his village, although they did not carry axes. They came forward, then stopped, and Konrad halted a few yards away.

"ullo ta ya, boy,' said one of them.

"ullo dere,' said the other.

Konrad looked from one to another, licking at his dry lips.

'Ain't seen ya afore,' continued the first man.

'Stranger 'round 'ere?' added the second man.

Konrad nodded.

'Where ya goin', boy?'

'Ya lost?'

Konrad kept staring at them.

'What's up wid 'im?' the first asked the second.

'Can't 'e talk?' the second suggested to the first.

'Dat right, boy?'

Konrad opened his mouth to speak, but no words would come. In his whole life, he had only ever spoken to one person, to Elyssa. He did not know how to talk to other people.

He shook his head.

'Stupid,' the first said to his companion.

'Very,' agreed the other.

The first pointed down the road in the direction from which they had come. 'Ya – go – dat – way?' he asked loudly, slowly.

Konrad decided that it was not him who was the stupid one, because it was obvious that was the way he had been heading.

'Yes,' he replied.

'Where–' the second one began slowly, loudly, '–ta?' he finished, not so slowly, not so loudly.

Konrad shrugged.

'Why doncha come wid us?' said the first one. 'We're goin' back. We'll show ya de way.'

'The way to what?' Konrad asked.

'Ta where ya goin'.'

'But I don't know where I'm going.'

'Den ya lucky we met, 'cos we'll take ya where ya wanna go.'

'Where?'

'Inta town, 'course,' added the second man.

Konrad began to feel suspicious. The strangers seemed far too friendly. Maybe that was the way that other people behaved, however. It was only those in the village who had treated him so badly.

'Bin catchin' rabbits, boy?' said the first. 'Dat's a fine buck, ya got dere. Take it ta town an' ya'd sell it fer a good price. Tree shillin's.'

'Three!' said Konrad, astonished.

'More,' added the second man, quickly, thinking that Konrad believed it was not enough. 'More dan tree. Four. Five!'

Five shillings was a fortune. Even three shillings was far more than he had accumulated in a lifetime of saving – then lost in a second. He wished that he had not eaten the other rabbit.

'Ya right, Carl,' agreed the first stranger, looking at the dead rabbit again. 'Five shillin's. How 'bout dat, boy? We'll take ya inta town, show ya where ta get de best price fer ya rabbit.'

'Ya catch it near 'ere?' asked the second man, the one named Carl.

Konrad nodded, not wanting to say where.

Carl laughed. 'By de river, wus it? Near de bridge?'

'Yes.'

'We knows all de best places fer all de animals,' said Carl, who then added to his companion, "e tinks we wanna steal his rabbit, Heinz. Dat's what 'e tinks.'

'Doncha worry, boy,' said Heinz. 'We hunt bigger game dan dat.'

Konrad nodded again, more slowly, unconvinced.

'We's only tryin' ta 'elp ya, boy,' Heinz continued. 'Ya look like ya wanna good meal, good clothes. Ya can find whatever ya wanna get in town. We only wanna 'elp. Ya don' know us, so ya don' wanna trust us. Why doncha follow behind us?'

Carl looked at his companion. 'I don' know 'bout ya, Heinz, but I wanna beer. I'm buyin'.'

They both turned and began walking back the way they had come. Carl glanced over his shoulder.

'An' I'll buy ya one,' he said.

Konrad waited until they had gone twenty yards, then he followed.

CHAPTER EIGHT

THERE WAS A wooden gate across the road into town, not far from the first buildings. At first Konrad assumed this must be some kind of defence, then he saw that the barrier was far too flimsy to fulfil such a function.

A uniformed guard stood by the gate, and he was collecting money from people who wished to enter or leave the town.

Konrad halted and watched as Carl and Heinz paid, then went through the opened gate. Carl beckoned to him, and he walked towards the barrier.

The guard leaned against the gate, watching as he approached, looking him up and down. 'Tree pence,' he told Konrad.

'Just to go in the town?'

'Na,' said the guard, yawning. 'Fer usin' de road.'

'But I haven't got three pence.'

'Tough. Den I ain't openin' de gate. Nobody 'cept de baron gets past dis gate widout payin' – an' dat's 'cos it's 'is road.'

'Dere,' said Carl, reaching into his pocket. 'Tree pence.' He handed it to the guard.

Konrad was astonished.

'Thank you,' he said. 'Thank you. I'll pay you back, I will, I will.'

'I know ya will,' said Carl, who turned and walked to where Heinz was waiting. They carried on up the road.

The guard swung the gate open just enough for Konrad to squeeze through. "ave a nice day,' he said.

The town seemed enormous, far larger than the village had been. There were so many people around, as many in the streets as had inhabited the whole of the village. And there were many more streets, all of which were cobble-stoned. Everything was on a much larger scale, with more buildings, which were bigger too.

As he walked up the central street, a few paces behind Heinz and Carl, Konrad gazed at everything in wonder and bewilderment.

No one took any notice of him. Had a stranger arrived in the village, however, everyone would have known about it and stared at the newcomer. Here, it seemed, travellers must have been a familiar sight. Also, there were so many people that they could not have known all the others who lived there.

People from one end of the town would be strangers to those from the other end.

He noticed the enclosed wagon that had sped past about an hour ago. There was an emblem painted on the side of the vehicle, some kind of tower, which Konrad guessed must have been a castle. The horses had gone from their traces, but the four-wheeled contraption was halted outside what could only be a tavern. It was bigger than Adolf Brandenheimer's inn, and in a much better state of repair.

After all the years he had spent within one, Konrad would have recognized an inn anywhere; but as if in confirmation, a huge sign hung above the entrance. The wooden placard boldly displayed an overflowing tankard of ale in proclamation of the nature of the establishment.

He had already observed that many of the other buildings carried similar signs displaying their wares – the baker, the butcher, the vegetable merchant, the blacksmith.

The village had been so small that everyone knew which buildings were owned by traders and what they sold. The town was so much larger that people must have easily become lost in its bewildering maze of streets, and so they needed the signs above the vendors to tell them that they had found what they were searching for.

Konrad expected his new companions to go into the tavern, but they did not. They continued further through the town, past even more merchants, into what must have been the market square. On the corner, although not as big as the first one, stood another inn!

Konrad found it hard to understand why there should be two alehouses. Then he guessed the reason: it was because one tavern would not be large enough for all those who wished to frequent a drinking house.

The town was far larger than he could ever have imagined. As he surveyed the area, he noticed that the fields which surrounded the town were so far away from the central square that it was almost impossible to see them because of all the buildings.

'Dis is it,' Konrad heard a voice say. 'Ya wanna drink?'

He had been so busy staring around that he had not been paying very much attention to the two men he had followed from the forest. Heinz was no longer in sight; he must have already entered the tavern. Carl had paused in the entrance; it was he who had called to Konrad.

Konrad nodded and stepped forward.

'Betta put de knife 'way,' Carl told him. 'It don' look very friendly.'

Konrad glanced down at his right hand, at the dagger still gripped there. He had not realized that he was holding it, and he tucked it into his belt before following Carl into the building.

It felt strange entering through the front door. He had always used the back entrance of Brandenheimer's tavern. He glanced around, noticing the rough wooden tables and stools, recognizing the familiar smells of spilled beer and fresh straw on the floor. From the rear came the odours of meat roasting and of ale brewing.

Heinz was already standing by a high wooden table, behind which three huge barrels lay propped on their sides.

The landlord was at one of the barrels, turning the tap to fill a pewter stein. He passed it to Heinz, noticed Carl, turned and began to fill another stein.

Carl said something to Heinz, and they both looked at Konrad, who still stood in the doorway staring around. Carl took the second beer, holding it towards Konrad.

'Come on!' he said, and he set the tankard on the table between himself and Heinz. 'An' anudda,' he added, to the landlord.

He threw a few coins onto the table, and the innkeeper returned to the barrel for a third stein.

Hesitantly, Konrad entered the tavern. One or two of the men already inside studied him for a moment before turning their attention back to their ale. Konrad walked over to Heinz and Carl, and glanced down at the stein of beer. *His* stein of beer.

He had never been allowed to drink Brandenheimer's ale, although that had not stopped him from doing so whenever the tavern owner was out of sight. Brandenheimer had even hated Konrad drinking water.

'Who's ya friend, Carl?' asked the landlord, setting down the final pewter stein and counting the coins from the wet table into his palm.

'Met 'im in de forest,' said Carl, taking a mouthful of his ale.

Konrad licked at his dry lips, picked up his tankard with both hands, raised it to his mouth.

'But 'e ain't na friend,' said Heinz, putting his own stein on the table, turning to face Konrad.

'Dat's right,' agreed Carl, and he also set down his ale and faced Konrad.

Before he could take a first sip of his beer, Konrad knew what was going to happen. Even as realization came, he knew he would be too late to do anything about it.

But that did not stop him trying. He twisted around, hurling his full tankard directly at Carl's face. He leapt away from the table, his hand reaching down for his dagger.

He was not fast enough. Heinz seized his wrist, and a moment later Carl punched him in the stomach. Konrad doubled up in pain and surprise.

Heinz grabbed him by the hair, yanking him upright. Carl held a knife to Konrad's throat, pressing the point into the soft flesh below his chin.

'Na,' said Carl, wiping the thrown beer from his face, "e ain't na friend.'

And Heinz said, "e's a poacher...'

KONRAD LAY ON the stone floor, watching the shafts of dawn light shine through the airblocks far above, and again he wondered what would become of him.

He had been right to be suspicious of Heinz and Carl, and he ought to have trusted his instincts. Because he had not done so, he had ended up being thrown down into one of the cellars of the inn.

He had told them he did not know it was a crime to snare rabbits, had asked what they planned to do and what would happen to him. The traitors were in no mood for conversation. All they would say was that his fate would be decided tomorrow. He had also overheard one of the two promising the innkeeper a share of the reward for letting them keep their captive locked in the tavern overnight.

In the village, Wilhelm Kastring had been the law. Anyone who committed an offence was taken before him. They would have to pay a fine, be given a beating, be made to work without pay for a certain length of time, or be put in the stocks – or some combination of all these punishments, depending upon what it was that they had done.

What was this town's punishment for poaching a rabbit? No, two rabbits. If it were a fine, he could not pay. The only way he could make restitution would be through working. Perhaps he would be sentenced to a whipping. He was used to that.

He heard the door being unlocked, and more light flooded the darkened cellar.

'Get up 'ere!' a voice ordered.

Konrad obeyed. He stood and walked towards the steps in the corner, climbing up to ground level. Heinz and Carl were waiting for him, both with knives in their hands. The knife that Carl now held was Konrad's.

'Good blade,' he said, seeing that Konrad had noticed. 'Far ta good fer a poacher.'

'Turn 'round!' Heinz ordered. "ands behind yer back!'

Konrad did so, and he felt his wrists being bound together.

'What's happening?' he asked. 'What are you going to do to me?'

'We ain't gonna do nothin', boy,' Heinz told him.

'Na,' said Carl. 'Someone else is!' Then he laughed.

He sheathed his knife, Konrad's knife, grabbed Konrad's shoulder and forced him through the inn. They passed a table on which his quiver and the dead rabbit lay, and Heinz picked them both up. Then they all went out into the street.

Despite the earliness of the hour, plenty of people were already in the square. There were not as many as yesterday, but when they saw that Konrad was a prisoner they paid much more attention to him than previously.

'Who ya got dere?' someone called.

'Yeah, wot's 'e dun?' yelled someone else.

'Stick 'round an' find out!' Carl shouted back.

He and Heinz both grinned. They stared up one of the streets, in the direction of the morning sun. They were look-ing for someone, and Konrad guessed who it must be – his judge...

After a few minutes, Konrad heard the sound of hooves in the distance. It came from the east, and it was the sound of more than one horse; several riders were approaching the square. Carl dragged him out towards the middle of the road, Heinz shoving him in the back.

A few seconds later, the first of the riders appeared around the corner, quickly followed by five more. There was also a retinue on foot, another dozen people, including two dog handlers, each of whom held two chained hounds.

Four of the horsemen were soldiers, garbed in blue-plumed helmets and polished breastplates, wearing swords at their hips, each carrying a shield emblazoned with the same crest – a blue dragon.

The fifth rider was a woman, richly dressed in colourful and expensive fabrics. She rode sidesaddle, and a servant girl walked beside her, holding a long-handled parasol aloft to keep the sun from the woman's face – even though her face was almost covered by a silk scarf.

Leading the procession was the man who Heinz and Carl must have been waiting for. His outfit put the woman's to shame. He was clad in satin and suede, trimmed with lace, all of different shades of blue – from his dark blue leather boots to his pale blue cap, and the feather in the band which was of an even paler hue. Only the hawk perched on his right wrist was not blue, but its hood was.

More people had arrived on the streets, and they cheered as the horseman rode past, bowing as he went. He ignored them, his nose in the air. He was riding directly towards where Konrad and his captors were standing.

'Baron!' said Heinz.

'Baron!' echoed Carl.

They both knelt, dragging Konrad down with them.

The rider twitched at his reins with his left hand, and his horse changed direction slightly, to go around the trio blocking his path.

'What is it?' asked the baron, not even bothering to look at them.

'A criminal, my lord!' cried Carl.

'Ah!' The baron glanced down for the first time. He halted his mount, and everyone in the procession behind him also stopped.

Konrad looked up at the baron. It was hard to tell his age because he was overweight, and he needed a huge horse to support him, but he was probably in his late thirties, his fat cheeks clean shaven.

Konrad only had a moment to glance at the rider, because then Carl forced his head right down, so that his hair brushed against the dirty cobbles. Upside down, he saw another horse enter the square from the opposite direction.

It was a white horse, and it was being led by a man on foot. A packhorse followed the white horse, and the man walked towards the tavern, tied up both his animals and went into the inn. It was hard to tell at such an angle, but it seemed as though the newcomer had been wearing a black helmet which completely covered his face.

While Konrad was watching the new arrival, the baron had been quizzing his captors. 'What has he done?'

"'e's a poacher, baron. 'e trapped two uv ya rabbits. Look. 'e skinned an' ate dis one, an' dis is de udda one. Dese are 'is snares.'

'An' 'e's a thief, Baron. Dis quiver, see? 'e musta stolen it.'

'Landlord!' came a loud voice from within the tavern. The helmeted rider had found the inn empty. Everyone was out in the square, watching what was happening there.

'What have you to say for yourself, thief?' asked the baron.

Konrad's head was jerked upwards, and he found himself looking at the baron again.

'I was hungry,' he explained. 'That's all. I trapped a rabbit because I was hungry. I didn't know it was a crime. I'm a stranger here. I'll pay for it.'

"'e ain't got na money,' said Heinz.

'Silence!' the baron commanded. His eyes returned to Konrad. 'You're a stranger, I accept that. Perhaps the law is different where you come from. But while you are here you must obey my law. You stole from me.'

'I didn't mean to!'

'Silence! You say you were hungry. I understand that. We all get hungry if we haven't eaten for two or three hours. I would certainly not blame you for trapping and eating a rabbit. But you trapped two. Have you anything to say?'

Konrad opened his mouth to speak, but he could not think of any excuse or justification, and all he said was, 'I'm sorry.'

'It's too late for apologies,' the baron told him. 'I'm going hunting now. When I return, you will be hung.'

KONRAD STARED AT the baron in utter bewilderment. Had he survived the massacre at the village only to be hung for trapping two rabbits?

The hell beasts had been unable to kill him, but they were only savage marauders, senseless brutes. When it came to cruelty and treachery, they were no match for the most dangerous creatures of all – humans.

'You can't hang him,' said a voice from the entrance to the tavern.

The voice was not loud, but because of the silence in the square it was heard by everyone – and everyone turned to look at the newcomer.

He did indeed wear a black helmet. The visor had been swung up so that he could drink his tankard of ale, but his face was in shadow. He was clad all in black: his chainmail surcoat was made of black metal rings on black leather. A black scabbard hung from his black belt, and even the hilt of his sword was black – as were his woollen breeches and short leather boots.

'What do you mean?' demanded the baron. 'Who are you? What right do you have to interfere?'

The baron glanced back towards his four mounted troopers, as if making sure that they were still there to back up his words. 'This is no concern of yours,' he continued, 'whoever you are.'

'He's allowed a defence,' said the man in black.

'Defence? Defence! He's a criminal. What defence can he possibly have?'

'He can defend himself.'

'He just did. And not very well!'

The baron looked around at the townspeople, and several took the hint and laughed appreciatively. He kept looking at the crowd, and more and more people joined in the chorus of laughter.

The newcomer sipped at his beer, waiting for silence. 'He has a right to trial by combat,' he said, once that silence had fallen.

The baron stared at him in astonishment. 'Trial by combat?' he repeated, incredulously. 'But he's a – a peasant!'

'That's a mere technicality. I think you'll find that under a codicil to the rules of chivalry, as decided by the court of Emperor Magnus in the year 2325, the right to trial by combat is granted to anyone in possession of their own blade.' The man in black took another mouthful of ale, then glanced at Konrad. 'Do you have your own blade, lad?'

Konrad had hardly been paying any attention to what was going on. He was still too stunned by the baron's death sentence, but he automatically replied, 'Yes.'

'Na,' said Heinz.

'Na,' said Carl.

'See?' said the baron. 'The word of two of my most reliable citizens against that of a poacher and a thief. I know who I choose to believe.'

'If he didn't have a blade,' said the man, 'then how did he slit open that rabbit? With his teeth?'

'Did he have a blade?' the baron demanded.

'Er...' said Heinz.

'Ah...' said Carl, and he displayed Konrad's knife. '...Yeah.'

'All right, all right,' said the baron. He gazed at the strange blade of the knife. 'But no peasant can own such a knife. He must have stolen it.'

Which was true, thought Konrad.

'He has a blade,' said the man in the black helmet, 'therefore he has a right to trial by combat.'

'No!' protested the baron. 'The rules of chivalry govern the conduct between gentlemen, knights, men of honour. Not peasants! And a blade is a sword, not a knife!'

'A blade is a blade,' said the newcomer. 'The accused has the right to trial by combat. You must either free him or grant him his rights. You can't hang him.'

'Don't tell me what I can't do!' the baron cried angrily.

He reached for the sword at his hip, and the hawk fell from his wrist. Squealing and flapping its wings, it dangled upside down from the cord that linked its leg to the baron's gauntlet.

One of the men on foot rushed to rescue the bird, transferring it to the leather padding around his own wrist; the baron allowed the chain to be detached from his glove.

'I was merely advising you as to the strict letter of the law,' said the black figure. 'But if you're scared...'

'Scared? Me!' The baron forced a laugh. 'What have I to be scared of?' He sat up straighter in the saddle, staring around at the populace of the town, his town.

'You are the Emperor's appointed representative in this region, so it is your duty to ensure that his laws are obeyed – to the letter. The accused is entitled to trial by combat, and therefore it is up to you to accept the challenge.'

'Me? You mean I have to fight – him?' The baron gestured contemptuously at Konrad.

'You don't have to,' said the man in black. 'If you wish, you may appoint a champion. But I'm sure you will prefer to carry out your judicial functions personally. The choice of weapons is, naturally, yours. Your reputation has travelled far, baron, and I believe you were once a celebrated duellist. You killed fifteen men, am I correct?'

'Sixteen,' the baron corrected.

'Of course you were younger then and not so…' There was no need for the man to finish what he was saying; the word 'fat' was the obvious conclusion to the sentence.

'I'm a match for any man!' declared the baron. 'As for a peasant – ha!'

'Then you accept the challenge?'

'Yes, yes, yes! Let's get on with it. I'll kill the thief now, while there's still time to go hunting before lunch.'

He beckoned to the nearest soldier. 'Give the criminal your sword.'

Konrad found himself back on his feet, his hands cut free. The trooper handed him a sword.

With difficulty, the baron dismounted from his horse. He drew his sword and walked slowly towards Konrad. 'If you have a god, then say your prayers.'

'Pause a moment, baron, if you will,' said the newcomer. 'You have declined to appoint a deputy, but the accused is also permitted the right to nominate a champion.'

The baron frowned, then shook his head. 'I'm fed up with you interfering. You're trying to delay the administration of justice. There's no one here to act as his champion. Let me get on with it and kill him.'

'What do you say, lad?' the man said to Konrad. 'Do you wish to fight, or would you care to nominate a champion?'

Konrad looked at the sword in his hand, looked at the baron, looked at the stranger in black, then it dawned on him what was expected. 'I nominate you,' he said.

'I accept.'

'Hey, what is this?' demanded the baron, turning to face the man. 'Who are you?'

In reply, the newcomer removed his black helmet. His cropped hair was snow white, as was his shorn beard. His head and face were completely tattooed, black lines etched indelibly into his skin to give him the appearance of an animal – a dog or a fox. No – a wolf...

'You!' cried the baron, taking several steps back.

'Me,' agreed the tattooed man.

'I'm glad you haven't forgotten, Otto. I said that we'd meet again, and I know how disappointed you'd have been if I hadn't kept my promise. I'm a man of my word. Unlike you.'

The baron glanced around quickly, anxiously, as though searching for some means of escape. He looked up at his mounted soldiers, obviously wanting to call for their aid, but unwilling to do so because it would make him look a weakling in front of the townspeople.

'Wolf,' he said, sheathing his sword and walking towards the white-haired man, 'it's good to see you again after all these years. We've had our misunderstandings in the past, and it seems this is another of them!'

He laughed, and the nervous edge to the sound was readily apparent.

Wolf set his helmet down and drew his sword, and the metal of the blade was as black as the rest of his outfit. He still held his beer stein in his left hand, and he took a drink.

'Let's go somewhere and talk this over,' said the baron. He had lowered his voice, so that the crowd could not overhear; but Konrad was the closest person to the two antagonists, and so he heard every word.

'I can pay you now,' the baron continued. 'I can pay you more, a lot more. We can sort everything out, I promise. You can't be serious about this. You aren't going to fight me for a poacher!'

'No.'

The baron relaxed slightly. 'I knew you'd see reason, Wolf.'

'I intend to fight you for myself. Pray to Ulric, for all the good it'll do you.'

'You won't get away with it!' the baron hissed. 'Even if I die, my men will kill you!'

Wolf glanced past the baron, towards the soldiers, then at the woman who had been watching all these events in silence, and he shook his head. 'I don't think so.'

'What do you want, Wolf?'

'Justice. You have accepted a challenge, Otto. Are you going to back off like the lying, treacherous coward that you really are?'

The baron looked over his shoulder, and everyone in the square looked back at him. 'What can I do, Wolf?'

'You can die, Otto, you can die.'

'I've killed sixteen men in duels, Wolf! You will be number seventeen!'

So saying, the baron took a step backwards, drew his sword again, then lunged forward with the blade aimed at Wolf's stomach. For someone so obese, he moved with an alacrity which demonstrated the skills that he must once have possessed.

The man in black casually sidestepped, and he took a sip of ale as the sword flashed past him.

The baron swung his weapon at his opponent's head. Wolf's sword whirled up, blocking the blow. Their blades were locked together above them, their faces a few inches apart.

For the first time Wolf allowed a flicker of emotion to register on his features. He grinned, showing his teeth – his pointed teeth!

'I'm not here to fight you, Otto,' he said. 'I'm here to execute you.'

His sword forced the baron's steel backwards, and the baron followed in retreat. Then the black blade sliced swiftly down and forward, straight into the baron's chest. The baron stared down at his satin shirt, where the blue was becoming red.

Wolf withdrew his sword, and the baron slid onto the cobbles. By the time his head hit the ground he was dead.

Wolf glanced around, at the woman on horseback, at the troopers, and the baron's retinue, at the crowd, at Konrad. No one moved. He raised the beer stein to his lips, emptying it.

'Pick him up,' said the woman, speaking for the first time. 'Put him on his horse.'

She watched as the body of the baron was draped over the saddle of his mount.

'Take him back to the fort,' she ordered. 'Let's get on with the hunt.' All the time her eyes had been on the tattooed stranger. 'Will you dine with me tonight, Wolf? Perhaps I'll be able to repay some of what my brother owes you.' She glanced at the body of the baron. 'And I think that I am also in your debt now. Will you acept my invitation?'

'Perhaps,' answered Wolf.

His reply seemed to satisfy the woman. While the baron's corpse returned the way it had come, all the others in the procession continued in the direction they had been originally going.

'Give him back his things,' Wolf commanded.

The soldier had already retrieved his sword from Konrad, who now found himself holding his knife, his quiver, his snares, the fur of the rabbit he had skinned and the body of the one he had not.

Wolf leaned his blood-smeared sword against the wall. 'Clean that,' he said to Konrad.

He turned, picked up his helmet and walked back into the tavern.

'More ale!' he commanded.

CHAPTER NINE

NOW THAT THERE was nothing to see, the crowd had dispersed, and there was no sign of Heinz and Carl.

Konrad used the skinned rabbit pelt to wipe the blood from Wolf's sword. When he had finished, he threw the stained skin into the street, picked up the black blade and carried it into the tavern. It was very long and broad, heavier than any weapon he had ever lifted.

Wolf was standing at the table near the barrels, drinking from a stein. He had removed his chainmail, beneath which he wore a black leather tunic. Bands of black fur were wrapped around each wrist, like amulets. A tight black chain encircled his neck – not a fine chain, but one with very heavy links.

His black helmet lay next to him. Seeing it with the visor pulled down, Konrad realized that it was shaped like the head of a wolf. It had metal fangs growing from the muzzle-shaped visor, and the holes where a wolf's eyes should have been were positioned for the wearer to see out.

Konrad held the sword towards the man, hilt-first. Wolf glanced at the blade, quickly inspecting it for signs of gore, then accepted and sheathed it.

'Thank you,' said Konrad.

'For what?' said Wolf, not even looking at him.

'For saving my life.'

'That was incidental.'

'Not to me.'

Wolf turned and studied him for the first time, and Konrad saw his glance move from side as he gazed at Konrad's eyes.

'I suppose not,' said Wolf. 'Your life is worthless to me or anyone else, but worth everything to you.'

'I was lucky you came along.'

'Lucky?' said Wolf. He smiled, showing his pointed teeth. 'There's no such thing as luck.'

Although he had noticed the sharpened teeth earlier, at more distance, Konrad could not but help taking a backward step.

Wolf laughed out loud. He was taller that Konrad, over six feet, his limbs strongly muscled. His white hair was deceptive; he could have been no older than the baron.

'Another beer!' he said to the landlord, who was standing as far as possible behind the table. 'And one for my friend.'

The innkeeper was the man who had allowed Konrad to be locked in his cellar, and Wolf's words reminded him of what the landlord had said yesterday – when he had asked Heinz and Carl who their friend was. This was different, however, a lot different. Konrad had been suspicious of the two men, yet Wolf had already proved himself. But a friend?

Konrad asked, 'What you said out there, that anyone who carried a blade was entitled to trial by combat, is that correct?'

'I very much doubt it. The law is different for the rich. Always has been, always will be.' Wolf shrugged. 'Let's see your knife.'

Konrad passed him the dagger, and Wolf examined the many-curved blade.

'It's called a kris,' he said. 'It was made thousands and thousands of miles away, beyond far Cathay.' He handed it back. 'But I don't suppose that's where you got it from.' He took a mouthful of beer. 'What's your name, lad?'

'Konrad.'

'That it? Just Konrad, no other name?'

Konrad nodded.

So did Wolf. 'You look too poor to own more than one name. Here.' He passed over a stein of ale, and Konrad drank thirstily.

'Drink can be a dangerous thing, Konrad. Look what it did to me.' He gestured towards his face and his mouth. 'I got drunk one week and decided to make myself look like my name. So I had my face tattooed and my teeth filed. It seemed like a good idea at the time. Let that be a warning to you, lad.'

Konrad nodded again; but he had no intention of ever letting that happen to him. Wolf might have regretted what he had done to his appearance, yet it did not look out of place. On someone else, the tattoos could easily have appeared comical. But the black lines accentuated Wolf's features, and even the sharpened teeth seemed to suit his character: he was a warrior.

'Let me have a look at the quiver.'

Konrad passed it to him, and watched as Wolf studied the gold design emblazoned on the black leather: the mailed fist between the two crossed arrows.

'Where did you get this?'

'I was given it.'

'Who by?'

'Elyssa Kastring. She's the daughter – *was* the daughter – of the lord of our village. It belonged to him.'

'Was?'

Konrad hesitated. 'She's dead,' he said, quickly.

Wolf looked at him, waiting.

'Do you recognize the coat of arms?' asked Konrad, trying to change the subject.

'No. How far is this village?'

'Not far.'

'What's it called?'

'The village.'

Wolf rolled his eyes. They were ice blue. 'It must have a name. People who live here call this place "the town", but it has a name, Ferlangen. So what's your village called?'

'Ferlangen?' said Konrad. 'This is Ferlangen?'

'Yes.'

'And that man you killed? The baron. You called him Otto.'

'Otto Kreishmier, Baron of Ferlangen. You've heard of him?'

'He was to have married Elyssa.'

Wolf took another swig of ale. 'And she gave you the quiver? Well, it's a small world, or so they say.' He wiped his mouth with the back of his hand. 'But from what I've seen of it, that's far from true.'

Konrad was thinking about the repulsive Baron Kreishmier and how Elyssa would have married him, had she lived. It was an awful prospect for the girl to have faced, but better than being dead.

'Why did you want to kill him?' Konrad asked.

'Because he cheated me out of some money several years ago. He ought to have killed me, but he thought he was being merciful. Mercy is for cowards, Konrad, always remember that.'

'And that was why you came back today, for revenge?'

'No. Midnight threw a shoe, and this was the nearest place with a farrier. Some might say it was luck that I encountered Kreishmier, but not me. And certainly not him. I told him I had returned to kill him, but that wasn't true. We met, I saw an opportunity to avenge myself, and I took it. That's all there was to it.'

Konrad was not sure whether or not to believe Wolf. 'How did the baron cheat you?' he asked.

'You're full of questions, lad. I've always found that the best policy is to say nothing but hear everything.'

'How can I hear without asking?'

Wolf smiled for a moment. 'Some years ago, I helped Otto in a minor territorial dispute concerning the lands between here and the next town. Thanks to my intervention, matters were settled in his favour, but he declined to pay me the agreed sum for my professional services.'

'You're a mercenary!'

'I prefer the term "soldier of fortune" myself.' He studied Konrad, looking him up and down. 'I have a proposal for you, Konrad. I have given you your life, all of it. And I want you to give five years of it back to me.'

'What do you mean?'

'I need a new squire. I need you.'

Konrad stared, but said nothing for several seconds. 'If I say "no"?'

'That's up to you, lad. You can travel to the next town, then the next, but how long until you get into trouble again and end up dangling from the end of a rope?'

Konrad shrugged, and he drank some beer so that he need not reply.

'What do you say? Five years of your life, five years of adventure at the far ends of the world, five years of risk and danger.'

'Do I get paid?'

'Pay? That's for merchants and traders, shopkeepers and peasants. You'll share whatever is mine, lad. Riches and rewards and ransoms, they can be all ours. I've won fortunes greater than your wildest dreams, and I will again.'

Konrad had never been paid before, so he supposed it would make no difference if he earned nothing from Wolf.

'You must have had another squire,' he said. 'What happened to him?'

'He had an argument in a darkened alley with a knife – and lost. It was his own foolishness that killed him. But I don't think you're foolish, Konrad, so what's your answer? If you say "yes", there's no turning back. I will own you for five years, five years to this very day. Own you the same way as I own my horse, my sword. But I'm a good master, I swear. What do you say?'

What else was there to say except, 'Yes.'

'Good!' Wolf plucked the beer stein from Konrad's hands. 'No more ale for you, lad. I'm the one who does the drinking. My name is Wolfgang von Neuwald, but you will call me "sir"' Now pay the landlord, then take Midnight to be shod.'

'But I haven't any money,' said Konrad, and he glanced at the innkeeper.

'Na charge,' muttered the man, guiltily, not meeting Konrad's eyes. 'On de house.'

'That's what I like to hear!' said Wolf. 'In that case, let me have another!'

Konrad left the tavern and went out into the street, wondering what he had agreed to – and why. He looked back over his shoulder. There was nothing to stop him leaving, he supposed. Five years. That was forever!

But what was the alternative? He had nothing else to do, nowhere to go, and he did not have to stay with Wolf for that long. If he wished, what was there to prevent him leaving tomorrow?

He walked up to where the huge white stallion was tethered. At a distance, it had looked very sleek and well-groomed. On a closer inspection, Konrad observed that the animal had several scars on its flesh and that one of its ears was missing.

He reached for the reins. The stallion snorted and bared its teeth. It backed away, then reared up on its hind legs and lunged forward. Konrad sprang back rapidly, and the flailing hooves narrowly missed his head.

'Midnight!' yelled a voice from the tavern doorway. 'It's all right. He's with us now.'

The horse became still. Konrad glanced around and saw Wolf leaning against the doorpost, sipping at his beer.

Warily, Konrad stepped forward and unhitched the reins. Cautiously, he stroked the animal's powerful neck. 'Good boy,' he said. 'Good boy.'

He knew where the blacksmith was, having seen it on his route into town yesterday. Slowly, he led the horse in that direction, the animal favouring its right hind leg, the one without an iron shoe.

While the horse was being shod, Konrad went through into the next part of the building, not wanting to be too near the animal if it did not take kindly to what what was being done. He found himself in a disused storeroom of some kind. He wandered around, looking at all the rusty old pieces of metal that hung from the walls or lay on the dirty floor.

Then, suddenly, he sensed something...

'WHAT'S DAT SMELL?' said a voice.

'Smells lika poacher ta me,' replied another voice.

Heinz and Carl appeared in the entrance, one from either side of the wide door. They were both holding knives, and Konrad reached for his own blade – his kris...

'An' dere 'e be!' said Carl.

"'ullo, boy!' said Heinz.

'What do you want?' Konrad demanded.

Carl's left hand had been behind his back, and now he showed what he had been hiding there. It was a rope.

'We wanna do what de baron said,' he replied. 'We gonna 'ang ya!'

'He wus good to us, boy, wus de baron. An' 'cos of ya 'e's dead. Dat ain't right.'

The two men walked slowly into the darkened building.

'You're not going to hang me!' said Konrad, stepping back.

'Den we cut ya inta pieces.'

'Dis time yer friend ain't gonna save ya, boy.'

Because he was inside the dark storeroom, Konrad could see the two men better than they could see him.

He ran straight at Heinz, yelling as loudly as he could, slamming his head into the man's chest, knocking him aside, and driving his dagger once, twice into his opponent's waist.

He fell on top of Heinz, striking a third time, then rolled swiftly away.

But Heinz did not roll away, not even slowly. He lay where he had fallen, bleeding heavily from the wound in his side.

Before Konrad could rise, Carl was upon him, slamming him down – but hitting him with the hand that held the rope, not the knife.

They grappled with each other, over and over in the dirt. Carl had dropped the rope, and now his left hand gripped Konrad's right wrist – while Konrad's left held his opponent's knife hand.

Carl was bigger, heavier, and his weight made all the difference. He managed to keep himself on top, sitting astride Konrad's midriff, leaning across and pinning both Konrad's hands to the ground. Konrad's dagger slipped from his grip.

'Got ya!' jeered Carl. 'Ya gonna die slow, real slow.'

Konrad tried to wriggle free, but he was held immobile. He brought his knees back, hard, thudding them against his enemy's back, but he was unable to shift Carl from his position.

'I've got money,' said Konrad.

'Ya ain't got na money.'

'Not me. The man with the tattooed face. I know where he keeps it. But I need help to get it from him.'

'Ya lyin'!'

'No! Trust me. We can get the money together. If I'm lying, you can kill me then.'

'Kill 'im now, Carl!' called Heinz, who had managed to raise himself on his elbows and was trying to staunch the flow of blood with his hands.

'If you kill me, you'll never get the money.'

"ow we get it den?'

'Na, Carl!'

'Shut it!' shouted Carl, glancing around at his wounded companion. And as he turned, the grip of his legs around Konrad weakened for a moment. Only a moment – but it was enough.

With all his reserves of strength, Konrad jerked his hips up, unseating Carl for an instant. Then Konrad twisted his whole body – and Carl overbalanced, toppling to the floor.

It took another fraction of a second to seize the fallen kris, and then it was Konrad's turn to leap onto his opponent.

And when he leapt, it was with his knife already stabbing down. The blade thrust into Carl's chest, slid between two ribs, down into the heart. Blood spurted. Carl groaned, and writhed – then became silent and still.

'That took long enough,' said a voice from a few yards away.

Konrad jumped swiftly up, spinning around, holding the knife defensively – and he saw Wolf watching him from the doorway.

'How long have you been there?'

'Long enough. You're promising, lad, I'll give you that. But under my guidance you'll get better, a lot better. Kill the other one, then let's go.'

'Na, pliz!' begged Heinz.

'Kill him?' said Konrad.

'He was going to kill you,' said Wolf. 'Never leave a wounded enemy. Or any kind of enemy. That was Kreishmier's mistake, remember?'

Konrad looked over at Heinz, who was trying to crawl away.

A minute ago Konrad would willingly have slain the man, but that had been in the heat of combat.

He glanced back at Carl, feeling absolutely nothing. Carl was the only man he had ever killed. Beastman or human, if they were enemies they died. But the pathetic figure of Heinz seemed no threat.

'I can't,' Konrad protested. 'Not in cold blood.'

'Pretend he's a rabbit.' Wolf held up the dead rabbit. In his other hand he carried the black quiver, which Konrad had also left in the tavern. 'Hurry up!'

'I can't,' Konrad repeated.

Wolf sighed. 'All right. I suppose it is your first day. I'll kill him.'

He passed the quiver to Konrad, then drew his sword. 'I'll show you the best way to do it. It's quick and involves the least effort. What you do is place the tip of your sword here–'

'Na!' pleaded Heinz.

'–then simply...'

Konrad shut his eyes, but he could not shut his ears to the helpless victim's agonized death scream.

'Clean this,' said Wolf, handing Konrad his sword.

Konrad knelt over Heinz's corpse, to wipe the sword and his knife on the dead man's stained tunic.

'If I hadn't managed to get him off me,' he said, nodding towards the body, 'what would you have done? Would you have helped me?'

Wolf shrugged his broad shoulders. 'I don't want to make a habit of rescuing you, lad. I hope you won't become a liability to me.'

Konrad wondered how much of a habit cleaning the black blade would become – and what other liabilities lay ahead of him.

'Search them both,' Wolf told him, once he had his sword back. 'See if they've got any money.'

'Eleven pence,' answered Konrad, after checking both the corpses.

'Is that all? Killing people like them, it's more bother than it's worth. All that effort for nothing.' He shook his head sadly.

Konrad said nothing, even though he considered all the effort had been his. He had done the fighting. Wolf had merely finished off a wounded man.

'I hope,' Wolf added, 'that you were only playing for time when you made that proposal about robbing me. In any case, you were wrong about what you said: I find myself somewhat financially embarrassed at present.'

'What?'

'I haven't any money.' Wolf swung the rabbit by its hind legs. 'Let's hope the farrier will accept this in exchange for shoeing Midnight. If not, that's his problem.'

He gestured towards the two corpses. 'Anything they have that'll fit you, take it. Choose yourself a pair of boots. I can't have my squire going around barefoot, it creates a bad impression. Strip them of everything else, maybe there's something we can sell for a few more pennies. Then hide the bodies at the back, under those sacks.'

Konrad did as he was told.

'What about that woman,' he asked, 'Kreishmier's sister? She said she'd reward you.'

Wolf shook his head. 'I trust Marlena even less than I did her brother. She invited me to dinner, but the first course would have been poison. I pity the man she marries now that Otto is dead.' He smiled as if remembering. 'Hurry up. Let's go.'

'Where are we going?'

'To your village.'

'BUT THERE'S NOTHING there,' Konrad had said.

Although it had not seemed of much significance when he had first examined it, the reason that Wolf wanted to visit Konrad's village must have been connected with the black leather quiver. But when Konrad had briefly explained what had happened two days earlier, he found that Wolf was even more anxious to travel there.

Wolf had traded their money and the dead men's daggers for some provisions, bread and cooked fowl that they could eat on the journey. Konrad had wrapped the clothes from the two corpses into a bundle and tied it to the back of the packhorse.

Wolf had climbed onto the back of his white stallion. Konrad led the grey packhorse.

The pack animal was laden down with Wolf's belongings, which seemed to consist mainly of weapons and armour. Heinz and Carl had not carried their bows and arrows when they attacked, and so Konrad was unable to rearm himself. There was no room on the laden packhorse for Konrad to ride. Wolf never suggested it, and Konrad remained silent.

He had only ever been on horseback a few times, and that was on Elyssa's mount when she had given him a few riding lessons. He had not been keen on the idea, but the girl had insisted. As usual, she had her way.

The only route that Konrad knew to return to the village was back along the river. But Wolf asked directions from the driver of the wagon that had overtaken Konrad the previous day. It was called a stagecoach, he discovered.

Although the coaches had never been there, and Konrad did not even know whether the village had a name, from his description the driver was able to suggest where it might lie and recommend the best route.

They left the town on the road by which Wolf had arrived. Each highway must have been gated, because there was also a barrier across this road. When the guard saw Wolf coming, he immediately swung the gate wide open. He stood well away, gave a nervous smile, then ventured a salute as the horseman rode by.

'Tell me everything that happened to you,' said Wolf, when they turned onto another road a few minutes later, 'from the very beginning.'

As they walked through the forest, Konrad did so. He began by relating how he had finally decided to leave the village, but that by the time he had departed it was too late in the day to travel very far. He told how he had spent the night in a hollow tree and been awoken by the sounds of hordes of impossible creatures passing by his hiding place.

He had narrated the full story, taking it right up to the moment when he had fired his last black arrow into Skullface's heart, then fled from the manor and found himself in the river.

Wolf had occasionally asked him to go over some part of the narrative for further emphasis, or requested more detail on a particular point, but for the main part he listened in absolute silence and without any change in his expression.

By the time he had finished, Konrad's heart was pounding within his chest and he was covered with sweat from having lived his ordeal all over again.

He waited for some reaction from Wolf, but several minutes passed and the rider remained silent.

'Do you believe me?' Konrad prompted.

'What you say is impossible,' Wolf replied, after another minute or two had gone by, 'although the individual details are possible. Those ratmen you encountered, for example, they were skaven. Few people believe they exist, very few have ever seen them – and even fewer have lived to tell the tale. From the vividness and accuracy of all your descriptions, I know that you must be telling the truth – or that you believe you are.'

'You think it was all some kind of... of dream?'

'A delusion? It could well be.'

'What about all these?' said Konrad, displaying some of his wounds. 'Are these delusions?'

'They could be psychosomatic.'

'What's that?'

Wolf grinned. 'It's the longest word I know, lad. No matter, we will soon discover the truth. And you say this occurred two days ago, on Sigmar's holy day?'

'Yes. Everyone in the village worships Sigmar – or did worship him, I mean.'

'I'm pleased to hear it. I belong to the Cult of Sigmar. When I was younger, I planned to join the Order of the Anvil. Imagine that!' He laughed briefly.

Konrad did not know what he was talking about.

'Me, a monk!' continued Wolf. 'I bet you thought I was going to say that I hoped to become a Templar, one of the Knights of the Fiery Heart.'

Konrad thought it was best to make no response, but Wolf did not seem to notice.

'You say everyone in the village worshipped Sigmar?'

'Yes, I think so.'

'That's unusual for around here. Ulric has many, many followers in this region. The cult is centred on Middenheim, which is the largest city near here – not that it's near, of course.'

'Of course,' agreed Konrad, totally baffled.

'I suppose you might have thought I was also a follower of Ulric. After all, he's the god of battle and also the patron of wolves. His emblem is the head of a wolf. But I have no insignia on my shield, I prefer to remain a – lone wolf.' Wolf grinned, baring his sharp teeth.

Konrad had heard the name of Ulric earlier today, when Wolf had made reference to him before killing Baron Krieshmier.

But he had first heard of Ulric from Elyssa. He must have been another god.

'It can't be coincidence that all these events you describe,' Wolf added, 'if indeed they occurred, took place on Sigmar's holy day – because there is no such thing as coincidence.'

Wolf lapsed into silence, and Konrad waited for him to continue. He did not.

'About Sigmar,' began Konrad, several minutes later.

'What about Sigmar?'

'He's a god?'

'Yes.'

'He founded the Empire?'

'Yes.'

Konrad licked at his dry lips before proceeding hesitantly: 'Well – er – who was Sigmar, and what is the Empire?'

Wolf reined in his horse, and he stared down at Konrad in total amazement. 'Are you trying to be funny, lad?' he said, angrily, 'Because if so…'

'No, no,' Konrad assured him. 'I don't know. I mean – I don't know about Sigmar. I don't. Really.'

'If it was almost anyone else but you,' said Wolf, 'I'd think they were lying. But...'

He ran his free hand through his white hair, and he sighed. He climbed off his horse, untied his water bottle from the saddle, and pointed to a patch of grass by the roadside.

'Let's sit down. It's time you were educated.'

They sat about a yard apart. Wolf drank a mouthful of water, then passed the leather skin to Konrad, who took a long swig before handing it back.

'Sigmar,' said Wolf, 'lived two and a half thousand years ago. In those days, the humans in this part of the world were more primitive and barbaric than today – although if you'd been to some of the places I have, you'd find that hard to believe. The land was fought over by humans and goblinoids: goblins, hobgoblins, orcs. (From your description, those you saw playing football were probably orcs.) These were the traditional enemies of the dwarfs, who like the goblins are a much older race than man. Sigmar was the son of a tribal chief, the leader of the Unberogens. According to legend, his birth was marked by a twin-tailed fireball appearing in the sky, and by very bad storms, the worst in memory. This fireball, a comet, is one of the insignia of Sigmar. When he was only fifteen, Sigmar single-handedly wiped out a band of goblins and rescued their dwarf captives. These prisoners included Kargan Ironbeard, who was the king of one of their clans. Sigmar was rewarded with Kargan's own double-headed warhammer. In the dwarf tongue this was called "Ghal-maraz", which in our language translates as "Skull-splitter". This magical weapon enabled Sigmar to become the most powerful and famous of all human warriors, and he built up a huge and mighty army. When his father died, Sigmar became chief and in a titanic duel he killed his main rival, the leader of the Teutognens. Sigmar was thus able to unite all eight of the divided human tribes – and that is the other insignia of Sigmar: an eight-pointed star, two overlapping squares, to represent the eight human tribes. Sigmar led his troops in a total war against the goblin hordes, intending to sweep them from the region and claim it for mankind. And he succeeded.

'Victory was achieved at a great battle in Stirland. (That's far to the south of here, lad, but we'll deal with your geography lesson later.) The goblinoids, however, were not totally defeated, because their armies turned their attention to the dwarfs – and this time, victory was theirs. The dwarfs were forced to retreat to their ancient homelands, leaving a few hundred of their number as a rearguard. A messenger brought

Sigmar the news, and he marched his legions into the Black Mountains. Then came the battle of Black Fire Pass, when the orcs and goblins were trapped between the humans and the dwarf rearguard. With his mighty warhammer swinging, splitting skulls, Sigmar was at the head of his troops as they totally annihilated the enemy. That was the day Sigmar became known as "Hammer of the Goblins" – Sigmar Heldenhammer. Thanks to Sigmar's intervention, the centuries-old war between goblin and dwarf was finally over. Sigmar was able to establish the Empire, and its foundation marked the date when the calendar begins, year one. Sigmar was crowned emperor in Reikdorf, which is now Altdorf, the capital. (And my home city.) Half a century after he became Emperor, Sigmar vanished. He set out to return Ghal-maraz to the dwarfs, the warhammer with which he had founded the Empire. When he reached Black Fire Pass, he went on alone. He was never seen again, or not by any human, and the dwarfs have never told what happened to him – if, indeed, they know. And that, lad, is who Sigmar was.'

Wolf drank deep from the leather bottle.

Konrad's head was reeling with everything he had heard: goblins and orcs and dwarfs – legendary events – mythical heroes – ancient battles...

'I had no idea,' he said.

'What have you been doing all your life?'

Konrad shrugged, because he had no real answer.

'Your parents never told you?'

'I had no parents, none that I knew. That's why I have no family name – because I have no family. For as long as I can remember, up until the day I left the village, all I ever did was work in a tavern.'

'I can think of worse work.' Wolf raised an imaginary beer stein to his lips.

'I can't.'

'All right,' said Wolf, 'let's proceed. That's the history, now the geography. Do you know where we are?'

'Between Ferlangen and the village,' replied Konrad. He was certain of that – assuming the coach driver had given them the right directions. 'And in the Empire.'

'Is that it?'

Konrad nodded. 'That's it.'

'Fetch me a stick.'

'A stick?'

'Yes, you know what a stick is?'

That was one thing that Konrad did know. He stood up, walked into the forest, returned soon after with a straight piece of wood about two feet long. Wolf took it and began drawing in the dirt of the road.

'This isn't to scale, you understand, but I don't think that will make a great deal of difference. We live on the world, right?' He drew a large square.

'Right,' agreed Konrad.

'And the Old World is a small part of the world.' He drew a small square within the larger one. 'Right?'

'Right.'

'And the Empire is a small part of the Old World.' He drew an even smaller square within the small one. 'Right?'

'Right.'

Wolf rubbed away what he had drawn with the sole of his boot, then drew another design, a circle.

'The Empire,' he said, and he pointed. 'Here, all around the west, the south, the east, the Empire is surrounded by mountains. To the north-east lies the land of Kislev, and to the north is the ocean – the Sea of Claws. Altdorf, the capital, is here, over to the west. Middenheim would be around here.'

'That's near, you said?'

'There's near – and there's near. It's not as near as your village, shall we say. Middenheim was where I last stayed for more than a night. I must admit that I like it there – maybe because it's known as the City of the White Wolf! Middenheim is the largest city in this part of the Empire, although it isn't a part of this province. Which is Ostland, here.' Wolf pointed towards the north-east, near where he had said Kislev was.

'And the capital of the Grand Principality of Ostland,' he continued, 'is Wolfenburg. A good name for a city, huh? It's smaller than Middenheim, and probably further from here. But Middenheim is a city state, not the capital of a province.'

Konrad stared into the dirt drawing, at the patterns that Wolf had marked in the dust, and he tried to make sense of the lines and crosses and what had been said – but without much success.

'This is where we are now,' added Wolf, jabbing the stick into the ground, 'between the Middle Mountains and the coast, in the Forest of Shadows. See?'

'Yes,' agreed Konrad, although he did not.

'Good.' Wolf threw the stick over his shoulder. 'That's all there is to it. Let's have something to eat.'

CHAPTER TEN

KONRAD WAS SURPRISED at how soon they reached the village –
or at least where the village had been.

There was nothing left of it. The invaders had set fire to
everything, but fire alone could not have so totally devastated
the area.

Where there had once been houses, homes, buildings there
was – nothing.

Wood and straw would have burned, but not stone and
brick. Yet stone and brick had vanished, as had the cobbled
road that led up to the manor house.

Everything had been totally obliterated from the face of the
earth, and all that remained was dust and ashes, dark scars
upon the landscape to mark where once hundreds of people
had lived – and died.

There was no sign of the invaders or their victims, not so
much as a single body. Hundreds of humans had died, thousands of inhumans. Where were their remains? Surely the
other predators from the woods could not have devoured
them all so swiftly. Such an unnatural feast should have
lasted for weeks.

But, Konrad realized, whatever supernatural force had demolished and disintegrated solid rock and stone would have had little difficulty in destroying flesh and bones.

The wooden bridge over the river was still there, intact, as though it were not a part of the village and therefore beyond the boundary of annihilation.

Wolf led the way across the river, and Konrad followed, leading the packhorse. Once they reached the other side, they halted. Wolf gazed at the scene of total desolation.

'I believe you,' he said.

But Konrad did not believe it. How could everything have vanished so absolutely?

All that remained were shadows burned into the ground. If it were not for those unnatural traces etched into the landscape, it would be as though the village had never existed.

Konrad shook his head in utter bewilderment. All he could say was, 'How…'

'You saw the beastmen attack, lad, the beastmen and their unholy allies. But beyond them, far more malignant forces were at work. Their minions were here to kill all the people, all the livestock. Once that had been accomplished, they were expendable. After all life had been wiped out, every trace of human existence also had to be eliminated. For that, greater and more unspeakable powers were called into action.'

In the few hours since they had met, much of what Wolf had said was incomprehensible because most of it was beyond Konrad's experience. But this was not: he knew about the village. He had lived here all his life. He had been here when the attack had commenced. Even so, Wolf's references were too oblique.

'What do you mean?' he asked, gazing at the devastation.

'It's hard to explain,' said Wolf, 'and I don't think I should even try – because I'm not sure that I really know.'

Wolf, however, knew far more than Konrad did. He had travelled the world, he was infinitely more experienced.

'What are the beastmen?' asked Konrad. 'Where do they come from?'

'They are the essence of absolute evil. They have been corrupted beyond all redemption. Those around here are the remnants of the forces that attacked the Empire two hundred years ago, that were driven back by Magnus the Pious. Those descended from the survivors, and those benighted creatures that later swelled their ranks, have lived in isolated areas like the Forest of Shadows for many years. They've been growing bolder of late, their attacks against humans more frequent. But I've never seen anything like this. And I've seen more than I care to remember, I assure you.'

Wolf took a drink of water, then looked back in the direction they had come. 'The Empire is under attack again, both from within and without. Those who would undermine civilization from inside do so with subtlety and cunning. In a way, they are the most dangerous of enemies – but they are not the sort that can be fought on the field of battle, that can be driven back with real weapons, cold steel and hot blood. To play any part in this conflict, a warrior must go beyond the borders of the Empire. That was where I was bound when I met you this morning.'

As he spoke, Wolf gripped the hilt of his black sword. Then he nodded towards where the village had once stood. 'One of the reasons I was leaving was because things seemed too tame around here,' he added, and he smiled without humour, showing his sharpened teeth. 'Where was the place that this girl lived, the one who gave you that quiver?'

'Straight ahead,' said Konrad. 'Up the hill.'

Wolf dug his heels into Midnight's flanks, and they proceeded through the ravaged landscape. The buildings were but marks upon the ground, almost as insubstantial as those that Wolf had made with his stick a few hours previously.

And they would be erased as easily. The wind, the rain, the frost, the snow, and before too long there would be no trace of habitation. The trees would return, the creeping forest growing over this isolated outpost of humanity, claiming back the land that it had once possessed.

Konrad glanced at where the tavern had stood. The inn had been absolutely razed, as had the barn behind it. It was as though all of his previous existence had dissolved along with the buildings where he had spent so much of his life.

And he felt glad.

Leaving the village had been a new beginning to his life. Until then, he had not lived, merely existed. Now that there was no village, he had no past – and so his life really had begun anew.

As little of the manor house remained as the rest of the village, and that was very little at all. The ground was marked with scorched embers, as if someone had used charcoal to lay out the plans for the outer walls and for all the buildings within.

'Tell me again,' said Wolf.

'The lord of the manor was called Wilhelm Kastring. His daughter was named Elyssa. She found the bow, the quiver, the ten arrows in an old cellar. She gave them to me as a reward for saving her life, when I rescued her from a beastman. The bow broke, I used all the arrows, and the only thing that remains is the quiver. Why?'

Wolf did not answer, he merely held out his hand. Konrad gave him the quiver, and Wolf examined it very carefully: the strangely patterned black leather, the gold crest of a mailed fist and two crossed arrows.

'And that's the truth?' he asked.

'Yes.'

Wolf threw the quiver down into the dust, scattering the ashes. This had been the entrance to the manor house. It was here that Skullface had stood, here that the black arrow had pierced his heart – and here that he had examined the golden emblem in almost the same way that Wolf had done.

Konrad bent down to pick up the quiver.

'Leave it!' Wolf commanded. 'This is where it came from, so this is where it can remain.'

Konrad became still. 'But–' he began.

Wolf waved his arm disdainfully. 'A peasant's weapon,' he sneered.

Konrad looked down at the quiver, now grey from the ashes that had immolated the manor.

It was all he had left to remind him of Elyssa. But he did not need anything to remind him of the girl, he decided, not while he still had his memories. While he remembered, she lived on.

Just as the bridge over the river was still there, so the draw-bridge across the moat remained. As they crossed back over the wooden bridge, Konrad remembered.

'There's something else,' he said.

'What's that?'

'The day before all this happened, a stranger arrived in the village. A knight wearing bronze armour.'

Wolf halted, turned his horse and looked at Konrad, saying nothing but waiting for him to continue.

'He rode through the village at dawn, and it seemed as if he rode in total silence. It's hard to explain now. Only Elyssa and I saw him, I think, although many others should have done. It was as though time stood still while he was in the village.'

'What did he do?'

'Nothing. He rode up the road here – or what used to be the road – came to the manor house, then turned away and rode back.'

'His horse was also clad in bronze armour?'

'Yes.'

'His armour was spiked at each joint – elbows, knees, knuckles?'

'Yes.'

'Twin spikes on his helmet and also on his horse's?'

'Yes.'

'He had no insignia, no emblems on his accoutrements, no kind of identification?'

'No.'

Wolf's hands had tightened on his reins, and he said nothing else.

'Who was he?' asked Konrad.

Wolf looked all around, looked up at the sky, looked down at the ground, then when there was nowhere else to look he finally answered, 'My brother. He's my twin brother – or he was...'

KONRAD REMEMBERED HOW Elyssa had described the bronze knight as a ghost, and he said, 'You mean he's dead?'

'Worse than dead,' said Wolf. He was looking at Konrad, but his eyes were focused elsewhere – upon a different time.

Konrad remained silent. If Wolf had more to add, then he would do so.

Wolf stroked his horse's neck then finally spoke again, 'Midnight also has a twin, a jet black stallion. My father gave myself and my brother the horses when we came of age. That's what he rides now, hidden beneath all that armour. He? Maybe I mean "it".'

He took a drink of water, wiped his mouth with the back of his hand.

'Families, Konrad, families.' Wolf slowly shook his head. 'You're lucky you never had one. That way you can never be betrayed by the person closest to you.'

Konrad suddenly felt icy cold, and he shivered, because Wolf's words brought to the surface what had been hovering just below the level of his consciousness – how he had foreseen that he, too, would be betrayed by the one who was most close to him.

But that was impossible now. Elyssa was dead.

Konrad's attention was suddenly distracted, and he turned his head towards the forest. There was nothing visible – but he could see...

'Beastmen!' he warned, because that was the only word he knew to describe the three hell-spawned creatures that were about to descend upon them.

Wolf had drawn his sword instantly, and he looked all around, but no danger was yet apparent. He glanced at Konrad, frowning, clearly not believing him.

Konrad's knife was in his hand as he scanned the hill above where the manor had been, and he watched the forest beyond that.

Then Midnight snorted and moved uneasily, his equine senses also detecting the unseen peril within the woods. A second later, the trio of death burst into the open, hurtling down the hill at an impossible speed!

Where most beastmen were shambling, clumsy monsters, these were sleek and muscular, clad in lightweight armour, carrying shiny curved swords and gleaming oval shields. Their bodies were humanoid, their fur striped with crimson and yellow patterns; their faces were fanged, their heads horned.

And they moved so fast because they flew!

Great wings grew from their backs which enabled them to glide down the slope far faster than any creature could run. The wings were those of birds; but instead of being feathered, they were covered with scales – each of which glinted in the sunlight.

'Looks like trouble,' commented Wolf, as he swiftly reached for his helmet. But he realized that there was no time to cover his head, and instead he grabbed his shield for protection.

A moment later the first of the three flying things swooped towards Konrad. The lad threw himself down and rolled away, feeling a cold draught of air by his face as a sword sliced past his cheek, narrowly missing him.

Then the second beast also dived at him, and this time he was hit – but only by the kick of a foot against his shoulder. Yet that foot was taloned, and the vicious spikes ripped through his tunic and into his flesh. He kept rolling, hoping to avoid the third creature which was also arrowing towards him.

Wolf urged his horse forward, to block the attack. He ducked, but thrust his sword upwards at the same time as he dug his heels into Midnight's flanks. The horse reared up, raising the tip of the black blade higher – and the attacker became even more red, slit open from throat to waist as it slid along the point of the sword.

It plunged to the ground and lay there screaming hideously, until Midnight's lashing hooves silenced it.

By then, the first two had wheeled about and were returning for another assault. As before, they both dived at Konrad. He was back on his feet, but was forced to throw himself to the ground again in order to avoid being split in half by a sword stroke.

This time, as he fell onto his back, Konrad lashed out with his knife and felt the blade make contact with the flying flesh. The thing dropped its weapon, and blood rained down from its slashed arm.

But the second survivor was also plummeting down at Konrad, its crimson and gold wings folded back.

Again, Wolf came to his rescue, Midnight springing between the creature and its target. Wolf jabbed his blade upwards. The attacker blocked the thrust with its shield and veered away.

'They don't seem to like you, lad!' yelled Wolf, as the red devils looped and then dived again.

Konrad was back on his feet, and he rushed towards the fallen sword, bending down to pick it up.

'No!' warned Wolf.

Konrad already had his fingers around the hilt – and he felt a surge of power rush from his hand, up his arm, and into his whole body. He glanced at Wolf, wondering what was wrong.

He lifted the weapon. It had appeared heavy, but it did not feel so. Yet he took it in both hands, instinctively aware that this was how its innate energy would flow more quickly through him, into every muscle and nerve, each bone and sinew.

The second flying monster, the one still armed, descended rapidly towards him. It spat and snarled as it skimmed lower, its sword raised. Konrad stood his ground, his own sword also lifted, holding it steady in both his hands. He saw where the creature was aiming, knew that its weapon would begin to strike to the left, but pull back as it veered away, and then the vital blow would be made to the right...

Konrad did not flinch as the sword sliced at him. Then, when it was suddenly withdrawn as he had visualized, he leapt upwards, lashing out. The creature tried to avoid the strike, bringing up its shield defensively, but Konrad's blow ripped away half one of its wings. The assailant tumbled to the ground.

Something flashed through the air close to Konrad's head. A knife. The other brute, although having lost its sword, was not disarmed. As it flew down at Konrad, it pulled another throwing knife from behind its shield.

The second knife darted towards him, and he sprang aside.

The blade whistled by his neck, and Konrad struck out with his sword. The attacker pulled back, beating its wings furiously, raising itself aloft and out of range. It drew a third knife from its shield.

Then Wolf hurled his own round shield at the thing, sending it spinning through the sky and into the creature's midriff. It lost its momentum, and its gaudy wings stopped beating. It dropped.

Wolf sprang from the back of his horse and sprinted in pursuit. He soon reached the stricken being, his black sword plunging swiftly down, then rising up red.

By now, Konrad had turned towards the beast that he had wounded, which was up off the ground and onto its clawed feet. Spitting venom, shrieking out its inhuman fury, it raced at him.

The two swords clashed, blade against blade, spraying sparks.

His opponent was taller than Konrad, stronger, heavier. He should have been forced back by this superior strength, but instead he found new power deep within himself – a source of strength that was tapped by the very weapon he held.

He should have been in great pain from his wound, which was deep if not serious. But he could feel nothing. The energy from the sword was like a soothing balm.

As they tested their physical prowess, pressing against one another, Konrad gazed into the eyes of his enemy – and saw that they were exactly like those of the beastman he had slain two days ago, the one whose skin he had worn. Its eyes were also all white, as if without any pupil. But still the thing could see.

They threw each other back, freeing their weapons. And then they fought.

Konrad had never used a sword, but he was able to parry every blow, anticipating where the blade would fall each time. He was on the defensive, however, driven back at each stroke, unable to attempt a strike of his own.

Pressing home its advantage, the renegade became more frenzied in its attacks, its blade chopping up and down, from the left and from the right. It snarled and growled, its slavering jaws snapping ferociously with every stroke.

Then, as with its very first sword stroke, Konrad caught the blade with his own. The weapons were locked together, but he was forced back, back, back.

He felt the hot foul breath of his attacker, saw its nostrils twitch as it scented victory.

Konrad had been wielding his weapon in both hands, but now he let go with his left, trying to keep back the whole force of his antagonist with but his right arm.

As his left hand reached for the knife in his belt, the creature swung its shield to knock him aside. Konrad ducked and backed away, gripped the bone hilt of his dagger, then sprang forwards, thrusting upwards with the kris. He buried the blade into his opponent's chin, driving it up through the jaw, the tongue, into the top of its skull.

The thing refused to accept that it was defeated, and it continued trying to force Konrad back. So he simply moved away, and the brute crashed to the ground. Its arms flailed wildly, swinging both sword and shield, carving up the ground, as though trying to dig its own grave. But its dying limbs became weaker and weaker, until they ceased moving. The aerial marauder lay dead, its blood staining the dry earth.

'I'm impressed,' said Wolf, who was leaning on his sword, watching.

His own sword still raised, Konrad stared at him.

'Drop it,' Wolf told him.

Almost against his will, Konrad took a step towards Wolf.

'Drop it!'

He obeyed, managing to open his fingers and let the weapon fall. He gazed at the creature that he had slain, then bent down to retrieve his knife from its throat.

'Ah!' he yelled, feeling the agony in his left shoulder. Three streams of blood trickled down his back from the claw marks.

'Take off your tunic,' said Wolf, going to the packhorse and tearing off some strips of fabric from one of the bundles tied there. He poured water over Konrad's wound, then bound it up.

'Why were they after you?' the warrior asked.

'Me?'

'You. It was you they were trying to kill, not me.'

Konrad said nothing.

'And how were you aware of them before they even showed themselves?' Wolf asked, once he was finished.

Konrad remained silent, glancing down at the ground, realizing that Wolf was staring at his eyes – his different eyes...

'Here,' said Wolf, and he handed Konrad his sword. 'I think you know what to do by now.'

Konrad took the blade, and he glanced around at the three dead red menaces. 'What are they?'

'Beastmen.'

'Do I strip them?'

'No! Don't even touch them. Use a rag to clean my sword, something from one of those two this morning.'

Konrad realized this was what his bandage was made from; it had been part of Carl's shirt. He did as he was told, while Wolf retrieved his shield.

Then they quit the dust and the ashes of the village, leaving the bodies of their dead attackers where they had fallen.

'Is THIS SAFE?' asked Konrad uneasily, when they finally camped for the night.

They had spent most of the day in silence and in travelling. Wolf would say no more about his brother, and he refused to speak about the beasts that had attacked them, and so Konrad had not even tried asking questions on such a trivial matter as their destination.

He did not like the idea of sleeping out in the forest, but there seemed no alternative. It was either that or continue through the woods during the dark.

Wolf merely shrugged.

'Should one of us stay awake, on guard?'

'You can if you want, but what good do you think it would do? And I've always thought I'd like to die in my sleep.'

Konrad gazed at him in the twilight. It was hard to know when Wolf was joking or not. It seemed that he could never remain serious for very long.

Konrad had thought that they might have lit a fire. That would have kept the animals of the woods at bay, but he knew it would have been no deterrent to those creatures who were far more of a danger. Instead, the flames would have drawn attention to their whereabouts.

'It's been quite a day for you,' Wolf remarked.

Konrad nodded, tentatively touching his wounded shoulder. It still throbbed, but was no longer as painful as it had been.

Then he stroked his throat, thinking of how he had escaped being hung. He could remember that last year in the village the miller's son had been found guilty of murder. He had been involved in a dispute over the weight of a sack of flour, which resulted in a farmer being killed. Wilhelm Kastring had sentenced him to death, and he had been hanged.

But there was a great difference between being hung for murder and being given the same punishment for snaring rabbits.

'Were they really going to hang me?'

'You heard what Krieshmier said.'

'For two rabbits?'

'What else should they have done? Put you in jail? That would have meant feeding you, paying someone to guard you. It was easier to kill you – and much cheaper.'

Wolf yawned, then continued, 'But you haven't lived until you've been sentenced to death, lad. I've lost count of the number of times it's happened to me. There are still warrants out for my arrest in some places, and a price on my head. And, believe me, being condemned to death is better than being jailed.'

Wolf unfastened his leather jerkin, and even in the gloom Konrad could see that his chest was criss-crossed with the traces of ancient lacerations. There were so many of them that there was more scar tissue than undamaged flesh. Konrad's own old wounds were nothing but scratches in comparison.

'That's what my captors did for amusement – but it didn't make me laugh.'

Wolf touched the links around his neck. 'This is the chain that once held me captive. I wear it to remind me – not that I could ever forget. And I will never, never be taken prisoner again.'

He stared at Konrad. 'If ever it seems likely that you're going to become a hostage, choose to slit your own throat instead. If there's life, they say, there's hope. That isn't true.'

'You lived,' said Konrad. 'Whatever happened, you escaped, you survived.'

'Sometimes I don't think so.'

Konrad knew that this was another of Wolf's enigmatic remarks, and that he would not elaborate further, so he asked: 'But who's going to try and capture me?'

Wolf let go of the chain and fastened his tunic. 'They'll try and catch you if they can't kill you – and twice today they couldn't kill you. No, three times. They tried to hang you, then murder you, and then the beastmen attacked. Is your life always so interesting?'

'Perhaps those three attacked because I survived the village massacre,' said Konrad. 'But I didn't see any like them in the attack.'

'There are many types of beastmen, lad, and more and more with every passing season, it seems. Some look like animals but have the intelligence of men; some look like men but have the brains of slugs.'

'And you think there's some connection between the beastmen and what happened to me in Ferlangen?'

But Wolf was already turning his head towards the woods, and at the same time Konrad saw a movement between the trees. He grabbed for his knife, but Wolf left his black sword sheathed as he stood up.

'We have company,' he said, and he walked in the direction of the silent intruder.

But there was more than one, Konrad noticed, as he also rose. Through the dark trees, he saw several even darker shadows glide past.

He caught glimpses of fur, of glinting feral eyes.

He watched as Wolf melted into the gloom and joined the animals.

Wolf, Konrad thought, wolves…

The creatures of the night were wolves, yet Wolf had no fear because he must have had some kind of affinity with them. It was not only his name, and his altered appearance, which were lupine.

Konrad strained his eyes, leaning forward but daring to go no nearer, and he caught sight of Wolf down on his haunches, stroking the head of one of the animals. It seemed as though he was talking to it.

After a few minutes, Wolf returned. 'We also have our allies,' he said. 'You can sleep easily, lad, our guard dogs will be on watch.'

Konrad had so many questions, but he realized there was very little that Wolf would have answered.

He sat down, and he shivered.

'Cold?'

'Yes,' said Konrad, although he did not know whether it was the chill of the night air or fear of the wolves that had made him tremble.

'How's the shoulder?'

Konrad flexed his arm, winced. 'Sore.'

'Good. That means it's healing. And you'd better start wrapping up warm and wearing those boots.'

'But it's summer.'

'Where we're going, they don't have summer.'

'Where's that?'

'To Kislev,' said Wolf. 'And beyond.'

CHAPTER ELEVEN

THEY TRAVELLED FOR many days, and Konrad walked all the way.

During the day, there was never any trace of the wolves; but they were there every night. Konrad did not know whether they were the same animal, which paralleled their course during the light, or whether it was a different pack each time that darkness fell. He did not even know whether they were real wolves, or some kind of spectral beasts that Wolf had conjured up for their protection.

He did not ask. Wolf did not say.

And every evening, at dusk, Wolf would step into the trees that ringed their camp. There, he would commune with the pack that prowled the dark forest for their defence. Konrad could have gone closer, could have attempted to find out what was happening; but if Wolf did indeed talk to the creatures whose name he bore, Konrad preferred not to know.

Initially, he was uneasy knowing that such animals were so close. But after the first few nights, he slept well, comfortable in the knowledge that an unseen circle of defenders stood between them and the other creatures of the woods. Either that, or he was exhausted by the journey.

Konrad's earlier uncertainies about staying with Wolf had
faded to the back of his mind. He had known that there was
more to his existence than the village, that he would go on to
live another life and do other things. If nothing else, serving
as Wolf's squire was a start, a new beginning.

He was not sure what a squire was supposed to do. As yet,
his only function had been to clean Wolf's sword. There must
have been more to it than that, but he suspected that he
would only find out exactly what his work entailed once they
reached Kislev.

This was something else that he was unsure whether he
wanted to know, and he was happy to keep on walking. Every
step he took was another step further away from the village.

On their journey, they passed through several other villages
and towns. They never stayed overnight, but Wolf was always
able to find something on his packhorse that he could
exchange for a few rations. He never stopped at an inn; all he
drank was water.

'I think you're safe by now,' Wolf said, one evening.

'Safe from what?' Konrad asked.

'From your wound.'

By this time, Konrad had almost fogotten his injury. Three
long scabs marked his shoulder, and he no longer wore a
bandage.

'It's nothing,' said Konrad.

'It looks like nothing,' Wolf told him. 'But far more trivial
injuries can be fatal. The beastmen must have some kind of
venom that gets into a wound. At first it doesn't hurt, and
sometimes people don't even know they've been cut. Then
the pain begins to build up, slowly, remorselessly, until they
die in screaming agony. I've seen men chop off their own
wounded arms to try and end the torture. But it never did any
good.'

From then on, Konrad inspected the scabs on his shoulder
several times a day, watching for some sign of poisoning. He
never found any – and if he had, it would have been too late…

The road upon which they travelled was no wider than the
one into Ferlangen, and in a much worse state of repair, but
Wolf had told him that it was one of the major routes within

the Empire. The land of Kislev lay beyond the Empire, but Konrad was confused by Wolf's references until he discovered that both the country and its capital shared the same name.

They were eastward bound for Erengrad, which was on the coast of Kislev. Following the road in the other direction, however, would have brought them to Middenheim. Middenheim was at the crossroads of the Empire. By turning south at Middenheim, they would have been heading for Altdorf, the capital. But continuing westwards, they would have reached the coast again at a port called Marienburg.

The coastline between Erengrad and Marienburg marked the northern boundary of the Empire. Above lay the Sea of Claws. Each port was also beyond the edge of the Empire, in another land.

Studying the various maps that Wolf drew in the dust for him, Konrad finally began to make some sense of all the names and places that he heard.

The road from Erengrad led west to Marienburg, but he also discovered that Kislev was linked to Marienburg by river. From the capital of Kislev, a river flowed all the way west to Altdorf, where it became the River Reik and turned northwards towards the sea.

'Everything is connected,' Wolf said, gazing down into one of the patterns he had drawn in the dust, as he traced a line along the road connecting Marienburg to Middenhiem to Erengrad, then followed the river back from Kislev to Altdorf to Marienburg.

'It was only a few years ago that I was shown such a map. A real map, drawn on parchment. Until then, I didn't even know what a map was. But suddenly so much fell into place. I'd been to all those places, and finally I was able to see the overall structure, the links between them. What happens in one part of the Empire affects what happens elsewhere, even if it's a thousand miles away. Similarly, whatever happens anywhere in the Old World affects the Empire.'

Konrad was not sure that he understood fully, but that was not unusual.

Every so often, they reached a toll gate on the highway, similar to the ones he had seen at Ferlangen.

Armed soldiers guarded each barrier, but Wolf was never asked for payment. After he had exchanged a few words with the men on duty, the gate was always swung open or raised to let him and Konrad through.

They had been allowed out of Ferlangen because the toll keeper was scared, Konrad knew; yet this was not the case along the Middenheim to Erengrad road. The veteran troops who patrolled the route did not look as though they were scared of anything.

They must have been chosen for their strength and valour, because Konrad was aware that the woods beyond the road were full of beastmen. And the further east they travelled, the greater the number of such creatures he could sense lurking in the decayed depths of the forest.

'Do they let us through because you're heading to Kislev to fight the beastmen?' Konrad asked, after they had passed through yet another barrier.

'No,' said Wolf, 'but that's not a bad guess. Troops on their way to help defend Kislev don't have to pay road tolls, of course. And freelancers may also be given a road warrant. But I don't need one.'

'Why's that?'

'Because I used to work for the toughest, most feared outfit in the whole of the Empire. Wherever we rode, strong men quaked in fear. No one was safe from us. No one ever escaped.'

'What were you?'

'An Imperial tax collector!' laughed Wolf. 'Which means, of course, that I never have to pay any taxes or dues anywhere within the Empire. The lads on the toll gates, they are in a similar line of work, part of the same brotherhood, and so I know the passwords and don't have to pay. Neither do you.'

'Thanks.'

'Don't mention it.'

Konrad obeyed; he did not mention it. He simply kept on walking. They only stopped to eat, to sleep, to trade, to graze the horses, or when the summer rain was too heavy. Until, finally, they reached Kislev.

***

THERE WAS NO border, no boundary to mark the end of the Empire and the beginning of a new land. The first time Konrad realized they were in Kislev was when the forest suddenly ended and Wolf pointed to the city that lay ahead of them.

'Erengrad,' he said.

The city was a fortress, enclosed by high wooden walls. A few towers could be seen above the walls, but nothing else. A wide expanse of woodland had been totally cleared around the city. There could be no attack here without the guards in the watchtowers giving warning, no invasion without the thick walls being breached.

Although fascinated by the city walls, which stretched almost as far as he could see, Konrad's attention was drawn to the north – to the sea.

They had been moving nearer to the coast throughout their journey. Without the forest blocking the view, for the first time ever he was able to see the ocean.

And he could not believe it.

There was more than a mile of land in between, which in itself was amazing enough. He had never seen such a huge expanse denuded of trees and not replaced by habitation. Throughout his life, Konrad had been surrounded by thick foliage, never able to see further than a few hundred yards uphill or into a valley.

But beyond the clearing, past the slope that led down to the coast, was the sea.

The absolute vastness that lay before him, the total nothingness between himself and the horizon, literally took his breath away.

It was a clear day, and the sun was reflected in the ripples of the blue ocean. A few sails were visible on the water, ships sailing to and from the port.

Konrad stood motionless, gazing in awe, feeling the cold wind from the ocean blow over his face and through his hair.

'It's only water,' Wolf told him.

'But... there's so much of it.'

'And there's even more of it underneath!'

'Where does it end?'

'It doesn't. It goes on forever. The waters that lap against this shore are the same as the waves that roll against the coasts of Araby and Lustria, Cathay and Nippon. It is all part of the same pattern, Konrad. And so are we. We are all pawns in the cosmic scheme.'

Konrad began to feel dizzy staring at infinity, and he had to turn away, to look around and focus on what he knew and recognized – the Forest of Shadows. That had seemed as though it went on forever, but from Wolf he had learned it was only a part of the woodlands which covered most of the Empire: the Reikwald Forest, the Laurelorn Forest, the Drak Wald Forest, the Great Forest...

'Come on,' said Wolf. 'We may have reached Erengrad, but we're still only halfway there.'

'Halfway where?'

But Wolf did not answer; Konrad should have learned that by now.

They continued towards the city. The road from the Empire led to a pair of bronze gates. Huge although they were, the gates were dwarfed by the walls in which they were set. The gates did not swing open for Wolf as easily as the toll barriers on the highway had done.

The guards at the entrance to the city wore furs on top of their armour, and most of them had thick, drooping moustaches. They watched suspiciously as Wolf dismounted. Leaving Konrad to look after his horse, he walked towards the guardhouse.

Konrad watched for several minutes as discussions took place, with much gesturing and pointing. An officer was called from the guardhouse, and there was more debate and gesticulating.

Then the door was opened very slightly, and an official from the city emerged to conduct the arbitration at a higher level.

One of the troops strode over towards Konrad, inspecting him carefully, stepped towards Midnight, then jumped back swiftly when the white stallion snorted and reared up, and he went to examine what the packhorse was carrying. Apparently satisfied, he returned to the gate where the negotiations were continuing.

Finally, there were smiles and nods, handshakes and salutes.

Wolf returned. 'Bloody foreigners!' he complained, as he climbed into Midnight's saddle. 'As if I wasn't here to help them.' He shook his head, sighed, then added, 'In we go.'

One of the bronze doors had been opened wider to admit them. Wolf rode through, Konrad followed, and the pack-horse followed him.

Konrad had been amazed by Ferlangen, at how it was so much bigger than the village. But Erengrad was far, far larger than Ferlangen had been – and he was utterly overwhelmed by all the sights and sounds of the city.

Erengrad stood at the mouth of a river, Wolf had said. The only river that Konrad knew was the one that had flowed through the village, but there was no comparison between that and the River Lynsk. It was like the difference between a drop of dew and a thunderstorm.

The Lynsk was so wide that there was even an island in the middle, an island far larger than Ferlangen, which until today had been the biggest town Konrad had ever seen.

It was here that all the ships from the Empire and the rest of the world berthed, where cargoes were transhipped to and from the river craft which carried them up and down the waterways of Kislev.

Yet the city of Kislev itself, Konrad knew from Wolf's lessons, could not be reached by river from Erengrad. It lay south of the upper reaches of the Lynsk, to which it was joined by road.

Konrad had been impressed by the bridge near Ferlangen. It had been built of stone, whereas the one by the village had merely been made of wood.

The bridge that had to be traversed to reach the dock area of Erengrad was only constructed of wood – but what a bridge! Most of it was built upon wooden pilings which had been driven into the river bed, but the centre section of the span could be raised like a drawbridge in order to admit the tallest of ships into the lagoon beyond.

Wolf left Konrad to look after the horses while he went in search of – something or other. As usual, he would not say.

While he was gone, Konrad gazed and gawped at all the fantastic sights on view. The ships which were larger than houses; the sailors from a dozen strange lands, all dressed in weird clothes and speaking even more bizarre languages; the stevedores loading cargoes which he did not recognize and could not even guess at.

After a while, two men stopped by Konrad. They were both small, barefoot, clad in loose white shirts and baggy breeches. Their eyes were narrow, their complexions very sallow, their hair thick, black and straight. They must have been mariners from a distant country.

One of them spoke to Konrad, talking in a language that he could not understand.

The foreigner's words were very fast, hardly sounding like human speech.

Konrad shook his head to indicate his lack of comprehension, and he wondered what the men wanted. Maybe they were asking for directions, or perhaps they were trying to sell him something.

When he did not reply, they looked at one another, gesturing wildly and chattering rapidly.

Midnight snorted and tried to move forward. Konrad turned, pulling on the reins and attempting to restrain the powerful horse.

His attention was distracted for a moment as the white stallion suddenly reared up, his hooves flashing.

And in that moment, the two sailors both drew their knives, long and narrow and razor-sharp.

Although his back was turned, there was no need for Konrad to look. He dropped both horses' bridles and swiftly reached for his own dagger. He now knew who the men were – they were his deadly foes.

Midnight's front legs kicked, his hooves punching the air like the fists of a boxer. One of the two attackers backed quickly away, ducking aside, trying to avoid the flailing hooves.

But the other sprang towards Konrad, yelling an incomprehensible war cry. Konrad yelled back, roaring out his own anger.

The two blades sliced through the air as the opponents came within range. Each initial whirling stroke missed by the thickness of a man's skin, as both leaned aside.

Then the antagonists were upon one another, each left hand gripping the enemy's right wrist as they struggled for supremacy.

They were evenly matched: Konrad was taller, but his attacker was heavier.

There was an abrupt scream, a desperate and despairing shriek that could only have been a death cry. It was the other foreign sailor. He had fallen victim to Midnight's deadly hooves and lay on the quayside, trampled by the white stallion.

For an instant Konrad and his opponent forgot their own duel and glanced over at the crushed corpse. Then their eyes met again – and Konrad grinned.

'Now it's your turn,' he hissed.

The mariner did not know what Konrad was saying, but he could not have failed to guess the meaning of the words. He spat back a retort, and then grappled with even more ferocity, trying to force Konrad's knife to drop, while pressing his own blade towards his enemy's throat.

A moment before it happened, Konrad saw that the man was about to relax his grip, pretending to weaken. When he did so, Konrad started to press forward, as if deceived – but before he could pull back, he found himself flying through the air...

He thudded down on his back, his breath knocked out of him. There was no time to wonder what had happened, because his foe was diving down upon him. Neither was there time for Konrad to search for his dagger, which he had dropped during his unexpected flight.

He rolled aside, avoiding the plunging knife, but the sailor managed to land on top of him and prevent his escape. Entwined, they twisted over in the dirt, fighting for control of the single blade.

As they struggled together, Konrad became aware of a circle of legs all around them. They were being watched, he realized. A small crowd had built up, a gang of seamen and dockers who were laughing and cheering. It was as if Konrad and his assailant fought for the amusement of the spectators, instead of for their very lives.

Over and over they rolled – and rolled over the edge of the quay and dropped into the waters of the dock.

They hit the river together, still fighting, and sank into the cold depths. Below the surface, they parted. In the darkness of the murky water, Konrad saw the sailor coming at him again, the knife aimed at his chest.

The thrust seemed very slow, as if in a dream, but the water also slowed Konrad's response. He managed to deflect his enemy's arm, twisted it – and the knife fell free, drifting down to the riverbed. The sailor tried to catch his weapon, while Konrad tried to catch the sailor.

It was Konrad who succeeded. He grabbed the man around the throat with both his hands, and he squeezed. A stream of bubbles erupted from the seaman's mouth.

Konrad kicked, driving himself through the water – and he smashed his opponent's head against one the wooden pilings of the dock.

Then he did it again, and again. No more bubbles of air came from the man's mouth. Instead, the water became stained red from his cracked skull. He struggled desperately, but Konrad refused to release his grip.

Another slow slam against the submerged tree trunk, and then the man became limp and still. One more silent strike against the ancient wood, another stream of blood, and finally Konrad let go.

The dead figure sank, and Konrad thrust himself upwards. His head broke the surface, and he sucked greedily at the air. He heard voices above him, some cheering, some jeering.

He looked up to see about a dozen people staring down at him from the dockside. One of them was Wolf.

Twenty yards away, a series of wooden steps led down towards the river. He swam towards them and hauled himself out of the water.

He stared at the surface. It was thanks to Elyssa, he realized, that he was not still down in the depths. It was she who had taught him to swim.

He removed his boots and emptied out the water before climbing back up to the quay.

A man was waiting for him at the top of the steps. He was holding his knife, and Konrad became still. The man laughed, then said something in an unknown language. He offered the rippled dagger to Konrad, hilt first. In his other hand he held a fistful of coins.

When Konrad accepted his knife, the man clenched his other hand, laughed again, then turned and strode away. It seemed that he had won many crowns betting on Konrad to win.

Konrad saw that Wolf was with a slightly-built, fair-haired man who was inspecting the packhorse's teeth. He walked towards them, his feet squelching, water dripping from his sodden clothes.

It did not take much to deduce that Wolf was trying to sell the grey horse. He kept praising the animal and pointing out its good features, while the man kept shaking his head and indicating aspects that were less than good.

'Vell, I dunno,' said the stranger.

'But I do know,' Wolf assured him. 'This is a good horse, Stephan. Years of work ahead of him. He's solid, reliable, healthy. What more do you want?'

'Vhat more do I vant? I vant a fair deal, Volf.'

'There are plenty of other people who would pay more than I'm asking.'

'Vhy don't you ask them?'

'But I don't want your money, you know that. My price is a boat ride. That's all. It costs you nothing. It's as though I'm giving you the horse.'

'I carry you, it means I can't carry someone else.'

'You know it's a bargain, Stephan. I have to get up river – and I'm going there to defend Kislev.'

'Ha! You're trying to appeal to my patriotism now?'

'Yes.'

Stephan stepped back and studied the packhorse. He was still shaking his head, although more slowly. 'You, your horse, your servant, to Bolgasgrad?'

'Praag.'

'Very vell,' he sighed.

The two men spat in their palms, slapped their hands together, and the bargain was struck.

'Put my horse on board with you,' said Stephan. 'Ve sail vith the tide.' He turned and walked back in the direction from which he had come.

Wolf turned to study Konrad, then glanced at the dead sailor who lay on the quay. 'Can't leave you alone for a minute, can I?' he said.

'I wasn't doing anything. They attacked me.'

'You don't seem very popular, lad. They don't seem to like you, do they?'

'They?' said Konrad, knowing that Wolf was not referring to the two foreign sailors. 'Who?'

Wolf did not reply, instead he said, 'Ever been on a boat?'

Konrad shook his head. He had not, and he was not sure that he wanted to.

'We're going to Praag by river. You'll find it's better than walking.' Wolf looked Konrad up and down. 'Or swimming. Let's find Stephan's boat before he changes his mind.' He climbed onto Midnight's back.

They located the boat, berthed against one of the wharves. Wolf dismounted and led Midnight on board, while Konrad almost had to drag the packhorse along the gangplank. The crew watched, laughing, but made no offers of help.

'Get yourself dry,' Wolf told him, after they had tied the horses on deck.

'What happens in Praag?' Konrad asked, as he sat wrapped in an old blanket. 'We fight beastmen?'

During their journey to Erengrad, Wolf had spoken more about the history of the Empire and the way that it was again under threat from inhuman incursions. Kislev stood as a barrier between the Empire and the invaders – the beastmen and all their foul allies.

If Kislev fell, then the Empire would be overwhelmed. This was what Magnus the Pious had feared, some two hundred years ago. Kislev had been in danger then, and Praag had fallen to the death raiders from the north. The forces of the Empire had come to the aid of their neighbour, and finally the fiendish legions had been thrown back. In gratitude, Tsar Alexis and Emperor Magnus had sworn a pact of allegiance between their lands.

And now that pact was being put to its strongest test. The marauding hordes were back in strength, ravaging the towns of Kislev, destroying villages, plundering trading posts, devastating military camps. If they succeeded in Kislev, the Empire would be their next target.

Wolf had already spoken about the enemy within the border, but the renegades that laid siege to Kislev were the enemy beyond the border.

'The Emperor has sent troops to defend Kislev,' said Konrad, as they stood at the stern of the riverboat and watched all the activity in the port, 'that's what you told me.'

'And I told you the truth.'

'Is that why you're here? Why I'm here?'

'In a way.'

'What way?'

Wolf shrugged his shoulders. 'I could have offered my services to the Empire, enlisted in the war against the incursion. I've done that before, when I was younger, more idealistic. But I have to think of my future. If I must risk my life, more than my life, I want to make sure I'm well rewarded. I'm a professional soldier, one of the best, and people pay a good price for my services. I work where I want, when I want.'

Konrad frowned, confused. 'So you're not here to fight the beastmen?'

'Yes, yes! Kislev should be a rich country, but it hasn't been able to exploit its wealth properly. All these creatures that keep overunning the territory, they're bad for business. I'm here to stop that. And so are you, Konrad. We'll be helping against the invasion – and also earning ourselves some modest compensation. Wars make people rich, lad, usually the wrong sort of people. But here's a war that will make us rich. Also, we're fighting for a good cause.' He smiled, his pointed teeth glinting. 'Sometimes, life can be just perfect.'

THEY BECAME GUARDS at a gold mine. The mine was located in the World's Edge Mountains, near Belyevorta Pass. Traces of

ore had been found for centuries in a river running through
this part of the mountains, but the lode had only been discovered fifty years ago.

Although it was on the very frontier of established human
settlement, the mine had flourished – until the invaders had
swept down from the Northern Wastes again, more and more
of them every year. They came from the lands of ice and snow,
as though the hell where they had been spawned were a
region of frozen wilderness.

These incursions severely affected production at the mine,
and the owners – who included the tsar – had established
their own private army.

Wolf had worked as a mercenary there before, but he had
no intention of remaining in such a lowly position. He knew
the man who was the head of the military garrison – and
within two months he had replaced him.

There was no need to offer violence; words were sufficient
inducement. All Wolf did was make reference to the various
thefts and robberies that the other man had organized during
his years at the mine. Wolf suggested that retirement was a
preferable option to assassination, but that he should first
appoint Wolf as his successor.

Security for the entire operation was not merely a matter of
defending the workings from the attacks of beastmen. They
were but one of the threats. All they wanted was to kill and
destroy, they were not after the gold.

Bandits and robbers and thieves would raid the mine,
ambush the gold shipments. They also had to be kept under
control. So did the miners themselves. It was they who were
in the best position to steal from the mine, through working
in the narrow shafts, digging up the ore-bearing rock and
finding the occasional nugget which they could hide about
their person.

Such thefts had to be stopped, because they affected Wolf's
own income, his share of the output that he appropriated
before shipping the gold down to Kislev.

The owners of the mine knew that the guards took a cut,
and that was reflected in the low amount they were paid. But
so long as the private army did not grow too greedy, their

masters were not too concerned. They had few other expenses, and whatever they derived from the mine was pure profit.

The majority of miners were slaves, convicted prisoners serving out their jail terms. Most of their sentences were for life – or for death – because few survived long enough to become free.

As for the mercenary army, many were not much different from the prisoners they guarded. They were on the run from justice. Only by heading north, to the limits of civilization, were they able to avoid being captured and convicted. They were unskilled as soldiers, and their life expectancy was even less than the mine workers.

Others were the roughest, most vicious combat troops in the Old World. They came to Kislev because here there was always fighting, always danger, and the rewards could be considerable – if one survived to spend them. The mine guards included soldiers from every part of the Empire, and from far beyond.

Each was an expert in killing, and Konrad learned from them all.

A deposed prince from one of the Tilean City States taught him how to fence. Swordplay was more than mere strength, it was skill and speed and cunning. Konrad could fight a duel like a gentleman, knew all the rules of chivalry which must always be obeyed in an affair of honour.

And a street brawler from Bretonnia who had never heard the word 'honour' showed him how to fight dirty, how to use anything available as a weapon, how to scratch and gouge and maim and murder with his bare hands if he had nothing else.

Konrad's techniques became more refined when a slim fellow who claimed to come from Nippon also demonstrated how to kill with just his hands – or his feet. He learned to fight without a weapon against an armed opponent, and how to win. This was an ancient art from the distant East, where every land seemed to have its own variety of weaponless combat. Konrad remembered how he had been thrown by one of the sailors who had attacked him in Erengrad – but that man had been unskilled and had become a victim of the kris.

Wolf disapproved of the bow as a weapon, but not the crossbow, and a mercenary from the Estalian kingdoms educated Konrad into its method; a warrior from Araby sharpened Konrad's knife skills, introducing him to a variety of throwing blades; a giant of a man from Norsca showed him how to use a spear and throw a javelin; a knight from Albion taught him how to ride; and there were more, so many more.

Not all those employed by the mining company were human. Many dwarfs worked there as engineers. It was they who built the new tunnels, who used gunpowder to blast away the rocks in the deep underground passages. And it was one of these who became Konrad's axe tutor, teaching him how to fight with every type from a small handaxe to a huge double-bladed weapon, the techniques of close combat with a hatchet in each hand, and the best way to handle a halberd.

When Konrad's right arm was severely injured during a renegade attack, Wolf said, 'What good is a right-hand man without a right hand? And that is where I want you in every battle, protecting my right.'

Although Wolf had originally taken on Konrad as his squire, Konrad had never been a servant. The two had soon become comrades-in-arms, but Wolf had never acknowledged the fact until now.

'And who protects my right?' asked Konrad, glancing at his bound and rigid arm. It had been tended by an elf who possessed curative skills. Wolf hated all magic and magicians, and a healer was the only type of sorcerer he permitted in the mining camp.

Konrad remembered Elyssa, the way she had soothed his wounds the first time that they met – but it did not take much for him to remember Elyssa...

Wolf had laughed, then he said, 'Anyone can fight. It takes no brains to kill. They might even be a disadvantage. But our intelligence is what sets us apart from the animals – and from the beastmen. Books contain the knowledge of the world, and it is by knowledge that we grow. While your arm is healing, you will do something useful. You will learn to read and write.'

Konrad was reluctant, but he found himself a tutor. His name was Matthew, a student at the university in Praag who had made his way to the mine during the summer vacation, hoping to earn some money to pay his next year's fees.

Matthew had begun his journey by boat, but been robbed and thrown overboard by the crew. After that, he travelled on foot, and somehow managed to reach the encampment safely. Armed only with a marline-spike from the riverboat, his feat in successfully crossing the wilderness alone made him famous for a few days.

Konrad called him 'Matthew Marlinespike,' and he returned the following summer, travelling with a supply convoy. By the third year, Konrad could read and write fully – and Matthew had also passed his final examinations to become a lawyer. He brought his pupil a special graduation scroll, which declared that Konrad had proved himself 'a worthy scholar.'

At the same time as his first lessons, Konrad had also learned to fight with his left arm – to use a sword or a mace, to throw a spear or a dagger.

'There are two ways of fighting a wild, unorganized rabble like the beastmen,' Wolf once said. 'You can have a trained and disciplined army, like the forces that the Emperor sends from Altdorf, like the Graf sends from Middenheim. Or you can have a force that is even more wild, more unorganized – a legion of individuals.'

Such was the battalion that Wolf had built up: an army of individuals who fought together to throw back the encroachments from the north. But however many of the enemy were killed, there were always more to replace them.

'It's as though their dead are reborn,' Konrad had said.

'You're getting the hang of it at last,' Wolf replied, and for once Konrad knew that he was not joking.

Konrad had learned to kill, to kill quickly and efficiently. But there was never any fear of making himself redundant. However fast he became, however many he destroyed, there was always another of the enemy to be slain.

There were long periods of inaction, of dull routine when there was nothing to be done except clean his armour and polish his weapons – and Wolf's. And then the scouts would report a pack of marauders approaching the area, and the boredom will be transformed into sudden frantic action.

Yet Konrad never saw an attack that even remotely resembled the assault on the village. Never again did he witness such uniformity of purpose, such determination, such overwhelming force, so many different types of creature united with one intent.

As had happened at the village once the inhabitants had all been massacred, on many an occasion the creatures would start to fight amongst themselves – but this was while they were still in combat with their human foes.

They would frequently attack an apparent comrade because it offered an easier target. Or they would fall upon and devour a wounded ally. They seemed to be mindless, nothing but killing machines.

They were lower than animals, because they did not have any instinct for self-preservation, allowing themselves to be slaughtered by the hundred just so that one human might die.

Yet that was only the way it appeared, because there was often a reason for their reckless tactics – hard although that purpose might be to deduce. Scores of warriors would be sacrificed simply to create a diversion, or to test new fortifications around the mine.

Wolf had referred to them as wild and unorganized. The former was certainly true, but not necessarily the latter. Sometimes Konrad would notice certain creatures that stood back during attacks, watching from a vantage point, as if directing the berserk hordes.

The beastmen had their own army, and so they also had their own generals.

Konrad learned to recognize the different types of deadly opponent, learned what they were known as. There were countless creatures for which no name had yet been found; there were so many types, so many variations; and there were more of them all the time.

When they turned upon each other, it seemed as if they must kill, that they did not care who or what died. But much more often, it was evident that the only reason for their existence was to destroy human life.

Konrad knew how to kill them all.

FIVE LONG WINTERS went by.

Five cold, hard, tough winters.

In which Konrad became colder, harder, tougher.

BOOK TWO

CHAPTER TWELVE

SPRING CAME, AND the thaw, and the weather became less harsh – while the attacks from the north were renewed with even more ferocity.

Konrad had been with Wolf for almost five years, but he saw no sign of any fortune. And he was sure that Wolf had not made much money as leader of the mercenary army. Elyssa had taught Konrad to count, and he had been forced to improve his arithmetic when Wolf had entrusted him with some of the payments to the troops.

Whatever money Wolf had made from his percentage of the gold output, he must have lost by increasing the number of soldiers under him. The workings had not been invaded for two years; no miner had been killed by enemy action for even longer.

The volume of gold reaching Kislev had more than doubled since Wolf had been in command, yet he had recruited more than double the manpower – far more than was needed to keep the enemy at bay and to protect the shipments of ore.

Meanwhile, Wolf's other tactics proved ever more successful. His army had grown much more skilful, was destroying many more of the foe than previously – and was even launching attacks upon the northern abominations, taking the battle to the enemy. No longer on the defensive, they were pressing the beastmen back. And while the invaders made no progress in Kislev, the Empire remained safe.

The mine was far bigger than Konrad's native village had been. Like a small town, it had to provide everything required for all those who worked there. The miners were almost like slaves, but they were never chained. They were free to escape if they wanted to take their chances against the besieging beastmen. Some tried, but very few could have made it – even those who had bought their way out of the mine with smuggled gold.

The mercenaries demanded amusement, they required entertaining when they were off duty. Wolf arranged for as many diversions as they needed, all of which cost his troops dearly. If they spent their money drinking and whoring or lost it gambling, then they would never earn enough to leave.

The same seemed true in Wolf's own case, that he would be unable to leave because he would never have sufficient funds. In the beginning, he had said that he intended to make money out of the campaign, because that was what happened during wars. He planned to earn a fortune. This far, however, it was impossible for Wolf to have accumulated more than a handful of crowns. Whenever he had but one such gold coin, he spent it all at the tavern.

And if Wolf never left the area of the mine, Konrad wondered if he himself ever would. He had a horse, clothes, armour, weapons – but they were not his. He belonged to Wolf, and so whatever he possessed also belonged to Wolf. He never had anything of his own. Whatever he needed, he had to ask Wolf.

When Wolf was in a good mood, if they had won a spectacular victory over the beastmen, he would buy Konrad a drink. Only one.

It had been a few weeks since the last battle with the beastmen, however, when Wolf asked Konrad to meet him in the tavern. It was late, but the place was very busy, and Konrad bumped into a dwarf as soon as he entered the inn. The dwarf spilled half his drink – spilled it over Konrad's trousers.

'Fool!' snarled the dwarf.

Dwarfs were notoriously short-tempered, and this one was no exception. He must have been one of those who operated the mine. He was less than five feet tall, his red hair long and wild, his face lined with dirt. The engineers could never rid themselves of the dust in which they worked.

Unlike most dwarfs, this one was unbearded. His leather clothes were worn away at the knees and elbows, from crawling through narrow tunnels. Most people wore a knife on their belt, but the dwarf carried a hammer and a set of metal chisels. Slung over his shoulder was a pickaxe, as though he was ready to start tunnelling any minute.

It was impossible to tell his age, because dwarfs lived much longer than humans – or they did in most parts of the world. In a mine surrounded by enemies, no one could plan on living very long.

Konrad shrugged, half-apologetically. That seemed sufficient. It was as much the dwarf's fault as his.

'You spilled my beer!' the dwarf complained. 'Buy me another!'

As Wolf's right-hand man, Konrad frequently had to keep the peace between the different factions in the camp. The last thing he wanted was to cause any trouble. He would gladly have bought the dwarf a drink, but for one reason: he had no money, he never had any money.

He glanced around the tavern, taking a few steps as he tried to see if Wolf was sitting in the far corner. The dwarf thought Konrad was trying to leave, and grabbed him by the arm. Konrad whirled around, his hand instinctively going to the hilt of his kris. But he held back from drawing his weapon. Instead he spat out a word, a dwarf obscenity that he had learned from his axe tutor.

The dwarf hurled the remains of his beer at Konrad – plus the tankard. And himself...

Konrad was sent flying, tripped over a stool, and landed flat on his back. He tried to rise, but suddenly the dwarf's pickaxe was against his throat, pinning him down.

It was only a drink, Konrad told himself, only a spilled drink. Many lives had been lost for reasons as insignificant – but they had not been taken by him. Konrad could have freed himself in under two heartbeats – and one of those would have been his assailant's last. But he lay still, staring up at the dwarf. Their eyes locked.

After a few seconds, the dwarf muttered something, then turned away. Konrad stood up and glanced around for Wolf.

He was seated in the far corner, as Konrad had expected. He looked at the younger man's beer-soaked clothes, but said nothing. There was a tankard of ale already waiting for Konrad.

Before he could reach for it, a short, stocky figure sat down next to Wolf.

'This is Anvila,' said Wolf. 'And this is Konrad.'

Konrad gazed at the dwarf who had just floored him. The dwarf sipped at his new beer stein and returned his stare. Konrad took a drink of his own ale.

'You might have noticed,' said Wolf, 'that Anvila is a dwarf. Did you know that thousands of years ago, the dwarfs used to live around here? The World's Edge Mountains were their homeland, although this was about as far north as they came. Am I right?'

Anvila shrugged and took a swig of beer.

'What do dwarfs do, Konrad?' said Wolf.

It was Konrad's turn to shrug and swig his ale.

'They dig holes, tunnels, passages,' said Wolf, answering his own question. 'You just can't stop them. It's what they do now, and it's what they did thousands of years ago. You could travel from here to Karaz-a-Karak, and not see the light of day. There was a network of tunnels all the way south, many of which still exist. When I first worked as a mercenary here, I heard of an ancient dwarf temple. You know what's in it?'

'No,' said Konrad.

'Treasure. That's why I really came back here. I knew that there must be some truth behind the legends, and there is. There's a fortune waiting for us in these mountains. It was lost when most of the subterranean passages were blocked by earthquakes, covered by volcanoes. And it's a fortune that doesn't have to be dug up by hundreds of miners. We're going to take it – you, me and Anvila.'

'Oh,' said Konrad.

'Try to contain your enthusiasm,' said Wolf. 'We've done more than enough around here – for the company, for Kislev, for the Empire – far more than our share. Now it's time to reap the rewards. It involves venturing through enemy territory.

'We could fight our way through, although that would mean drawing attention to ourselves, and also having to divide the booty among more people – if any of us survived. But that isn't necessary, because a small party should be able to sneak by. We leave tomorrow, at midnight.'

'Do I have a choice?'

Wolf grinned, and Konrad knew that he did not.

'Anything else he should know?' asked Wolf.

'No,' replied Anvila, speaking for the first time since he had sat down. He drained his tankard and set it down on the table, then stood up.

'Until midnight tomorrow,' said Wolf, raising his beer stein in a toast.

Anvila turned and left the crowded tavern.

'This is what I've been waiting for, planning for,' said Wolf. 'Things didn't work out to start with, I admit. I spent too much time killing invaders when I should have been thinking of myself. But this is where it all becomes worthwhile. It's hard to communicate with the dwarfs, and it's taken a long time to get through to Anvila. We've combined our knowledge, worked out where we think the temple must be, and she'll be able to locate it exactly once we get there.'

'She?' said Konrad.

'That's right – she. In order to prove herself here, she's had to be twice as good at her job as any of the male dwarfs, twice as tough as they are.'

'But... she's a woman.'

'So? That only matters if you're another dwarf. Anvila's clever, too. She was taught at some kind of university the dwarfs have at Karaz-a-Karak, and while she was there she studied many historical documents relating to the tunnels.'

If she was clever, wondered Konrad, why was she working in a mine? But he did not ask.

IT HAD BEEN bad enough allowing a dwarf to get the better of him – but a female dwarf...

Konrad was still thinking of this the following evening, as he lay next to Krysten.

At first, he had not understood why there had been such a violent reaction when he had sworn at the dwarf. That was when Konrad thought it had been a male he was dealing with. But now that he knew Anvila was a woman, he felt guilty for having used such an expression.

It was already dark, the room lit with a few candles. Soon it would be time to leave. There would be no returning – and he also felt guilty about Krysten.

She had managed without him before, and she would do so again. It was not even as though she kept herself for him exclusively. They were friends, no more than that.

He slipped out of bed slowly so as not to wake her, and he caught sight of her reflection in the mirror on the wall. He had brought the mirror from Praag as a gift for the girl. She could sell it if she wished; it was worth a lot out here. He gazed at her nude body, at the mane of blonde hair flowing on the pillow. She would be fine.

He had always regretted bringing the mirror. It reminded him too much of Elyssa and her mirror – just as Krysten, no matter how different, always reminded him of his first love, his only love.

It was almost five years since Elyssa had died. Konrad had believed that his memories would inevitably fade, but that had not happened. Instead, there was seldom a day that he did not think of the girl.

Whenever he was with another woman, her eyes became the same hypnotic black as Elyssa's, her flesh as soft and white as hers. He still dreamed of her, although in his dreams she was not as she was – but how she would have been had she survived.

The dreams were not always pleasant. Sometimes Elyssa was his torturer, or she was trying to murder him, and Konrad remembered his premonition of how she would cause his destruction.

But whenever he woke from such a dream, he was convinced that Elyssa was still truly alive. When he became fully awake, however, he realized that dreams and reality bore little similarity.

After what had happened five years ago, the only place where Elyssa lived on was in his mind. She was forever a part of him. The only way she could destroy him was if he plotted his own death, and he had no intention of doing that.

As he passed the candlelit mirror, Konrad saw his image in the glass. He had always tried to avoid his reflection, for fear that one day he might see his younger self staring back at him. But that was a lifetime ago, and it seemed to be someone else's lifetime. He was far different from the person he had once been. No longer a youth, he was truly a man. Like his former self, he was tall and lean; but now his limbs were rippled with muscles, and his body was marked with the scars from many a battle.

He pulled his white leather headband over his scalp, tugging his two braids of hair in front of his ears, and began to dress. It was summer, and he did not need his thick furs. Nor did he need the few jewels and trinkets he had collected over the years. His breastplate and chainmail, his helmet and gauntlets, his buckler and sword, his axe and his faithful kris – they were all a warrior needed

He noticed the scroll that Matthew Marlinespike had once given him. It had been worth nothing then, and by now it was torn and stained with wine, but Konrad tucked it into his boot.

He kept wishing that Krysten would wake – but hoping that she would not. He kissed her cheek and found it wet with tears. She knew he was leaving, he realized, and she also knew that he would not return.

THEY TRAVELLED BY night, heading north, using only the light of Mannslieb and Morrslieb to guide them. Progress was slow because of the dark and the harsh terrain, and it became slower the further they went.

There were no tracks through the mountains, and they had to go on foot, leading their own mounts and the three pack-horses. Anvila was usually in front, because she had better night vision. Dwarfs were used to working in dim light, deep underground, and their eyes were large by human standards.

Wolf followed Anvila, and Konrad followed him. Every moment he was alert, watching for danger. He could still remember that when he lived in the village night was the time that the beastmen were on the prowl. Out here, however, night and day were equally as bad. Light or dark, the creatures could attack at any time. When they had destroyed the village it had been during the day.

Almost five years ago... In a few more days it would be the eighteenth of Sigmarzeit, by the calendar of the Empire – the first day of summer, which was the same by any calendar. That had been the day when the inhabitants of the valley had been annihilated. Two days later, he had agreed to serve Wolf for five years.

Wolf had made no reference to the approaching anniversary, and Konrad wondered what would happen on that day. Would he have to remind him of the date? Then what?

Every day, they made camp, hiding away among the rocks. Every night, they advanced fewer miles. Their route became steeper, narrower, more precarious.

It would have been easier to leave the horses, but Wolf was worried about the animals being discovered. He also claimed that they would be needed to transport all the treasures, just as they were needed now to carry Anvila's equipment: picks and shovels and spades, strange measuring devices and barrels of gunpowder.

Konrad was very uneasy about the black powder. It was not natural, such explosions which imitated thunderbolts. Although it was used primarily for mining, Wolf had encouraged experiments whereby the powder could be used for weapons, creating detonations in the paths of attacking beastmen.

It seemed that Anvila had been one of the dwarfs who had helped Wolf, but she had more sense than to prove the worth of her own inventions. Several mercenaries had been killed in such research, although Wolf had always chosen the most expendable to test these modern developments.

Others of Wolf's army possessed guns of various types, but Konrad had never been impressed by such armament. As in so many other things, he had probably been influenced by Wolf. Guns were the only combat weapons in which Konrad had not become proficient. They delivered little in the way of killing power, and seemed as dangerous to the user as to the enemy. Neither had larger artillery pieces yet proved their worth.

Konrad knew no more about their expedition deep into the ancient mountains than he had done when Wolf first proposed the scheme. Little was said during the journey, because any sound was magnified by the rocks. The horses' hooves were bound with fabric to silence their steps.

Even at the best of times dwarfs were laconic, which meant that Anvila said hardly a word throughout the trek. Konrad wondered what she was thinking, whether she believed in Wolf's expedition or whether she was here for her own motives. He did not trust her, and he knew that the dwarf did not like him – which was fine by Konrad.

As for their mission, Konrad did not know what to think. Buried treasure, hidden for thousands of years? It was possible, although not very probable. But it was not up to him to think. All he had to do was obey, to do whatever Wolf told him – for a few more days, at least.

In the beginning, Wolf had been concerned that they might be followed by some of the troops from the mine. If Wolf went missing, the other mercenaries must have suspected that he was up to something. But there had been no sign of pursuit.

Neither had there been any sign of the invaders. At first, that was a relief. If they ran into a band of marauders, they would be finished. Three of them could not hope to survive.

By now, however, Konrad was beginning to consider that something was wrong. The whole region was teeming with beastmen, and so they should at least have caught sight of one of the creatures. He presumed the reason that they had not was because the mountains were so desolate and barren. What was there here for the renegades?

Only the three of them...

Konrad could still see. His extra senses would warn him of danger – sometimes. His left eye was able to glimpse what would happen a fraction of a second before it actually did, and this had saved his life many times in the past five years, when he had been able to anticipate and avoid a blow which would have proved fatal.

Wolf, he was sure, was aware that Konrad had this gift, some kind of second sight. He must have suspected it from the day that Konrad had foreseen the attack by the trio of flying beastmen, but he had never made any explicit reference to Konrad's talent.

As ever, Konrad hoped that his erratic skill would not let him down when he most needed it. Throughout their climb, day or night, he was constantly vigilant.

Finally, the route became too dangerous to take in the dark, and so they continued during daylight. That was almost as bad.

'We'll have to leave the other horses here,' Wolf said. 'Midnight is the only one that can get through. You stay and guard them, Konrad. Anvila and I will go on. We're almost there.'

Konrad wondered how Wolf could tell. All the rocks and boulders and peaks looked the same. However, he was content to remain where he was. Mountains were not for humans, they were for eagles – and maybe for dwarfs.

He did not like the idea of Anvila being alone with Wolf, but Wolf ought to be able to take care of himself.

'How long do I wait?' asked Konrad.

'As long as it takes,' Wolf told him.

'Then what? Do I follow you?'

Wolf shrugged and turned away.

Anvila and Konrad looked at one another in silence, and then she also turned. Midnight was laden down with as much as he could carry. Wolf and Anvila were also like beasts of burden, with heavy bundles tied to their backs.

They headed on and up and were soon hidden by the thrusting rocks. Konrad kept watching, but he saw no sign of them throughout the rest of the day. Night finally fell, and he lay down and gazed at the stars. For some reason, as he fell asleep, he thought of the twin-tailed comet that had appeared when Sigmar had been born.

HE AWOKE WHILE it was still dark, his hand clutched even tighter around the carved handle of his trusty dagger. Carefully, slowly, he reached for the sword by his side.

There was danger, he could see...

But, his eyes still closed, he suddenly realized that he was not seeing danger for himself – it was Wolf and Anvila who were in deadly peril.

He sat up and stared around as best he could in the darkness, looking and listening, in case there was any immediate threat to himself. But the horses were still and silent, and their animal senses were usually aware of strange scents such as those of beastmen.

The image had already faded, but his mind had visualized both Wolf and Anvila. It was night where they were – and creeping up on them were several silent shapes, dark and deadly.

The ambush had not yet occurred, although it was about to. And there was nothing whatsoever that Konrad could do.

It was futile, impossible, he was far too far away, but even so, he filled his lungs and yelled out as loud as he could: 'Wolf..!'

His voice echoed through the mountains, bouncing back at him, magnified and distorted.

'Wolf!' he shouted again.

'WolfWolfWolf,' the mountains mocked. 'Wolf... Wolf... Wolf...'

'WOLF!' he bellowed.

Despite the darkness, he began making his way further up the mountain, following the route of the other two. He did not bother with any armour. It was too heavy, it would slow him down, and speed was vital. All he took was his sword and the twin-bladed battleaxe that he carried over his shoulder.

He could hardly see where he was going, but that scarcely made any difference, because he was only guessing which direction to take. Forward and upward he went, relying upon his instincts to lead him to the place that he had foreseen.

The sun rose, it grew lighter and he could see where he was going, but he hardly noticed – until he realized that the dawn meant it really was too late. The ambush must already have happened. Konrad hesitated only a second, and then he pressed on, harder and harder.

He was sweating profusely, and he threw off his fur jacket and the leggings around his breeches. His fingers and palms had been cut by the sharp rocks, and the blood made his hands slip as he reached for every grip.

It must have taken nearly three hours until he arrived at the killing zone. But all he saw were dead beastmen, and Midnight lying dead on his side. The stallion was no longer white but almost completely red with gore.

Konrad moved slowly through the huge grey rocks. A dozen of the enemy could have hidden behind each of them. But the only invaders he saw were corpses.

They were all goblins, he observed. Goblins were poor fighters, which was why so many of them must have died in the assault. These seemed smaller and more deformed than most. They had been stabbed and sliced and hacked, trampled by Midnight's hooves, and one lay with Anvila's pickaxe through its skull.

There was no sign of Wolf or Anvila amongst the dozens of bodies. Could they possibily have escaped? Or perhaps all this was Anvila's doing: she had led Wolf into a trap.

Konrad heard a scraping sound a few yards away, and he was instantly in a fighting crouch, sword poised in his right hand, knife in his left.

The noise was repeated, and he moved warily forward, realizing that it was coming from over the side of the sheer rock face. Cautiously, he went nearer, saw that there was a deep gap in the rock before the edge of the mountain – and the scrabbling was coming from there. He peered down.

'Don't just watch, fool, help me!'

It was Anvila. She must have fallen down the crevasse, but she was unable to climb up. Konrad found a rope among the pile of equipment that had been stacked for the night. He secured one end to a boulder, threw the other end into the ravine, then helped the dwarf reach level ground.

They glanced at each other. Anvila did not offer her thanks; Konrad did not ask if she was hurt.

The dwarf looked around, studying the bodies. 'Where's Wolf?'

'That's what I was going to ask you.'

'We were attacked in the dark. We fought. I slipped and fell. Last thing I saw was Wolf, in the moonlight, surrounded by goblins.'

She kicked one of the corpses. 'I hate grobi!' She kicked another.

'What happened to him?'

'Maybe they killed him, threw him off the mountain.'

'Or maybe,' said Konrad, 'they took him prisoner.'

That had always been Wolf's greatest fear. He had never wanted to become a captive again, not after the unspeakable tortures and mutilations he must have suffered previously. Wolf had never said who had captured him, when or where, but he had made it amply clear that he intended to kill himself rather than risk being made a hostage again.

It seemed that there had been no time for suicide.

'We've got to find him,' said Konrad. 'Where will they have taken him? Where were you heading?'

'The temple is reputed to be near here. We've already found one blocked tunnel, late yesterday.'

'The tunnels – that's where the goblins must live,' said Konrad. 'That's where they must have taken Wolf. How do we get in there?'

'Wait,' said Anvila. 'I admit that I like Wolf. For a human, he's all right by me. But there are only two of us, Konrad – and hundreds, maybe thousands of goblins. We don't know where he is, or even if he's alive. We don't stand a chance. The logical thing is for us to retreat.'

'What's logic got to do with it?'

The dwarf sighed. 'I suppose you're right, manling.'

'How do we get underground? Where's this temple?'

'Let's get my stuff.'

Anvila chose what she wanted from the bundles that had been abandoned when she and Wolf were attacked, and they shared the things between them – although Konrad made sure that he did not carry any of the small wooden gunpowder barrels.

They climbed further up the mountain, Anvila leading the way. Konrad noticed drops of blood on various rocks that they passed, but he said nothing.

The dwarf stopped several times, drawing out some marked sticks from her pack, setting them on the ground, sliding pieces of metal up and down them.

All hostility between human and dwarf was forgotten. They were allies now – exactly as Sigmar Heldenhammer and the dwarfs had fought together against the goblins twenty-five centuries ago.

'Come on, come on,' muttered Konrad impatiently. 'They could be killing him!'

And even as he spoke, he knew it would soon be true.

'Here,' Anvila said finally.

'Where?' he demanded, staring around.

The area looked no different: surrounded by peaks, scattered rocks lying everywhere, a few traces of vegetation, sparse clumps of grass, moss growing on boulders. There was no sign of a temple, of any structure that had been fabricated by a force other than nature's.

'There, manling,' she told him, and she pointed.

He followed the line of her finger, which was directed at a fissure in the mountain face. He moved closer, saw how dark it was within, a darkness that indicated a long deep passage.

He noticed a mark on the side of the rock, a bloody handprint. A human handprint. It could only have been Wolf's.

'I'm going in,' he said.

'Wait!'

'There's no time to wait.'

'It's too dark down there for a human,' Anvila told him. 'Light a torch.'

'Where–?'

But before he could finish his question, the dwarf had opened her pack and pulled out an oiled brand. It was the kind of thing a mining engineer always carried. She lit it with her tinderbox, passed it to Konrad.

'What about you?' he asked.

'You find him. I've other things to do.' She gestured to one of the powder barrels at her feet.

Konrad did not know what she meant, neither did he care. He had too much else to think about. He turned to go.

'Konrad!'

He looked back.

Anvila swore at him, the most obscene phrase in the Dwarf language – far worse than what he had said to her when they first met. 'Do that to the goblins!' she laughed grimly.

CHAPTER THIRTEEN

THE DWARF WOMAN'S fierce curse against the goblins rang in Konrad's ears, reminding him of the ancient enmity which existed between dwarf kind and the greenskins. Among the few books which Konrad had read since he had learned his letters was a very battered old copy of *The Life of Sigmar Heldenhammer* – which he had found tremendously exciting, an inspiration. The thought of the mighty Sigmar slaughtering goblins by the score, his huge warhammer dripping blood as it rose and fell repeatedly, gave him a renewed strength of purpose as he entered the dark fissure in the mountainside.

Sword in his right hand, the blazing torch in his left, Konrad ventured into the abyss, pressing between the rocks which led deep into the mountain.

He had never been in such a place before, and the stygian darkness sent a shiver down his backbone. The air was foul; it stank with the odour of goblins. The light from the fire in his hand caused eerie shadows to dance across the rocks on either side of him.

After a minute or two, he observed that no longer was he squeezing between a natural split in the rock face – the passage was lined with hewn stone blocks. They were carved with archaic symbols, faded runes.

Although he could not read the old language of the dwarfs, Konrad recognized the shapes of the runes from examples that his young tutor, Matthew Marlinespike, had shown him. The presence of these arcane symbols proved that this place must indeed have been the object of Wolf's quest – the ancient dwarf temple. Wolf had found his goal, but he had been hauled down here as a captive.

Beneath his feet, Konrad noticed steps, and he descended a long and twisting flight of stones which curved around and around until he seemed to be heading back in the direction he had come.

The torch offered little in the way of light. He could not see very far ahead, and the illumination was probably more of a hindrance than a help. It warned the goblins that he was on his way; they would see him before he saw them.

He suddenly found himself in a wider chamber, and he almost tripped on an object lying on the floor. It clanged as it slid away beneath his boot, and he glanced down. It was an old sword, rusty and chipped. He stared around, seeing more ancient weapons lying to either side: clubs and maces, spears and daggers, shields and all kinds of armour – and a bow.

He paused, his eyes fixed on the bow. It was short, very curved, unstrung. The string lay with it, notched at only one end. But a bow was useless without an arrow, and he was about to move on when he saw the single shaft.

Wolf had warned him to avoid all of the enemy weapons. Everything touched by the beastmen was possibly contaminated. The armour and armaments of the vanquished marauders were always destroyed, or left to rot with their fetid bodies.

However, goblins were not quite the same as beastmen, even if they were in league with the same Dark Powers. Despite his qualms, Konrad bent down to pick up the arrow, fearing that it would crumble in his fingers.

It did not. Beneath the dirt, the wood was still solid, the arrowhead still secured, the flights still feathered. The string of the bow, however, must have perished by now.

It had not. But it must surely snap when he slipped it into the other notch and it became stretched.

It did not. Konrad slid the arrow into his belt, transferred the sword to his left hand and also held the bow there, while his right took the flaming torch. The bow and arrow could not possibly be as old as the temple; they must have been recent goblin booty.

The chamber where he stood had three exits, three dark and uninviting tunnels. He examined them all, but there was no bloody handprint to mark the route he must take.

He continued forward, relying on his innate senses to choose the correct passage, and the walls narrowed once more as he went through into the darkness and silence.

His ears seemed to sing in the eerie blackness. But the silence did not last for long. He heard a terrible sound echoing along the tunnel. It was a scream. A human scream. Wolf's scream.

Konrad had been creeping uneasily through the gloom, but now he picked up speed, moving ever faster. He bruised his sides painfully several times, but he pressed on regardless, conscious only of the fact that Wolf was in dire need of him. He came to junctions, to points were the passage split in twain, but he never hesitated. Wolf's tortured cries were his guide. They grew louder...

And then, without warning, he was out of the tunnel. His footsteps no longer thudded back at him, and the light from the torch was swallowed up by the vastness of the underground cavern in which he found himself.

He saw all the dark hunched silhouettes ahead of him, and could see another shape in the distance, pale and straight, upright against the far wall. A sacrificial offering, one whose death would be slow and lingering. It had to be Wolf.

Hundreds of ugly faces turned towards Konrad, the flames of his torch reflected in their hundreds and hundreds of glinting red eyes. He had stumbled into a huge assembly of armed goblins, green-skinned horrors of the underworld.

The altar was raised high above floor level, and there stood the figure of Wolf's inhuman torturer. Draped in dark robes, the unholy priest was taller and less twisted than the other skulking shapes. In one hand, the shaman held his totem stick, hung with bones and topped by a human skull. In his other hand was a curved blade, blood dripping from its pointed tip.

'Wolf!' yelled Konrad.

'Konrad!' came the reply, not so loud, not so strong. And then, 'Kill me!'

Without hesitation, Konrad stretched his right arm back and hurled the blazing brand as high and as far as he could, into the heart of the temple. As it flew, tumbling over and over, illuminating the cavernous space with its flickering flame, he reached for the arrow in his belt, letting the sword drop from his left hand and raising the bow.

It was five years since Konrad had shot an arrow with such a bow, but the action was as natural as drawing breath. The arrow into the string, the string pulled back, the bow lifted, the shaft aimed – seeing where the arc of flight would take it.

He released the arrow, dropped the bow while the shaft was still in trajectory and glanced down for his sword – but it had vanished in the dark amidst all the debris.

He reached for the double-bladed waraxe slung across his back, then ran forward, the after-image of the torch showing him his route. His heavy axe was like a scythe, cutting down the autumn wheat – but his deadly harvest was of the goblins who dared block his way.

He had dispatched the first few before his arrow even found the shaman's right eye. Its death scream was lost among the cries of those who fell victim to the vengeful axe.

Using both hands, Konrad swung his weapon to and fro, back and forth, around and around. Flesh was slit and sliced; severed limbs flew; bones were crushed; ugly heads were smashed. The ground underfoot became slippery with goblin gore. He had succeeded in taking the creatures by surprise, but there were more and more of the enemy every instant, and it was growing dark. The light shed from the torch was too far away, rapidly fading, and then it was suddenly extinguished.

For the first time Konrad found himself being pressed back. His opponents were armed, they outnumbered him – and they could see in the dark. Still his mighty axe did its deadly work. The goblins pressed so close there was no way that he could miss. It was tiring work, but he was filled with an almost joyful strength and each dead foe seemed to invigorate him.

But without light, his left eye could give him no warning of the impending sword jabs which began to lacerate his body, and he realized it could not be more than a few seconds before he was struck a fatal blow. Strength alone would not be enough to carry him through, and he began to feel the keen edge of desperation urging him on to a suicidal recklessness. All would end here, in the bowels of the earth, deep below the cold borders of Kislev.

Suddenly he felt a distant rumble, a vibration through the soles of his feet, and a moment later the whole temple shook. Rocks fell from above, one crashing within a yard of where Konrad fought, flattening three goblins. There was dust everywhere, blinding and choking. This caused a lull in the fighting, and Konrad shook his head to clear a trickle of blood from his eyes. The rumbling sound still echoed in the distance. Could this be an earthquake?

He saw a flash of lightning cross his left eye, then streak across his right – and the two images merged within his brain, a vision of twin incandescent trails.

Then, abruptly, there was light all around! The temple was ablaze, as if ignited. But there was no fire, no heat.

The goblins yelled and screamed, holding their clawed hands over their eyes, trying to scuttle away from the sudden brilliance.

Konrad did not care where the light came from. He was too busy. The real killing had begun.

He strode through the creatures, and each swing of his heavy axe meant death for one of the hunched inhumans. Blood spurted onto him and spilled across the dirty stones that had not seen the light of day for thousands of years.

He felt a renewed surge of force flowing through his limbs, which reminded him of the energy he had sensed when he had used that beastman's sword, so many years ago. This was different, however, because the power came from deep within him. It was not some external and malign source of strength that would ultimately drain his vitality.

Instead, he had become absolutely revived. Like the heroic Sigmar of old, he was an invincible warrior destroying his despicable foes. The axe swung repeatedly, and as it swung its blades seemed to glow as if infused by some magic. Amid all the blood, Konrad felt exultant. This was so right; it was as though he had been born for this day. As the killing continued, he felt himself entering a trance-like state.

In his mind the double-headed hammer swung, slaughtering goblins with every sweep. No wonder the dwarfs called the weapon 'Ghal-maraz' – 'Skull-splitter.' This was the battle of Black Fire Pass, where the orcs and goblins were trapped between the humans and the dwarf rearguard. With his huge warhammer swinging, splitting skulls, Sigmar was at the head of his troops as they annihilated the enemy. For this was the day that he would become known as 'Hammer of the Goblins' – Sigmar Heldenhammer!

The massacre only ceased when every goblin was dead or mortally wounded or had managed to creep away into the darkness.

Eventually, emerging from his killing-trance, Konrad was able to lean on his now-stilled weapon, his magical energy beginning to wane.

But weariness could not dim his fierce pride in the outcome of the battle. A hundred goblins – perhaps two hundred – slain by one man!

Splattered with gore, Konrad made his way to where Wolf was tied. The tortured warrior hung from his wrists, naked, covered in even more blood – but it was red not green, Wolf's own blood, human blood. He was staring at Konrad, as though slightly afraid.

He looked different somehow, his body deformed. Perhaps it was twisted with pain, which was why his limbs appeared misshapen. Yet his face had also taken on a strange aspect, as if his jaw were elongated; and although his flesh was soaked with blood, it also seemed matted with thick hairs.

'Didn't you hear what I ordered?' Wolf said, his voice weak. 'You were supposed to kill me, not him.' He spat towards the supine body of the goblin priest. A ball of blood and spit landed on the corpse's ritually mutilated face.

'You can't rely on a bow – it's a peasant weapon,' Konrad replied, as he leaned his mighty warhammer against the wall… He paused, staring at the axe he had just put down, wondering what had made him believe it was a hammer. He rubbed at his eyes, wiping away the blood, then drew his kris to slice through the ropes that held Wolf.

As the last strand parted, the blade of the knife suddenly shattered into a hundred pieces. Konrad gazed at the handle, then let it fall.

'I thought you were going to slit your own throat before you were captured,' he said.

Wolf grimaced as he was helped down. 'Decided I'd rather slit a few of their throats,' he managed to say.

Then they heard the sound of heavy footsteps in the distance, and they both stared towards the tunnel entrances on the opposite side of the cavern.

Konrad was supporting Wolf, one arm around him. He reached for his blood-stained axe. They watched and waited, wondering what enemies would emerge from the dark passages.

The steps came nearer, louder, echoing, like a whole army on the march and preparing to attack. Then at last a small, solitary form appeared from one of the tunnel mouths.

'Where's all this treasure?' asked Anvila, and she stared around at the bare walls of the ancient temple.

THE TIME HAD *come once more. The human had escaped his nemesis five years ago, but that would not happen again.*

Instead of hiding, of venturing far away from the Powers that sought his elimination, he had remained at the very centre of the conflict.

It was almost as if he knew – and yet that was impossible.

He had finally been located and kept under observation until the omens for his death were most auspicious.

The hordes of darkness had been at odds with one another for too long, their energies wasted upon futile rivalries. Their divided armies had been destroyed and pushed back by the forces of humankind.

Lately, however, this had become a deliberate tactic. The more they retreated, the more human troops would be lured into the trap – and to their deaths.

The victory would be magnificent, and there would be much shedding of blood as tribute to the true gods.

This would be the final battle in Kislev. All resistance would be swept aside, the land ravaged, every trace of mortal life annihilated.

Then it would be the turn of the Empire.

The time had come once more.

CHAPTER FOURTEEN

KONRAD FELT TOTALLY exhausted and wished that he could simply close his eyes and sleep. Wolf lay unconscious on the floor, and Konrad envied him.

Wolf's wounds appeared worse than they were. They would heal in time, although his body would be even more scarred than before. But he now looked the same as he always had. The earlier change in his appearance must have been caused by the torture he had endured, unless Konrad had simply imagined it. Konrad's physical senses were never very reliable after the ferocity of combat. Fighting was a matter for instinct and reflex, not for the mind – why else had he been under the delusion that he had wielded a hammer instead of an axe?

The cuts inflicted upon Wolf had been designed to cause the greatest pain, but not to kill – not immediately. The goblins had wanted his death to be as slow and agonizing as possible.

Konrad stared at all the bodies scattered around the floor. The temple had become a charnel house.

At first, he had feared that the green hordes would be back, but he realized that the light kept them away.

The light...

The huge chamber had been lit by the ingenious dwarf, Anvila. The luminescence came from about halfway up one part of the cavern, radiating from what seemed at first to be a broad tunnel – but it was bright instead of dark, covered with a round piece of glass like a window.

'Dwarfs used to illuminate their subterranean temples by a series of lenses which diverted the light down from the surface, from the sun,' Anvila had explained. 'I found the lens above, but it was covered in tons of rock – which I blew away with that gunpowder.'

'Told you she was clever,' Wolf had muttered, then he had passed out.

Now Anvila was exploring the temple. Konrad did not think that she was looking for any of the treasure that Wolf had hoped for. If there had ever been any gold and jewels here, they must have been looted centuries ago.

Instead, she was inspecting the stones and the carvings, studying the entrances to the various passages that led away from the central area.

The chamber must have been carved out of the naked rock, then the floor and some of the walls lined with stone blocks. The floor was circular, some two hundred feet across, and the walls were curved, arching up to meet one another in a massive dome a hundred feet above the ground.

Eventually, Anvila came back and knelt by Wolf. She glanced up at the wall above him, seeing the ropes by which he had been tied.

'This was a dwarf temple, manlings,' she said, 'and now the goblins use it for their own vile rituals. This must have been some ceremony connected with the last day of spring.'

'Tomorrow is the first day of summer?' said Konrad, softly. He was remembering what had happened five years ago – but trying not to.

He gazed at the figure of the goblin shaman, the arrow embedded in its eye socket. He recalled the last arrow he had fired before this one, when he had aimed at the mysterious Skullface's heart. Konrad shook his head, not wanting to think of that either.

He had attempted to wipe the blood and gore from his body, but he was still very sticky. Now that Anvila was with Wolf, he went looking for some water. He did not find any, and he had no intention of leaving the light.

He gazed up at the huge piece of glass set in the rock. It was round and there seemed various rings inside it, circles of different sizes and thicknesses. The lens reminded him of a mirror.

He began to turn away, and as he did he caught a glimpse of movement in the glass above him. He looked back, watching as a shape within it became clearer, like a figure emerging from fog. He saw a rider, the image of a man on horseback. A man he could not fail to recognize.

The bronze warrior! The man that Wolf claimed was his twin brother...

Konrad stared in amazement, not believing what he could see, refusing to believe it. Only once had Wolf ever mentioned his brother, the day that he and Konrad had met. He had said that his twin was dead. It was five years since the bronze knight had ridden into the village, five years to this very day. Konrad recalled that the horseman had seemed like some supernatural entity.

Worse than dead – those had been Wolf's exact words when referring to his twin.

And Skullface had not died when an arrow had buried itself in his heart.

Was that because he had no beating heart, because he was no longer alive? He had not died because he was already dead.

Had the warrior in bronze really returned to haunt Konrad – or was he only the illusion that he appeared to be?

'Anvila!' he yelled, and he pointed up at the round glass. 'Can you see it?'

'Yes!' she shouted back.

'What does it mean?'

'It's a distant image, reflected and magnified by the lenses. The one on the surface must have fragmented, and by some phenomenon it's displaying a stray vision.'

'Is it real?'

'Yes.'

'Is he real?'

'Yes. He's probably a few miles away, near the edge of the mountains.'

As she spoke, the ghostly apparition faded into the mists of the lens and was gone.

'I have to follow him,' Konrad said, as he hurried back to where Anvila and Wolf were.

The dwarf looked at him, but she said nothing.

'I must go. It is… my destiny…'

Anvila shrugged. 'If it's that important, go.'

'What about Wolf? Can you take care of him, help him out of here?'

'Yes.'

'What about the goblins?'

'I'm a dwarf. These are the lands of my ancestors. I know how to deal with goblins.'

Konrad gazed down at Wolf, and Wolf's eyes flickered open.

Wolf licked at his lips and opened his mouth to speak. He uttered a single word, a hoarse sigh, and Konrad barely caught what was said. Wolf took a shallow breath before speaking again, the same word, much louder. Then he slipped into unconsciousness once more, as though the repeated word had been too much effort.

It was a word that Konrad had heard before, a word that was often spoken on the frontier, a word Konrad had even used himself – but he had never understood its true meaning. He glanced at Anvila, who showed no reaction and said nothing.

'I must go,' Konrad said.

'You said that. If you have to, then – go!'

He nodded and backed slowly away, making for the passage through which Anvila had entered the temple.

He had to leave, and yet he wanted to stay. He did not want to abandon Wolf and Anvila here. But what help could he be? The dwarf was confident that she could get Wolf out, away from the mountains.

There was nothing more that Konrad could learn from Wolf, his second teacher. Elyssa had been his first instructor, and she had died five years ago. Five years less a day.

And now the bronze warrior was nearby, and this was the same date upon which Konrad and Elyssa had originally seen him.

The was no such thing as coincidence – only fate.

Konrad must find the knight. Only then, he knew, would he begin to find his own true self.

Elyssa and Wolf had given him much, but he was the only one who could discover who he was – who he had been – and who he would become...

A final glance at Anvila, at Wolf, and then he spun around and entered the dark tunnel that would lead him up to the surface.

As he strode through the ancient passageway, Konrad remembered what Wolf had said.

'Chaos,' Wolf had whispered.

'Chaos!' Wolf had warned.

ABOUT THE AUTHOR

David Ferring was born on a small island called Britain, from which he escaped by running away to sea. His first writing job was typing out passenger menus, but he soon began making up imaginary dishes. Critical reaction to his early literary work was mixed, and he jumped ship in New York. Claiming to read Japanese, he was hired to translate the captions of scores of manga books. Instead, he made it all up.

He wrote his first Warhammer novel, *Konrad*, after he stopped producing gags for nightclub crooners in Las Vegas; *Shadowbreed* was written when he gave up devising plot-lines for an Australian soap opera; and *Warblade* was written one-handedly in Hong Kong, after he broke his right arm during a stunt in a Jackie Chan movie – and he'd only been on set to compose a few lines of dialogue for the European villain...

Now living on his native isle, David Ferring is still making up things.

The saga of Konrad continues in

SHADOWBREED

by David Ferring
Coming soon from the Black Library

KONRAD SAT UP abruptly, wincing at the pain that wracked his whole being. The sun burned fiercely down upon his naked body. His throat was drier than ever, his lips cracked, he was covered in a crust of blood. The embers of the fire still smouldered, and the wisps of grey smoke were the only sign of movement. Everything else was still and silent; everyone else was gone.

From the angle of the sun, it was at least three hours since dawn. He seldom slept that long, yet there had been plenty of catching up to do. Although he was no longer so totally exhausted, he felt as if he could easily have found some shade, closed his eyes and slept through the rest of the day.

He resisted the temptation and studied his wrist. The two serpent bites had scabbed over, as had the cut in his arm where one of the inhuman girls had sliced the flesh. The elf who had saved Konrad's arm now seemed to have also saved his life. According to Kastring, Konrad should have been dead. That was why the marauders had left him here; they believed that he was. It could only be the residual effects of the potent healing magic which had saved him.

He stood up and went to examine the creatures' camp. At first glance, there was hardly any sign that they had been here. Even the headless corpses of the sacrificial offerings were gone. The blood had been absorbed into the earth, baked by the early sun. The ground seemed very dry, and Konrad knelt down to touch it. It had no substance, was as lifeless as sand. The few clumps of grass and plants in the vicinity had become brown and brittle, were wilting away. The nearby trees were covered in fungus and rot, decayed like those where the Forest of Shadows was inhabited by beastmen.

Whatever the invaders touched became corrupted, even the ground upon which they trod.

Konrad fingered his lips, remembering the goblet from which he had drunk, remembering Kastring's lips, wondering if that was why his own were now cracked...

But it was the lack of water, he told himself, the raging thirst that consumed him. Drinking wine always made him very thirsty the next day, and he had been parched even before his first taste.

'It transpires that you are as tough as you look.'

Konrad whirled around. Kastring was a few yards away, mounted on a huge beast that must once have been a horse. Its skin was mottled, red and black, and its flanks were protected by armour; instead of hooves, it had taloned claws; its mouth was fanged like a dog's, and a single spiral of dark horn grew from the centre of its skull.

Despite his own grotesque appearance, Kastring did not look as frightening in the daylight as he had at night. The horns on his head seemed to be a part of his helmet, his grinning teeth were like a mask he wore over his face. His hair hung almost to his waist, and he was clad in black fur and red leather, as well as gleaming brass armour. His snake-hilted sword hung at his hip, his two-crested shield hung from his saddle.

Konrad backed away.

'Have no fear,' Kastring told him. 'I have no intention of killing you, I assure you. Not at present. I merely wish to invite you to join our expedition.'

'If I refuse…'

'That question does not arise. My request was more in the nature of a command. You should be dead. Because that seems not to be the case, you intrigue me. You will join us. You will amuse me with tales of Ferlangen. I was fatigued last night, I must admit, and so my conversation may not have been very spirited. For that I apologize. We will share many hours of discussion in future, until…'

'Until?'

'Until you die. All things must come to a conclusion, even life, especially life. We are born to die. It is not knowing when we shall meet our ultimate demise that makes our lives so interesting, I'm sure you agree? And your own life, I promise you, will be extremely interesting.'

Konrad sensed another figure behind him, and he turned. It was the surviving death dancer. She was clad now, wearing sandals and a short loose robe, her body cleansed of gore. Her hair was tied back, but was still the colour of blood; so were her eyes and her feral teeth.

Her forehead was marked with the main symbol that was on Kastring's shield; the cross with two bars had been carved into her flesh, leaving a vivid crimson scar. She looked far more gaunt, far less seductive than she had in the haunted moonlight, but no less terrifying.

The spiked band was still around her neck, but now she also wore a necklace through which her knife was looped. The necklace seemed to be made from bones, human finger-bones.

'I don't believe you have been formally introduced,' said Kastring. 'This is Silk. Or maybe Satin. I'm afraid I never could tell them apart. No matter. Like myself, she has no need to know your name. She does not speak Old Worlder, but you will learn to do everything that she commands. From now on, you and she will never be more than a yard apart. Perhaps much closer. She can be very pleasant company, I assure you. And then one day, maybe soon, maybe not, she will kill you.'

Kastring spoke to the girl, who nodded solemnly. All the time, her eyes were on Konrad, studying his naked body. When Kastring had finished speaking, she raised the blade of her knife, kissed it, and blew Konrad the kiss. He shuddered, staring at her lips and remembering her forked tongue and the way it had licked his blood last night.

'She appears to like you,' Kastring commented.

Konrad remained silent. It would not be him who died, he promised himself. His erstwhile torturer would be the first to meet death. Either her or Kastring...

'The Empire, Ostland, Ferlangen!' called Kastring, as he tugged at his mount's reins. 'Our beloved homeland awaits our return!' The horse reared up, caracolled, then galloped off towards the south-west.

'Any chance of some water?' said Konrad to his guard. 'Something to eat? Anything to wear?'

He saw her tail twitch. She spoke, a few grunted syllables, and pointed in the direction that Kastring had taken. Konrad kept watching her and remained motionless. The girl withdrew her knife and raised it at a throwing angle. She was too far away for him to reach before she could hurl the blade, but too near for the knife to miss if she threw it.

Konrad turned and followed the rider; his escort followed him.

He had walked from the Empire to Kislev, leading Wolf's packhorse. Now he walked back, this time with a deadly shadow close behind every step of the way.

It was a longer walk, because without any boat journey it was much further – and because there were so many interruptions for fighting battles, sacking villages, sacrificing captives...

Konrad saw very little of this, and he saw very few of Kastring's motley regiment. They were not like a regular army, taking orders, marching together. They split up into smaller units, choosing their own routes, then came together again for a raid or a massacre.

He was allowed to clothe himself with garments taken from the victims. They soon became ripped, sliced when Silk gave him an order that he did not immediately understand or when he did not respond with sufficient alacrity. His body was covered in tiny stab wounds, as if he had been bitten all over.

He had very little chance of escape, and even less chance of success. Every minute, Silk was within a few feet of him. And beyond her were Kastring's warriors and beastmen, each of whom was eager to kill, craving the offering they could make to their foul lord by spilling fresh blood. It was hard to judge how many there were in Kastring's band. The numbers were forever changing, increasing when they appeared to recruit new members from the areas through which they passed, declining after every clash of arms.

Sometimes they travelled by night, other times their journeys took place during the day. Often they would be on the move for a whole day and a night, then they would halt for a few days. Konrad never understood why. He never asked, and no one ever told him.

They carried few supplies with them. There were no baggage wagons, although there was one chariot. It was always well guarded, and Konrad realized that it must have borne the sacred brass armour which composed the altar.

The troops had to forage for food, or plunder from the farmsteads they destroyed. Most of them were on foot, which meant they could carry very little. A handful of warriors rode on horseback – horses that had begun to mutate in a similar fashion to their riders. These were an elite corps, true fighting men with professional weapons and armour.

They seemed oddly out of place amongst the rest of the warband. They were more like disciplined knights than berserk savages. They had their own warped code of chivalry, and it seemed their only destiny was to fight, that they honoured their chosen deity by the shedding of blood upon the field of battle – either their own blood or that of their vanquished foes. But then the opposite would happen: when the lesser moon was full, more blood sacrifices would take place, but on these occasions it would be helpless captives who were ritually tortured and foully murdered to satisfy the obscene cravings of the Chaos cult.

At the other end of the scale from the warrior knights were the brutal subhumans, dressed in rags, bearing whatever weaponry they had been able to steal. Between these two extremes lay the majority of Kastring's renegades, beings that were neither man nor monster, but some hideous combination of the two.

These were the kind that Konrad was most used to fighting on the frontier, fighting and killing: the creatures whose limbs had become weapons, who had extra eyes or ears or mouths, whose faces were set in their chests, who were part insect, with huge pincers for arms, who were part bird, with great wings on their backs, who were part reptile, with their flesh covered in scales, who had the heads of animals on human bodies – or human heads on bestial bodies.

Their bodies were predominantly red and black, the colours of blood and death; and their fur or feathers or fins or pelts or shells or hides would be striped or streaked or spotted with variations of these two hues. Many of them had eyes which were completely white, without any pupils. They seemed blind, but they could see.

And they were united under the same symbol, the same emblem that was on their banners, the same device that was on Kastring's shield, the same pattern that was on Silk's face – the vicious sign of Khorne, the god of blood.

Khorne, one of the four great powers of Chaos.

The runic design was the mark of death, as if it were the Huntsman of Souls' own unholy signature.

Silk proclaimed her allegiance to her dark lord with his rune emblazoned upon her forehead, and others of the creatures were similarly marked. Many of them had horns which were twisted into the design of Khorne's elaborate cross.

His devotees worshipped their lord through slaughter, through combat on the battlefield, through blood sacrifices. Every death was dedicated to the greater glory of Khorne, and it was not only enemies who could become such offerings. When a death was called for, then it could be the death of another cultist – as had happened when Silk slew Satin.

To Khorne's followers, everyone else was a potential sacrifice. They had no friends, no allies, only future victims. Every day that passed, it seemed more likely that Konrad would become the next blood offering. But until then, every day that he survived was another victory.

And the days went by, the weeks, the months... until the hideous regiment had crossed from Kislev into the Empire, every mile of their route marked by the death of another innocent – or the occasional ally.

Konrad found himself praying that the marauders would find enough victims, that they would slay someone else, anyone else, so long as he survived. He had to survive in order to kill both Silk and Kastring. At first, that was all he cared about, the central idea which kept him going as he took every step.

Krysten had receded to the back of his mind. Already he was beginning to forget the girl. He had known her less than a year, and whenever he tried to picture her it was always Elyssa whose image he saw. He did not want to remember her, because he felt he had betrayed her. Had he not gone off with Wolf and Anvila, then Krysten may have still been alive. She must surely have been dead by now. He hoped for her sake that she was, because the only reason the legions of the damned ever took captives was for torture and degradation and ultimate sacrifice.

He never felt in immediate danger himself. It was almost as if all the carnage and mayhem he witnessed had nothing to do with him, that he was watching from a distance, an uninvolved spectator to the events happening around him. Even his own punishments seemed to have very little to do with him. His body might be in pain, but his mind was elsewhere. He felt that he was simply travelling in the same direction as Khorne's warband. They shared the same route, and that was all they had in common.

Konrad was aware that this state of affairs could not continue, that something must happen – and something would happen. Reality would return when he came face to face with the inevitable death that Kastring had promised. Either that, or he would be awoken from his trance in some other fashion. He could not imagine what might prompt his reawakening, but he would recognize it when it occurred.

He was uncertain why Kastring was keeping him alive. He seemed to derive macabre pleasure from Konrad's long torment. Maybe they would reach Ferlangen, and there he would be finally executed in what Kastring believed was his home town. Kastring knew Konrad was a soldier, but he wanted him to die like some beast on a butcher's block.

'You are a veteran of many battles,' he remarked one evening, as he sat opposite Konrad and his tailed captor.

The girl was throwing Konrad scraps of food. His arms were tied behind his back, and he had to eat from the dirt. It was only a minor torture, but Kastring and the blood girl were vastly enjoying themselves.

'You have caused many deaths,' Kastring continued, 'and so your own death is of greater significance than that of someone who has not themselves taken life, not shed the blood of others. You are too valuable to sacrifice for no good reason. I do believe that I will save your demise as a celebration for some special occasion.'

He watched as Silk poured a trickle of water onto the ground, and Konrad thirstily lapped it up. Then he spoke to the girl, and suddenly her foot was pressing Konrad's head into the dirt, her dagger at the main artery in his throat.

'Or maybe I won't,' Kastring added. A few seconds later, he issued another command, and Silk released her prisoner.

Kastring delighted in the humiliation that Konrad suffered, that a warrior had become a slave, and that he was commanded by a female. Konrad felt only hatred, and it became deeper with every passing day. It was a cold calculating hatred, not the futile fury of impulse.

Silk and Satin had been too much for him on that very first night, when he had been weak and exhausted. He could have taken them both now, but there was only one.

He knew he could kill the girl; he could even kill Kastring; and often he considered that the price of his own death would be worth the payment. But then he would reason that he had too much else to do with his life, that ultimate revenge upon his enemies was not worth his own death. Not while he knew he would live through another night. And not while he was still awaiting the time he knew must come.

Several nights would pass without any sacrifice, and during that interval the number of captives held by the raiders would increase. And then the time of torture would arrive once more, he would be bound by the throat and wrists, and once more he would become the only hostage to witness the dawn.

That was the one time he was left alone, when Silk went off to play her part in the obscene ceremony. She would finally return to him, naked and covered in blood, excited by the pain and terror and final death she had inflicted upon her helpless victims. Despite her appearance, she was far more like an animal than a human. Her tail, her forked tongue, they were the manifestations of her true bestiality.

'Or possibly you should join us,' Kastring suggested on another occasion. He was in a good mood, having destroyed a small garrison of road wardens during the afternoon. 'We are always eager to recruit a good man. Although you need not be a man, of course, or even good...'

The idea was utterly repulsive, but Konrad pretended to consider it as he watched Kastring across the fire. It might keep him alive a little longer.

'What would I have to do?' he asked.

'Kill. You have done that before, I believe. But now you would kill in the sacred name of Khorne. You're a mercenary, I know, that is why you were in Kislev. You killed for money. What kind of reason is that? Would you not prefer to kill for a holy purpose, to glorify the greatest of the gods?'

It was not true that Konrad had killed for money. He had received hardly any payment during the years he had worked with Wolf, but that had not been his motivation. He did have a purpose in slaying, he had been protecting mankind's northern frontier against the incursions of the creatures from the frozen wastes, the realms of Chaos...

And now he was in the midst of those very creatures. He felt like a traitor to his race for being here, for being alive when so many others had died.

The heathens had broken through humanity's first line of defence, making their way across hundreds of miles of territory. Yet it had hardly been an infiltration. Kastring's raiders had burned a fiery trail into Ostland, the first province within the borders of the Empire. The savages had made no attempt to disguise their presence, and this had resulted in more and more opposition being directed against them.

At first, Konrad had wondered whether this was part of the master plan. Kastring's marauders were creating a diversion, drawing away the imperial troops while the massed legions of darkness prepared to invade elsewhere, striking at the larger townships. Yet such a scheme was far too organized for the blood clans.

Kastring appeared calculating and cunning, but he was no different from the creatures he commanded. All he craved was blood, all he wanted was to kill, to destroy.

That was how he maintained his authority, by providing his followers with enemies and with victims. The more troops lined up against them, the more opportunity there was for slaughter and the more prisoners there were available for sacrifice.

'Who do I have to kill?' Konrad asked, knowing what the inevitable answer would be.

'We have several suitable captives, I believe,' Kastring told him. 'Perhaps you would care inspect them, to choose the one which you wish to give to our great lord and master.'

KASTRING WAS RIGHT: Konrad had killed before, many many times. But he had never murdered. Now, it seemed, there was no alternative. If he did not take human life, then he would also become a victim. Even if he refused, that would not save the person he had to slay. The victim would die no matter what. Konrad must kill. But he could kill quick, giving the merciful release of instant death instead of the lingering agony of torture.

'They gonna kill us, sir?' asked the small figure tied up next to him.

He was about fifteen years old, his eyes wide with fear. He had been brought in with a group of other captives, militia from the nearest town. The others were taken elsewhere, but the youth had been dragged away from them and thrown down with Konrad. His clothing was stained with blood; his face was dirty and bruised, streaked with tears.

'No,' Konrad lied. 'If they wanted to do that, they'd have done it by now.'

'What's gonna happen to us?'

'I don't know,' he lied again.

Silk was squatting directly opposite the two captives, and she was grinning, humming a tuneless tune to herself, tapping the blade of her knife on her bone necklace.

'Where you from, sir? When they catch you?'

Konrad said nothing. He wanted to avoid any communication, because he knew from the look in the girl's red eyes that the youth had been chosen as the one he was to slaughter.

'They are gonna kill us, mister. I know it!'

'No,' said Konrad, trying to reassure him. 'They caught me a long while ago, and I'm still alive.'

'She wants to kill us,' the boy said, lowering his voice to a whisper. 'I can tell.'

Silk stared at him, but he looked at the ground and would not meet her gaze.

'She one of them "mutants"?' He spoke the word as though it were the first time he had dared use it.

Konrad realized that the youth knew far more of the world than he himself had done at a similar age; he had never heard of mutants until after he had left his native valley. The village had been overrun by them, and he had not even known what they were called.

Chaos mutants. The source of their deformities lay in the corrupted regions north of Kislev.

'I don't wanna die, sir!'

'Neither do I,' said Konrad, softly, thinking how the price of his own life was probably the boy's death.

He gazed up at the dark sky, lit only by the stars. Mannslieb would not rise for several hours, that was definite; the lesser moon was far less predictable, both in its hour and its phases, but it seemed that tonight Morrslieb would be full.

The frightened boy kept talking, asking questions. Konrad said as little as was necessary. Meanwhile, Silk watched and waited, then finally the irregularly shaped moon rose above the horizon – and a hideous scream broke the silence, a long ululating scream of absolute agony.

The assembled beastmen, the mutants, the warriors of Khorne had greeted the arrival of Morrslieb by sacrificing their first captive.

The boy gasped, and Silk laughed. Without her partner in torture, she was not always the main executioner, although seldom an evening of death went by without her taking some part in the orgy of mutilation.

From where Konrad sat, he could not see into the area where the altar had been erected. Since the first night, he had always been out of sight of the killing zone; but he had always been close enough to hear the ritual slayings.

Tonight, he was on the outskirts of the marauders' encampment, on the very edge of a wooded slope that led down to a valley beneath. Below him, he could hear the distant rush of water. As the blood ceremonies commenced, he tried to concentrate on the sounds of the river instead of the sounds of painful death.

There was screaming from the sacrifices in the distance, and screaming from the boy next to him.

'Stop it!' Konrad yelled, turning to the youth and shouting directly into his face. 'Shut up! Listen to me!'

The boy became silent, his eyes wide with fear. For the moment, he was more terrified of Konrad than the fate which awaited him.

'You'll be all right. We'll both be all right. That's why you're with me. That's why they took you away from the others. You're not to be killed. They haven't killed me. They won't kill you.'

The boy stared at him, and his expression hardened.

'You're one of them!' he accused, and he spat in Konrad's face. Then he turned away.

At least he was silent, thought Konrad. But he kept thinking about the boy's words: You're one of them...

In a way, he supposed it was true. He had been with the savages for many weeks. And if he were forced to kill the boy, that would indeed make him one of them – or almost.

Kastring had invited him to become one of Khorne's followers. If he slew before Khorne's effigy, would that serve as an initiation ceremony? No matter his motive, or his intention, would the slaughter be the first stage of his own descent into the abyss of bestial mutation? Kastring had begun as a man, a human. How had he started to change? Had it happened in the Chaos wastes, or could the mutation occur anywhere?

Konrad had considered that he could save his own life by taking that of another, by killing the boy; but did sacrificing before the shrine automatically mean acceptance of Khorne as his deity? In that case, his life would no longer be his own – he was lost forever. It was more than merely his life that was as stake: if he joined the barbarous clan, Khorne would also claim his immortal spirit.

He wished he knew more. Konrad had never been religious. There were so many gods who were worshipped within the Empire and Kislev, but he had never had much contact with any of their followers and rituals. He knew most about Sigmar Heldenhammer, who was venerated as a deity.

Wolf had belonged to the cult of Sigmar, and he always offered a prayer to the founder of the Empire before going into combat.

Silk rose to her feet. At the same time, Konrad became aware that there was silence. The last victim had died.

The last but one – or two...

The girl kicked off her sandals, shrugged out of her robe, let her necklace of fingerbones fall, untied her blood-red hair and shook it loose. She stood naked, armed with her knife; she was ready to kill. She spoke a few words. Konrad recognized the command. She was telling him to get up, but he ignored it. She sprang towards him, her blade at his throat. The tip drew blood. She repeated her order.

She would not kill him, he knew, but she was an expert in pain. With a few swift and accurate knife strokes, she could inflict excruciating agony. Instead, she transferred her attentions to the boy, jabbing him in the shoulder. He cried out in agony. She gestured for him to rise, and he obeyed. She swiftly cut away his garments, and he was naked, his hands still tied around his back.

She looked at Konrad, then she slowly drew the point of her blade diagonally down the boy's chest, right to left. He screamed as the blood began to flow. She did it again, left to right, her red eyes watching Konrad. She was carving the mark of Khorne on the boy, he realized, and she would continue unless Konrad obeyed. He did so; he stood up. But Silk did not cease her mutilation. With two rapid strokes, one to the left, one to the right, she completed the pattern. The boy's torso glistened with trickles of blood.

He swayed, as though he were about to faint, but he held himself upright. His screams had ceased, and now he sobbed. He was not badly hurt. Silk had not wanted him dead. Not yet. Now she stepped towards Konrad, and her knife flashed. He winced as she sliced his cheek for disobedience. Her blade kept working, and after a few seconds he was also naked. She growled a command, and Konrad began walking slowly towards the shrine. She pushed the boy, and he also began to move.

The worshippers awaited them, dark silhouettes who encircled the armoured effigy of Khorne. One of the shadows stepped forward.

'Delighted that you could accept our invitation,' said Kastring. 'Is this your guest?'

The boy stood motionless, dazed, his eyes fixed on the shrine, staring at the skulls and fresh heads at the feet of the seated brass figure.

'I'm going to kill you, Kastring,' Konrad hissed.

'You seem to misunderstand the situation,' Kastring replied. 'The only killing you are going to do involves this young gentleman. Neither do I believe this is the most appropriate time for you to threaten me. I'm the one who issues the threats. And, as I once promised, I will have you killed. Eventually.'

Silk's knife severed Konrad's bonds, and Kastring held out a dagger to him, hilt first. Konrad accepted the blade, and as he did he felt the tip of the girl's knife at the base of his skull. As Kastring stepped back, so did Silk.

Konrad and the boy were left in the centre of the area, in front of the altar. The ground beneath their feet was wet with blood. The boy turned away from the shrine to look at him, at the knife, then at Konrad's face.

'I knew you was one of them,' he said, very quietly, and he lowered his head.

Konrad wanted to deny the accusation, to tell him that he would dispatch him swiftly, whereas any of the others would have slain him slowly and horribly. But there was no point. He would only have been speaking for his own benefit, not the youth's.

The idolators began to chant their hymns of blood.

'Do it!' Kastring commanded, his voice louder than all the sacrilegious prayers.

Konrad gazed at the shadowed shape which had spoken, and he held the knife loosely in his hand, testing its balance, weighing it for its flight through the night – and into Kastring's throat.

Before he could act, the blade was suddenly knocked from his hand. Silk had hurled herself silently at him, and she shouldered him aside. Unbalanced, Konrad fell into the mud. He instantly rolled away, believing that the blood girl was about to dive on him. Instead, her target was the young Ostlander...

Her blade plunged into his chest, and his cry was terrible, long and ear-piercing. He fell, and Silk went down with him, her knife carving deep into his torso. After a few seconds, she sprang up. In one hand she held her knife, in the other was a lump of raw human flesh. It was the boy's heart.

His beating heart!

There was a roar of approval from the worshippers, and she reverently placed the gory organ at the feet of the brass figure.

Konrad had been unable to find the dagger and was back on his feet, and he became aware of a dark shape moving towards him. He heard a sword being drawn from its oiled scabbard, and he knew it was the sword with a coiled serpent as its hilt.

He backed slowly away, glancing quickly over his shoulder for another potential assassin. When he looked back a moment later, there was a slim figure between himself and Kastring.

It was Silk, but she was facing her leader, threatening him with the reddened blade she held.

Kastring halted, said something in the heathen language. Silk said nothing, but neither did she move aside.

'She does like you,' said Kastring. Then he forced a contemptuous laugh, sheathed his sword and turned away.

Silk looked at Konrad, and their eyes met. For some reason of her own, she had killed the boy when Konrad had refused, and she had defended him from Kastring's wrath. But she had also saved Kastring's life by knocking the dagger from Konrad's hand. Konrad had no idea why she had interfered in the ceremony, protecting him from Kastring. Whatever the reason, it must surely spell doom for both of them.

The dark shapes around them melted away into the deeper darkness, leaving them alone, alone with the body of the young Ostlander and the corpses of all the other victims who lay as gory offerings to Khorne's bronze altar.

As they gazed as each other, Konrad suddenly realized what she must once have been: human.

And he also knew that this was the moment he had been awaiting. It was the time of his awakening.

Konrad walked away and Silk followed. She was a pace behind him when he reached the spur of land above the river. He turned as the girl raised her knife, standing motionless while she thrust the point of the weapon into the trunk of the tree next to him. The blade glinted as it vibrated. Mannslieb had begun to rise, a sliver of brilliance on the horizon, already shedding a radiant light far greater than the dull glow created by Morrslieb. The river lay far below, and on the edge of his vision Konrad noticed another glimmer further down in the valley. It was also the reflection of moonlight on metal.

And he finally became aware of what he must do.

The girl pressed herself hard against him, turning her face up to his. No matter what, he hated her absolutely, but for a moment he remembered what he had thought when he first saw her and Satin: that they were the most beautiful women he had ever seen.

Until now he had always refused the temptations of her body, no matter what torments she inflicted upon him in reprisal. Because of tonight he owed her this one final tribute to her lost humanity, to her forgotten femininity.

Her flesh felt warm and soft, and that surprised him. He tried to ignore the blood on her skin, her feral eyes, her forked tongue and tail. He sank to the ground, allowing her to assume the ascendant role, as if still accepting his subservience to her.

She was at her least animal, he at his most. When she cried out, it was not the rutting call of some bestial mutant but the sounds a woman made at the peak of passion. He was the one who growled primitively, driven by his deepest instinct.

This was the way life was created, the way of Konrad's unknown origins, the way that Silk herself had begun her true existence, before her body had become corrupted by Chaos, her spirit stolen and twisted.

Konrad reached up to her, beyond her, and for the first time he allowed her lips to touch his. Again, so warm, so soft. They kissed – and it was the kiss of death.

Silk sighed as he slipped the dagger into her back and plunged it deep into her heart. Their eyes met for one last time, and the girl's were wet with tears. She leaned back and she smiled and she died as easily as if she were still human.

Konrad caught her as she fell, and he rolled free. He withdrew the blade and stared down into the valley, searching for what he had observed a few minutes ago, the glint of moonlight on armour.

On bronze armour...

Konrad's quest is concluded in WARBLADE.

More Warhammer from the Black Library

TROLLSLAYER
A Gotrek & Felix novel
by William King

High on the hill the scorched walled castle stood, a stone
spider clutching the hilltop with blasted stone feet. Before
the gaping maw of its broken gate hanged men dangled
on gibbets, flies caught in its single-strand web.

'Time for some bloodletting,' Gotrek said. He ran his
left hand through the massive red crest of hair that rose
above his shaven tattooed skull. His nose chain tinkled
gently, a strange counterpoint to his mad rumbling
laughter.

'I am a Slayer, manling. Born to die in battle. Fear has
no place in my life.'

*TROLLSLAYER IS THE first part of the death saga of Gotrek
Gurnisson, as retold by his travelling companion Felix Jaeger.
Set in the darkly gothic world of Warhammer, Trollslayer is
an episodic novel featuring some of the most extraordinary
adventures of this deadly pair of heroes. Monsters, daemons,
sorcerers, mutants, orcs, beastmen and worse are to be found
as Gotrek strives to achieve a noble death in battle. Felix, of
course, only has to survive to tell the tale.*

More Warhammer from the Black Library

SKAVENSLAYER
A Gotrek & Felix novel
by William King

'Beware! Skaven!' Felix shouted and saw them all reach
for their weapons. In moments, swords glittered in the
half-light of the burning city. From inside the tavern a
number of armoured figures spilled out into the gloom.
Felix was relieved to see the massive squat figure of
Gotrek among them. There was something enormously
reassuring about the immense axe clutched in the dwarf's
hands.

'I see you found our scuttling little friends, manling,'
Gotrek said, running his thumb along the blade of his axe
until a bright red bead of blood appeared.

'Yes, Felix gasped, struggling to get his breath back
before the combat began.

'Good. Let's get killing then!'

*SET IN THE MIGHTY city of Nuln, Gotrek and Felix are back in
SKAVENSLAYER, the second novel in this epic saga. Seeking
to undermine the very fabric of the Empire with their arcane
warp-sorcery, the skaven, twisted Chaos rat-men, are at large
in the reeking sewers beneath the ancient city. Led by Grey
Seer Thanquol, the servants of the Horned Rat are
determined to overthrow this bastion of humanity. Against
such forces, what possible threat can just two hard-bitten
adventurers pose?*

More Warhammer from the Black Library

DAEMONSLAYER
A Gotrek & Felix novel
by William King

The roar was so loud and so terrifying that Felix almost dropped his blade. He looked up and fought the urge to soil his britches. The most frightening thing he had ever seen had entered the hall and behind it he could see the leering heads of beastmen.

As he gazed on the creature in wonder and terror, Felix thought: this is the incarnate nightmare which has bedevilled my people since time began.

'Just remember,' Gotrek said from beside him, 'the daemon is mine!'

FRESH FROM THEIR adventures battling the foul servants of the rat-god in Nuln, Gotrek and Felix are now ready to join an expedition northwards in search of the long-lost dwarf hall of Karag Dum. Setting forth for the hideous Realms of Chaos in an experimental dwarf airship, Gotrek and Felix are sworn to succeed or die in the attempt. But greater and more sinister energies are coming into play, as a daemonic power is awoken to fulfil its ancient, deadly promise.

More Warhammer from the Black Library

DRAGONSLAYER
A Gotrek & Felix novel
by William King

The dragon opened its vast mouth. All the fires of hell burned within its jaws.

Insanely, Felix thought the creature looked almost as if it were smiling. Some strange impulse compelled him to throw himself between Gotrek and the creature just as it breathed. He fought back the desire to scream as a wall of flame hurtled towards him.

DRAGONSLAYER is the fourth epic instalment in the death-seeking saga of Gotrek and Felix. After the daring exploits revealed in Daemonslayer, the fearless duo find themselves pursued by the insidious and ruthless skaven-lord, Grey Seer Thanquol. Dragonslayer sees the fearless Troll Slayer and his sworn companion back aboard an arcane dwarf airship in a search for a golden hoard – and its deadly guardian.

More Warhammer from the Black Library

BEASTSLAYER
A Gotrek & Felix novel
by William King

At the last second before impact, the Slayer moved. He lashed out with his axe. A blow, as swift and irresistible as a thunderbolt, struck the Chaos warrior's steed's legs. The beast tumbled, blood fountaining from its sheared limbs. Its rider cartwheeled from the saddle and skidded across the hard-packed earth to land at Felix's feet with a crash like an earthquake hitting an ironmonger's shop.

STORM CLOUDS GATHER around the icy city of Praag as the foul hordes of Chaos lay ruinous siege to northern lands of Kislev. Only Gotrek Gurnisson, a death-seeking dwarf Slayer, and his sworn human companion, Felix Jaeger, stand between the ancient city and the forces of Darkness in this latest instalment of their epic quest.

More Warhammer from the Black Library

VAMPIRESLAYER
A Gotrek & Felix novel
by William King

Gotrek thundered through them like a raging bull. His axe left bloody corpses every time it struck, and it struck often, moving almost too fast for the human eye to follow. As Felix watched, the Slayer cut down two more assailants and dived headlong into the pack of men trying to force their way in through the door. Whoever wanted the talisman had brought a small army with him. It was not a reassuring thought, Felix decided, as he shouted a challenge and raced to join the carnage.

IN THE UNCEASING war against Chaos, the doom-seeking dwarf Gotrek and his human companion Felix are beset by a new, terrible foe. An evil is forming in darkest Sylvania which threatens to reach out and tear the heart from our band of intrepid heroes. The gripping saga of Gotrek & Felix continues in this epic tale of deadly battle and soul-rending tragedy.

More Warhammer from the Black Library

HAMMERS OF ULRIC
A Warhammer novel by Dan Abnett, Nik Vincent & James Wallis

Aric rode forward across the corpse-strewn ground and helped Gruber to his feet. The older warrior was speckled with blood, but alive.

'See to von Glick and watch the standard. Give me your horse,' Gruber said to Aric.

Aric dismounted and returned to the banner of Vess as Gruber galloped back into the brutal fray.

Von Glick lay next to the standard, which was still stuck upright in the bloody earth. The lifeless bodies of almost a dozen beastmen lay around him.

'L-let me see…' von Glick breathed. Aric knelt beside him and raised his head. 'So, Anspach's bold plan worked…' breathed the veteran warrior. 'He's pleased… I'll wager.'

Aric started to laugh, then stopped. The old man was dead.

IN THE SAVAGE world of Warhammer, dark powers gather around the ancient mountain-top city of Middenheim, the City of the White Wolf. Only the noble Templar Knights of Ulric and a few unlikely allies stand to defend her against the insidious servants of Death.

More Warhammer from the Black Library

DRACHENFELS
A Genevieve novel
by Kim Newman (writing as Jack Yeovil)

Now Conradin was dead. Sieur Jehan was dead. Heinroth was dead. Ueli was dead. And before the night was over, others – maybe all of the party – would be joining them. Genevieve hadn't thought about dying for a long time. Perhaps tonight Drachenfels would finish Chandagnac's Dark Kiss, and push her at last over the border between life and death.

DETLEF SIERCK, *the self-proclaimed greatest playwright in the world, has declared that his next production will be a recreation of the end of the Great Enchanter Drachenfels – to be staged at the very site of his death, the Fortress of Drachenfels itself. But the castle's dark walls still hide a terrible and deadly secret which may make the first night of Detlef's masterpiece the last of his life.*

WINE OF DREAMS
A Warhammer novel
by Brian Craig

The sword flew from Reinmar's hand and he just had time to think, as he was taken off his feet, that when he landed – flat on his back – he would be wide open to attack by a plunging dagger or flashing teeth. As the beastman leapt, Sigurd's arm lashed out in a great horizontal arc, the palm of his hand held flat. As it impacted with the beastman's neck Reinmar heard the snap that broke the creature's spine.

As soon as that, it was over. But it was not a victory. Now there was no possible room for doubt that there were monsters abroad in the hills.

DEEP WITHIN THE shadowy foothills of the Grey Mountains, a dark and deadly plot is uncovered by an innocent young merchant. A mysterious stranger leads young Reinmar Weiland to stumble upon the secrets of a sinister underworld hidden beneath the very feet of the unsuspecting Empire – and learn of a legendary elixir, the mysterious and forbidden Wine of Dreams.

More Warhammer from the Black Library

GILEAD'S BLOOD
A Warhammer novel
by Dan Abnett & Nik Vincent

Gilead got to his feet unsteadily. The dulled blade dropped from his hand with a clatter. 'You dare to speak to me of that?' he hissed. 'Galeth was one with me, my brother, my twin! We were one soul in two bodies! Do you not remember?'

Fithvael bowed his head. 'I do, lord. That is what they said of you…'

'And when he died, I was cut in two! Death entered my soul! Ten years I hunted for the murderer! Hunted for vengeance! And when I found it, even that pleasure did not slake the pain in my heart!'

GILEAD'S BLOOD FOLLOWS the saga of the doom-laden high elf, Gilead Lothain. Along with his faithful retainer Fithvael, Gilead, shadowfast warrior and the last of the line of Tor Anrok, travels the Warhammer world seeking revenge on the servants of Evil.

More Warhammer from the Black Library

REALM OF CHAOS
An anthology of Warhammer stories
edited by Marc Gascoigne
& Andy Jones

'MARKUS WAS confused; the stranger's words were baffling his pain-numbed mind. "Just who are you, foul spawned deviant?"

The warrior laughed again, slapping his hands on his knees. "I am called Estebar. My followers know me as the Master of Slaughter. And I have come for your soul."'
– **The Faithful Servant,** *by Gav Thorpe*

'THE WOLVES ARE running again. I can haear them panting in the darkness. I race through the forest, trying to out-pace them. Behind the wolves I sense another presence, something evil. I am in the place of blood again.' – **Dark Heart,** *by Jonathan Green*

IN THE DARK and gothic world of Warhammer, the ravaging armies of the Ruinous Powers sweep down from the savage north to assail the lands of men. REALM OF CHAOS is a searing collection of a dozen all-action fantasy short stories set in these desperate times.

More Warhammer from the Black Library

LORDS OF VALOUR
An anthology of Warhammer stories
edited by Marc Gascoigne
& Christian Dunn

'THE GOBLINS SHRIEKED their shrill war cries and charged, only to be met head-on by the vengeful dwarfs. In the confines of the tunnel, the grobi's weight of numbers counted for little. As they turned and fled, Grimli was all for going after them, but Dammaz laid a hand on his shoulder.

'"Our way lies down a different path," the Slayer said.'
– *from* **Ancestral Honour** *by Gav Thorpe*

'MOLLENS SNARLED WITH surprise. The hulking Reiklander advanced towards him, his own glistening blade held downwards. With a speed and grace which belied his hefty frame, the Reiklander leapt with a savage howl. Mollens twisted and struck. For one terrible moment the two men gazed helplessly into each other's eyes, then the Reiklander collapsed into the cold mud.' – *from* **The Judas Goat** *by Robert Earl*

IN THE GRIM world of Warhammer, the bloodthirsty followers of the Ruinous Powers ravage the land. But the human realms have their own defenders: noble warriors, sworn to fight to the death for those under their protection. From the pages of Inferno! magazine, LORDS OF VALOUR is a storming collection of all-action fantasy short stories that follows the never-ending war between the champions of darkness and light.

LET BATTLE COMMENCE!

NOW YOU can fight your way through the savage lands of the Empire and beyond with WARHAMMER, Games Workshop's game of fantasy battles. In a world of conflict, mighty armies clash to decide the fate of war-torn realms. In Warhammer, you and your opponents are the fearless commanders of these armies. The fate of your kingdoms rests on your shoulders as you control regiments of miniature soldiers, to do battle with terrifying monsters and fearless heroes.

To find out more about Warhammer, along with Games Workshop's whole range of exciting fantasy and science fiction games and miniatures, just call our specialist Trolls on the following numbers:

IN THE UK: 0115-91 40 000

IN THE US: 1-800-394-GAME

or visit us online at:

www.games-workshop.com